CAT AND MOUSE

Bucher began to suspect it was he who was being
toyed with; that he, not she, was the mouse in
their little game of cat and mouse—and icy chills
flushed in successive waves up his spine. He fixed
the mad woman with cold eyes, suddenly anxious
to terminate their confrontation with all possible
dispatch. Killing a woman went powerfully against
his grain—but this was no longer a woman, or
even human, only human-shaped insanity bent on
death and destruction.

"Nobody is going to kill Kleyr," he snarled softly.
"And especially not an insane slut like you."

"Oh, come now, Boo," she said, purring again.
"Isn't that what the bitch calls you? Boo?" She
laughed throatily, stretching a third time, combing
her long fingers through her silken hair and—too
quick almost to see, she sprang, screaming, the
Puerto Rican sun glinting brightly off the deadly
straight razor that appeared in her hand . . .

The Butcher Series

The Butcher
Suicide in San Juan
by Stuart Jason

PINNACLE BOOKS • NEW YORK CITY

THE BUTCHER: SUICIDE IN SAN JUAN

Copyright © 1975 by Script Representatives, Inc.

An original Pinnacle Books edition, published for the first time anywhere.

ISBN: 0-523-00726-4

First printing, October 1975

Cover illustration by Fred Love

Printed in the United States of America

PINNACLE BOOKS, INC.
275 Madison Avenue
New York, N.Y. 10016

SUICIDE IN SAN JUAN

PROLOGUE

"Whadda ya mean quit?" the other crime overlords had snarled at Bucher in angry alarm. *"You can't quit! Ain't nobody quits the Syndicate and lives! You know that! What's wrong with you all of a sudden anyway? You gone nuts or something? You got the whole East Coast Division sewed up tighter'n a drum: girly houses, wire services, racetracks, the numbers, the unions, everything—and you wanna quit? Huh-uh! Not never! Quit and how long you think you gonna live, huh? A day? Two days? A week if you're lucky? Huh-uh! You don't quit the Syndicate. You're the toughest, meanest sonofabitch we ever seen operate and you pack the fastest heater since John Dillinger came boiling down the pike, but quit the Syndicate and you're dead! Make book on it!*

Bucher had quit the Syndicate anyway; simply walked out and never went back. At the apex of the underworld success ladder, when his private coffers were repeatedly filling to overflowing, he had turned his back and walked away. And from that day forward his life style took on the aspects of a pressure-cooker existence, at times reminding him of a blood-gutsy Hollywood class-B extravaganza produced over the weekend on a shoestring budget. For the day he walked out on the Syndicate, his former business associates quietly placed a one hundred thousand dollar dead-only kill-price on his head. Moreover, when his back trail became strewn with the bodies of eager beaver gunsels trying to collect this kill-price, even the most blood-lustful killers lost interest in collecting the reward. That's when the Syndicate increased the kill-price to a cool quarter of a million dollars.

Not long after Bucher's break with the Syndicate, two neatly dressed young men from Washington located him in a Detroit hotel.

"Mr. Bucher," one of the young men had said. "With your intimate knowledge of organized crime, both in this country and abroad, you can be of invaluable service to your country. As a special secret agent . . ."

They offered him a contract, which he ignored; a badge for protection in emergencies, which he waved aside; a salary, which he laughed at. Yet in the end he had accepted their proposition because in it he saw the opportunity of atoning, in his own mind at least, for some of his grisly past.

Before leaving, two young men from Washington had given him a telephone number, exclusively his and never unattended, and the code name Iceman.

And thus Bucher, ex-crime overlord of the Syndicate's powerful East Coast Division, became a member of White Hat, a national security agency so super hush-hush no hint of its existence was ever found in the President's fiscal reports and budget requests to Congress.

Since his connecting with White Hat he had undertaken some peculiar, even weird, assignments; however, this current case, this Puerto Rican thing of supertankers vanishing without a trace in the Bermuda Triangle, was enough to give any itinerant gunslinger pause.

1

Bucher glanced at his watch on reaching the rented Dodge van in the Dorodo Beach Hotel's parking lot and grimaced sourly. It was six hours since his flight from New York had touched down at the San Juan airport, and with the passing of each hour, he had grown proportionately more disgruntled with this current assignment here in Puerto Rico. Nor did his mood alter for the better by recalling White Hat's director's sole purpose for urging him to accept the assignment.

"Because you're a catalyst, Mr. Bucher. Wherever you are, things soon begin happening, usually in our favor, and God alone knows how desperately we need something to begin happening in our favor with this vanishing super-tankers affair."

With effortless ease Bucher tooled the van out of the lot and onto the driveway leading to Highway 2 and San Juan, his destination a triple-X-rated strip joint named Dainty Dish in the older section of the city.

"Catalyst or not," he growled aloud to himself. "I still don't like it."

His dislike for the assignment was in no way related to his coming to Puerto Rico. In very truth, at any given point during the years since their separation, he would have gladly given anything to have been able to come to Puerto Rico knowing Kleyr Boriquen and her forgiveness awaited him. No, he disliked the assignment because he knew, perhaps with greater certainty than most, that knowledge was survival and this Puerto Rican-vanishing supertankers thing was related to matters, at least ostensibly, of which he had only a limited amount of hard knowledge; matters such as the mysterious Bermuda Triangle, the Puerto Rico Trench, Einstein's Unified Field Theory, seiche waves, tsunamis, antigravity warp, electromagnetism, ionization, the Sargasso Sea. Dammit! Terms such as magnetic anomalies, electromagnetic incomprehensibles, and atmospheric incongruities did not belong in the vocabulary of an itinerant gunslinger! And why the hell couldn't the "small international body of scientists" manning Puerto Rico's renowned Arecibo Observatory take care of their own damn problems?

Pondering the science-related aspects of the case as he was, and even in a temper, it was inevitable with Bucher that before long the sweet-painful memories of vivacious little Kleyr Boriquen, whose genius but a few years past had astounded, and delighted, the literati of the world's scientific community, would appear yet again to haunt him. Their few weeks of knowing each other had been a time of incredible happiness, and their last few days together, at Hibbings Summer Lodge in the Catskills, had been a time in which they found new joys in rediscovering the awesome mysteries of the intimate tenderness and affection they felt for each other.

It had also been a time of another discovery. By Bucher. About Kleyr. And he had chopped off their relationship as with a broadaxe. He had been wrong, wretchedly, miserably wrong in acting so ruthlessly, in treating her so terribly, but of this he remained ignorant until after the deed was done. The shock attendant to the discovery of his mistake had been so powerful at the time that even now, some eight years later, remnants of it returned and tormented him when thoughts of Kleyr filled his mind.

There are two separate sections of San Juan, Puerto Rico; metropolitian San Juan and Old San Juan, and coming in on Highway 2 by car from the west there is no reaching the second without going through the first. Thus it was that Bucher was entering the outskirts of metropolitan San Juan when that peculiar sensation one sometimes experiences from being the object of covert observation interrupted his reflections and brought to his attention the fact that the deep purple VW Bug behind him had been following him since his leaving the Dorodo Beach Hotel. He recalled having seen it not far from the parking lot. He studied the vehicle through the van's rearview mirror. With the Syndicate's quarter-million-dollar dead-only reward on his head, more than once he had encountered eager beaver gunsels in much more far out places of the world than Puerto Rico, hoping to collect it. As for the two people dimly visible behind the purple Bug's tinted windshield, there was a way of learning if they meant to make a bid for his scalp or not.

At the last second and without signaling, Bucher whipped the van into a vacant parking space along the curb, and the purple Bug shot past him without so much as a glance. Even so, Bucher dismounted from the van, entered the drugstore across the sidewalk, and took up a position at the front window, watching. But all to no avail. The purple Bug did not reappear. After thirty minutes Bucher returned to the van and continued toward his destination in Old San Juan, his second visit of the day.

Shortly after arriving at the airport, renting the van, and making a few purchases at a grocery and a furniture store, he had spent two hours prowling about the area, first locating the Dainty Dish, then driving here and there to familiarize himself with the street pattern. One of the outstanding features of Old San Juan was its exceptionally large number of boites, suggesting that with enough dedicated effort, tourist-bilking could become a major industry.

Before returning to the Dorodo Beach Hotel, he had circled around past the Dainty Dish once more just to be certain, and because of his knowledge of the area he now, on his second visit, drove directly to the place, parking against the curb across the narrow, somewhat grubby street directly in front of the main entrance.

According to one of the briefing sheets Bucher had seen during his preparation for coming to Puerto Rico, he was to take a seat at one of three specific tables as a means of identification when he entered the Dainty Dish. If number one was occupied, he was to take number two, if two was also occupied, then number three, and if all tables were in use when he entered, he was to stand at the bar until one of the three was vacated—which, he reflected dourly as he cased the joint from the cab of the van, is just about as damn cloak and daggerish-silly as anyone can get. Who, he wondered absently, had conjured up such a staggering masterpiece of originality?

The sun had been disappearing on the horizon as Bucher entered the city some time ago, and now as he checked his watch, he saw the time for him to put in an appearance inside the Dainty Dish was drawing nigh; unless he entered at the predetermined time that awful rigamarole with three tables would be wasted. Therefore, he stepped out of the van into the fragrant, flower-scented Puerto Rican dusk—but he did so cautiously, carefully surveying the surrounding area in all directions. The fact that the purple Bug had failed to reappear had not satisfied Bucher at all, and the more he thought about it, the more unlikely it seemed that the Bug would again be behind the van, trailing him from the Dorodo Beach Hotel all the way to the edge of the city, purely by chance. However, he saw nothing suspicious as he locked the van and crossed the street to his destination.

The Dainty Dish, according to White Hat's briefing information, catered mainly to tourists, the main attraction being sex acts performed by a nude man and woman on stage and in the view of all. The establishment remained open only because of heavy police payoffs, and was seldom patronized by Puerto Ricans. Regardless, Bucher did not anticipate with any relish what he expected to soon be witnessing. During his Syndicate days, he had not made a rigid practice of shunning these X-rated establishments, dollars and cents business being what it was, yet he had avoided watching "meat market" performers whenever convenient due to an inveterate embarrassment he always felt from watching two fellow human beings rut openly like two dumb brutes of the field. In his private opinion sex between a man and woman was indeed a thing of beauty when carried on in privacy, whether the privacy be in the house at home, in the backyard, in the forest, at some secluded beach or wherever, and just as long as only the two were involved. But the moment a third or more persons entered the picture, the thing of beauty became obscene pornography, period.

Bucher sauntered across the street to the Dainty Dish,

6

entered the vestibule and paid a weary-eyed jade the twenty-dollar cover charge. She indicated a door to her right. The walls around this door were festooned with placards proclaiming a "Battle of the Sexes" to take place between Mary Jo Philasheo and Dingus Koonilinges, and Bucher let out a small sound of disgust as he pushed open the door and entered. Luck was with him.

"I'm living right," he grinned wryly to himself at sight of table number one with nobody seated at it. Then, instinctively, he checked the place carefully with his eyes. A minute later he occupied the single chair at table number one and turned face-down the "Reserved" notice.

Surprisingly it did not have the usual garish lights and too-loud music usually found in "meat market" joints, but instead had a hushed atmosphere, the rather expensive furnishings and muted music creating an aura of genteel reserve and good taste. The room was huge, and at each end couples danced sedately on oblong mini-ballroom floors, with the remaining floor area, except for a dais in the exact center of the runway connecting it to a curtained stage at the far side of the room, occupied by tables for two and four persons. Each table was cleverly arranged among great potted elephant plants, tree ferns, rubber plants, and palms in a manner offering maximum concealment from neighboring prying eyes. The dais in the center was round, twelve feet across, and three feet above the floor, a height that would afford seated spectators the greatest advantage visually, and the runway connecting it to the curtained stage approximately four feet wide. Several patrons, all men and by the cut of their clothes and their loud voices from the U.S. proper, sat at tables arranged in a rough half-circle around the dais. Their occasional coarse laughter and flushed faces defined the eagerness with which they awaited the main event by Mary Jo Philasheo and Dingus Koonilinges.

One of these patrons in the half circle, a meaty-faced character in his mid-twenties with bull-shoulders and foghorn voice more often than not dominated the conversation. Neither those at the dais nor those dancing gave any particular notice when Bucher entered and took a table

7

heavily shadowed by an enormous fern—but those about the dais and those dancing were not the only patrons when Bucher entered. There was one other patron, an aging Syndicate torpedo named Surd Gulgar, seated in the room's most remote corner behind a brace of flourishing plants. During those brief seconds between Bucher's entry and his reaching his table, Gulgar recognized him, and the old killer's seamed face blanched in fear, his lips silently jerking out the words:

"The Butcher!"

Surd Gulgar was by no means a coward, for cowardice could never have withstood his years of organized crime, but neither was he a fool, for as such he also could never have survived those years; therefore when Surd Gulgar saw the dread Butcher enter the Dainty Dish and take a seat, he conducted himself in the manner he deemed most conducive to his continued longevity—he did nothing. Had this new arrival been a person other than Bucher, and had he posed the same potential threat as Bucher did to Gulgar's Syndicate boss Luigi Nappo, who sat at the dais gulping drinks and dominating the conversation, Surd Gulgar would have moved in at once and neutralized the potential threat. But against Bucher, he was not doing anything.

"God forbid!" he quavered, forefinger tugging at his suddenly too-tight shirt collar, other hand mopping his perspiring brow. "Ain't no bohunk in his right mind goin' up against the Butcher. Too many good boys already tried it and failed. Far as I'm concerned, the Red Cross can have that quarter-million reward on his head—the Red Cross'll get it before Surd Gulgar tries for it, and that's gospel fact. Surd Gulgar ain't tryin' nothin' with the Butcher." Nor was he unaware of the additional jeopardy to his continued well-being from Luigi Nappo, whom he was supposed to be body-guarding, if Luigi learned of Bucher's presence when he, Surd Gulgar, also knew of it and had done nothing. Again Gulgar mopped sweat. If harm came to Luigi through Gulgar's neglect, a quick death was the best he could hope for; Luigi's older brother and Syndicate *capo*, Big Jute Nappo, would make certain he ceased to live. Big Jute operated that way.

8

The wizened killer was approaching a state of nervous torment when the muted dance music was interrupted by slightly louder sound, a fanfare, and the huge room was blanketed by an expectant hush. Couples on the mini-ballroom floors at once forsook their dancing in anticipation of the voyeur delights from an all-out battle of the sexes between Mary Jo Philasheo and Dingus Koonilinges. Those patrons in the rough half-circle about the dais gulped their drinks excitedly and ordered more.

Bucher had no inkling as to the identity of his contact, nor what means this contact might use to communicate with him, so there was little he could do but continue to follow instructions, in spite of the intense scrutiny by a single eye fixed on him through a small part in the curtains concealing the stage at the far end of the dais runway. The scrutiny had been in progress almost five minutes when the fanfare sounded. With the fanfare, however, the eye vanished, and Bucher sat watching the patrons scurry for seats as near to the dais as possible.

A second fanfare sounded. Then it happened. The curtains hiding the stage were swept aside vigorously, and as the fanfare reached a crescendo, Mary Jo Philasheo gamboled into view adorned by a few of Puerto Rico's famous tiny pink orchids, and carrying a small bouquet of the flowers in one hand. Loud and lustful greetings acknowledged her appearance, plus a few impatient barbs from the women over the failure of Dingus Koonilinges to appear with her.

The young woman billed as Mary Jo Philasheo had dark masses of springy curls on her head, an olive complexion, was dainty-light on her feet and nymphian slender. Without question she could have doubled for any virile male's fantasy of erotic feminine perfection, from the tiny waist that flared gently over immaculate thighs to the outward, slightly up-jutting cone-shaped breasts the ripe plumpness of honeydew melons firm and tight with juice. Their jiggly accompaniment to her body movements could create riots. Those around the dais ogled and salivated, the women also approving but casting frequent glances toward the curtained stage in search of Dingus Koonilinges.

9

From his experience with Syndicate X-rated clubs, Bucher knew the performers who put on these acts never used their right names, but a name assigned them by the house for the length of their stay, a house name. Therefore, even before entering the Dainty Dish he had known the name of the nude young woman scheduled to rut in public was not Mary Jo Philasheo. But he had not known that her real name would be Kleyr Boriquen. And now that he did know, he sat as death, still as frozen stone, a black and terrible sickness forming around his heart, in his mouth the bitter-sour taste of galling defeat—and the canker of murderous hate.

For his own safety, Bucher's soul forbade him to become too emotionally overwrought from his discovery that Mary Jo Philasheo was really Kleyr Boriquen. But it was not an easy job. The emotions were tenacious. Only after repeated effort did Bucher realize the quickest means of assuaging them was to focus a part of his memory on the cause of the emotions, on Kleyr herself. Though not as she was at the moment. As she had been. To him. When they were together years ago. When they had compiled that incredibly silly and wonderful lexicon of theirs, a special lexicon of private words and terms, with private, intimate definitions that meant nothing to anyone but themselves.

The whole thing had been Kleyr's idea, really, stemming from her penchant to create new words and word forms, even in the midst of conversation. Not too meaningful to them personally, but one of the first of their words was born as she read a verbose magazine article larded with too many adverbs.

"The author of the article," she had told him, grinning impishly, "suffers from adverbosity." Thus her technique of "verboid remodelization" as she termed it, had created another word for their lexicon. And he had gone along with little comment until she had selected and bestowed upon him a pet nickname. A while passed before he ceased to cringe each time he heard it.

"Why Boo for god's sake?" he demanded.

"Why Boo for god's sake? Ha! Because to me you're

Boo because for me Boo fits you for god's sake, that's why Boo for god's sake."

It was here that he had the good sense to give up, for he also enjoyed the delight it gave her to spring words of her own manufacture on him, and it was not long after he received the nickname that she confessed to him contritely: "I can't help it, Boo. I'm just an impressionistic verbalizer of the semantic articulitis school with obsessive plethormania for anti-clichéikkiness." He had taken her seriously until he saw the merriment dancing in her eyes.

"But all that with Kleyr Boriquen was long ago and far away," Bucher growled to himself as he watched her now, in the Dainty Dish as Mary Jo Philasheo, mince down the runway toward the dais.

Luigi Nappo, meaty face bloated with drink and lust, lurched to his feet as she neared, grabbing at one of her ankles when she passed. But coarse, inflamed Luigi Nappo, at twenty-five filled with the fire and vinegar of youth, was not to be gainsaid by her adroit evasion, preferring instead to loudly acknowledge the assumption of a presumed game of catch-as-catch-can to now exist between him and the enticing feminine morsel on the dais. Remaining on the floor, he lumbered after her in drunken pursuit. She had no difficulty in evading the lout by the simple expedient of moving to the opposite side of the dais whenever he approached her, nor did his attempts to grab her interfere with her tossing individual tiny orchids from her bouquet into the excited audience. The bouquet was becoming depleted when she leaped lightly from the dais, gave a portly fellow an orchid and bussed his bald pate, then continued to trip gracefully among the spectators bestowing both orchids and kisses on the men, Bucher not fully aware of her design until she dropped an orchid on his table, pressed a second into his palm, and bent to kiss him, quickly whispering instead:

"Outside in two minutes."

Her breath against his lips, her nearness, but most of all an absence of any anger toward him, plus the aura of glad surprise to see him filled Bucher with a joy so fierce it bordered on the dangerous—and seconds later proved to

11

be dangerous for Luigi Nappo. For the instant Kleyr turned to continue her trek through the spectators, Nappo arrived at Bucher's table. This time Kleyr did not succeed in evading the man, who seized her nymphian body in a powerful bear hug.

"Haw!" he shouted exultantly, unaware that his oafish conduct sparked a powderkeg. "Gotcha! And I'm gonna have me some of yours, little babe!"

In a single flow of motion Bucher dropped the second orchid into his coat pocket, rose to his feet, the now-empty hand a balled fist heavily armored with brass knucks. An involuntary whimper of pain sprang from Luigi Nappo's thick lips when the vise crushing his shoulder spun him around . . . Kleyr deftly wriggled free, raced for the dais, leaped upon it, and as Surd Gulgar scurried from his corner to the men's room as an excuse for not going to Nappo's aid and thus facing Bucher, fled down the runway and disappeared behind the curtains as Bucher's mailed fist descended like a mace of doom. A guttural scream spewed from Nappo's wrecked face when Bucher dropped the man to the floor and quickly exited the Dainty Dish, anxious to be with Kleyr again. And anxious also to know why a brilliant radio astronomer like herself was cavorting about naked as the female half of a rut-in-public nightclub act. The cool springlike night air felt good on his face as he crossed the street toward his rented van.

"Psssssssst!"

Bucher turned toward the sound.

"What is it?" He well knew the sound came from Kleyr.

"Open the rear doors of the van." Her voice carried an undertone of mirth. "I've lost all my orchids."

Promptly he obeyed, and a moment later Kleyr Boriquen emerged from the lilac bushes, raced across the street, and dived head first into the rear of the Dodge.

"How's *that* for streaking? Caramba! Am I lucky; who put this mattress on the van floor? Get us away at once! There's a dead man in the Dainty Dish! At once! Go! Go!"

"Where to?" Bucher switched life into the van.

"Anywhere! Do you know the road past Rio Grande? Highway 3? But hurry! We'll go to Luquillo Beach."

Because of Puerto Rico's small size Bucher had been able to commit most of the main highways to memory from a map on the flight from New York. "I know Highway 3, yes." Bucher poured on the gas.

"Quickly then! We go!"

2

Bucher concentrated on his driving, keenly aware all of a sudden that the girl who knelt on the mattress behind him was the same person that a few years ago he dealt with so shamefully. They had left the older part of the city, passed through metropolitan San Juan and were on Highway 3 heading east when Kleyr's soft arms crept around Bucher's neck from behind.

"You low-down no-good worthless cruel and inhuman heartless son of a beast," she purred, nuzzling his neck. But she did not continue to purr. *"Damn you!"* she screamed. "Why?" She commenced pounding his shoulders with both fists. "Why? Damn you, *why?* Who was I to you at Hibbings Summer Lodge in the Catskills, eh? *Who was I, beast?* The original twenty-four hours a day shack job?" Her voice became choked and her anger flagged. Despite an explosive, tempestuous nature she had never been able to remain angry with Bucher longer than a few seconds.

"I've got it coming," Bucher said, slowing a bit and hugging the right side of the road. "Go ahead."

"W-Why did you do it, Boo? When I w-woke up that morning, I wanted to d-die."

"So did I," he told her honestly.

"W-What?"

"I wanted to die that morning too, when I found out." He could almost hear her thinking, weighing his words against the facts as she remembered them.

"Then w-why did you do it, Boo?" she pleaded, arms tightening about his neck. "And *don't* try to sell me the

13

idea I failed to please you as a woman." She frowned into the darkness behind Bucher, biting her lower lip, one moment not at all certain this was not the reason behind his conduct, the next moment positive it could not be. But— por Dios Jesus! she thought desperately. How could she have failed? When, except for odd moments, their entire first three days at the lodge in the Catskills had been spent in bed? And even when hunger drove them forth on the evening of the third day, he made arrangements with the wonderful old couple owning the lodge, the Hibbings, and thereafter all meals were delivered to their rooms. For over a week. And then ... and then she had awakened that morning, that terrible, horrifying morning to discover herself all alone, totally, completely, absolutely alone. No note of explanation. No anything, except a thick stack of hundred dollar bills on the nightstand. For services rendered, she had thought a few million times since that morning. For temporary use of my body. She had spent exactly one dollar and two cents of that money; the remainder of the money was now at her home in Arecibo in an alligator wallet he had bought her as a gift. But that day of his disappearance a dollar and two cents; ninety-eight cents plus four cents tax for a ten-foot length of stout hemp rope—but the Hibbings had grown suspicious, broken into her room, and cut her down, thwarting her attempt to end her agony and her life, both of which that day became and remained one for many months until, by power of will alone, she had forced herself to forget. Or so she had thought until tonight.

"Boo. Answer me. Why did you do it? We were in love, were we not? No man ... No woman ... No two people can ... can ..." She paused, gritted her teeth and tried again. "No two people can share what we shared with each other of ourselves and ... and the entire matter be a *damn commercial arrangement!*" One small hand thrust forward toward the windshield, pointing to a side road on the left. "There! Turn there. Take that road."

"That road doesn't go to Rio Grande and Luquillo Beach."

"So? I change my mind. We go instead to Loiza Aldea. I have cousins who live at Loiza Aldea."

Bucher braked the van obediently and wheeled it left onto another blacktop, but after a mile he let the vehicle drift onto the right shoulder of the road and coast to a stop. He had no idea what part Kleyr played in the disappearing supertankers matter, but now was a good time to find out—after he cleared up his own disappearance that morning so long ago. He patted the seat beside him.

"Come up here, Kleyr. We have some talking to do. About us." Viewed through the perspective of time some eight years later, his decision and subsequent action that particular morning at Hibbings Summer Lodge might appear foolish to her, or perhaps even ridiculous, but—

Kleyr crawled across the back of the single wide seat with Bucher helping, she laughing softly on seeing him remember her state of undress. "I told you I lost my orchids, Boo."

"About that morning, Kleyr ... about me leaving like that, without telling you . . ."

Kleyr nodded but said not a word, sat waiting, a bit breathless now that the greatest mystery of her life was about to be solved.

Bucher took a deep breath to start over—already it was not going as smoothly as he had hoped it might, goddammit.

"How long had we known each other when you were graduated from Cornell?"

"Three months. Three months and four days exactly the morning we drove up to the Catskills. Why?" Unknown to Kleyr, the trusting adoration in which she had held Bucher years ago was reappearing in her voice, and on recognizing it Bucher searched his brain for precise words. It was becoming more important to him by the second that she understand.

"How come during those three months you never told me you were Cornell's number one pride and joy genius? That because of this you attended as a special student?" Silently Bucher swore at himself; it was beginning to go even less smoothly than before, for Kleyr's puzzled expres-

15

sion clearly revealed she did not understand the tack he was taking.

"I—was there any urgency for me to tell you, Boo? I did not neglect to tell you with any intent to deceive, but . . . I was quite taken up with . . . I was quite happy in those days, and I . . . It didn't occur to me, Boo, that you might want to know. You see, I was not aware, until this minute, that you did not know, and since you never mentioned the matter . . . I didn't either. Is that the reason you left me? Because I didn't tell you?"

"Wait a minute, wait a minute, dammit, I'm doing this all wrong." Bucher massaged his face roughly with a big hand. "Do you remember that alligator wallet I bought you to carry your university pass, library cards, credit cards, that photostat of your birth certificate, and things?"

"I remember. Yes. I remember. What about the alligator wallet?"

"Well, the morning I suddenly left, I'd been to the bathroom—you were sound asleep—and when I went into the bathroom the alligator wallet was in your purse, which sat open on the chair near the door; where the night light was? Anyway, I was half asleep, and I must have brushed against the purse strap in passing the chair, because when I came out of the bathroom, the purse was on its side, and the wallet lay on the floor, open at that card holder containing the photostat of your birth certificate. When I picked the wallet up from the floor, I automatically glanced at the birth certificate. That's when I found out. That's when I learned the truth."

"The truth?" Her large limpid eyes beheld him in bafflement. "What truth, Boo?"

"The way you wore your clothes, your makeup, the way you acted and talked, and your having graduated from the university and all . . ."

"You left me because I graduated from . . . ?" She refused to believe and sat staring at him.

"No. Not that, Kleyr; Christ. The birth certificate . . . I damn near went into shock when I saw it."

"Boo. For heaven's sake. Saw *what?*"

Again Bucher took a deep breath, then let it go in a

16

rush. "When I saw I was in love with a child only fifteen years old."

Silence. Thick, heavy silence descended inside the Dodge van. In the feeble light from the dashboard, Kleyr's large limpid eyes held Bucher's transfixed, as she herself sat transfixed in a form of suspended animation, too stunned by his totally unexpected revelation to breathe until the desperate force of her oxygen-starved lungs lifted her chest in a long and tremulous intake of air. Yet she made no other move. Only sat, in effect suspended between past and present while through her mind flickered all the thousands of reasons, both possible and impossible, she had dwelt on over the years as being behind Bucher's strange behavior in the Catskills. And not once, never for one single instant, had it *ever* occurred to her that his concept of moral propriety might be the reason, that the precepts and tenets of the private code she knew he lived by forbade any sexual relationship with a fifteen-year-old girl. But his leaving her so abruptly, without a word, vanishing from her life without saying goodbye she did not understand. Though when he continued talking, she began to understand.

"I hated myself," he told her quietly. "Every time I saw a reflection of my face, my blasphemy and my shame and self-contempt multiplied a thousandfold." He lifted one of her small, delicate hands to his lips and kissed the fingertips. "You see, all my life in the Syndicate I'd done a lot of things that would gag a self-respecting hog, but when I broke with the Syndicate, I adopted what seemed to me to be a proper code of conduct to live by, and this code does not permit—"

"Your getting in bed with a fifteen-year-old girl?"

"That's right."

"Not even if you *love* her?"

"Especially if I love her. In my book there's no excuse for it. Nor forgiveness."

"Oh."

Again they sat in silence, now for a much longer time, each busy with memories of their past times together, and since Kleyr already knew much of the rigid do's and don'ts of his personal code of honor, she was quick to understand. Nor did she need to have an explanation for his not contacting her at a later time; her knowledge of the code gave her that, also. At last she released a soulful sigh, one that spoke of dead sorrows and new joys to come, and said, happiness visible in her large eyes, in the tempting tease of the smile flirting with her mouth:

"Then I forgive you, Boo." Eyes closed, lips held up to receive his kiss; "providing you ecstasize me right now and—"

Bucher lost no time in complying with this delightful condition of forgiveness, pleasantly surprised with himself at recalling after so long a time that the word "ecstasize" in their private lexicon of intimate expressions meant "kiss." When the "ecstasizing" necessitated a pause for breath, she continued talking from the point where she had stopped:

"—providing also that you frequently recall I am no longer fifteen years old." Her plump, cone-shaped breasts lifted with her deep breath, and she biffed him delicately on the chin with a small fist. "Thanks to you, lout, I am probably the most thoroughly un-earthquaked female in Puerto Rico today, if not in the Western Hemisphere." She laughed softly, a magnetic, throaty expression of inner joys, and squirmed closer in the snug circle of his arms.

"From all indications you were well on your way to being earthquaked, in public, with an audience yet, at the Dainty Dish tonight."

"Oh, mercy." She leaned back to look into his face. "These past few minutes I'd almost forgotten about that horrid place."

"You told me some guy was dead in there."

She nodded solemnly. "Dingus Koonilinges; his real name is Arnie something-or-other. I don't remember, really. Someone cut his throat." A small shudder quivered through her nude body. "And Martha's dressing room was a wreck. Martha Andrews; she's the Dainty Dish's Mary Jo Philasheo, poor dear."

Bucher started the van and pulled back onto the black-top, proceeding along the comparatively deserted road at

18

moderate speed. "What was in that second orchid you gave me tonight?"

"An address to tell you where to meet me later; the home of Dr. J. M. Philbrick, in Arecibo. He's a retired psychologist and writes these huge tomes medical schools are beginning to use as Bibles. I've known him all my life, and I thought if the police came or we got separated or something, we could always meet at Dr. Philbrick's home." She searched through his coat pocket until she found the orchid and unrolled a narrow strip from around the stem. "See?" She stuck the note back in his pocket and tossed the flower out the window.

"Then it was you watching me through the curtains on the stage."

"You saw me? Caramba! Yes, it was I. When I saw you enter, I almost fainted from surprise. I had just found Arnie's body and was terrified."

"And the real Mary Jo was not there?"

"You really believed me when I said she was gone, didn't you?" Kleyr marveled. "I mean, you believe there is another Mary Jo don't you, and that I'm not her?"

"Shouldn't I believe?"

"With me coming out naked like I did, not many men would."

"What's the name of this place we're headed for?"

"Loiza Aldea. I have cousins there and can get some clothes to wear home tomorrow." She looked over the top of the seat back into the rear of the van. "Why the mattress and the canned goods and all?"

"Against getting out in the boondocks somewhere without a bed. It has happened. The food and bottled water are just in case."

"Splendid. Aldea has a superb place for swimming. After we stop at my cousins', how about spending the night there?"

"How long had Arnie been dead?" Bucher wondered about the man getting killed in the Dainty Dish on the night he had visited the place.

Kleyr did not answer at once, but at last said: "I got the very distinct impression when I found the poor man that he had just the instant before quit kicking. Peculiar sounds had come from his dressing room and the door was ajar. That's the only reason I found him. The sounds and the door. But I can't imagine what on earth happened to Martha—Mary Jo. Her real name in Martha Andrews, Mrs. James Andrews. She's from Miami, Florida, where her three children are in boarding school. Her husband is in prison for bank robbery."

"You've known her long, then?"

"For several months. We met on one of the beaches at Arecibo; I didn't know then she was Mary Jo. Martha is one of those rare people everybody likes and who has never had an enemy in her life. We got to be good friends before I knew she worked at the Dainty Dish. I think she expected me to begin cold-shouldering her because of her job, but when I didn't ... well, as I say, we're good friends. She heard about the Mary Jo job while in Miami, and with her husband in prison and three children to support, she came to Puerto Rico and applied for it. Every cent she earns above barest living expenses goes to her children. Boo, she's not a bad person, not at all the type one would expect to be a Mary Jo at the Dainty Dish. It was at her insistence, by the way, that the owners of the Dainty Dish changed the two last names of her and her partner to Philasheo" and "Koonilinges." Before that they were billed as Mary Jo Fellatio and Dingus Cunnilingus."

"You say her dressing room was a wreck when you saw it?"

"A total wreck. It looked as if someone had torn the place apart searching for something."

Bucher had been waiting ever since she'd jumped into the van for her to say something about vanished supertankers and related reasons for his being in Puerto Rico and now, at long last, she did, but she approached the subject obliquely.

"I work with the Arecibo Observatory in Barrio Esperanza, here in Puerto Rico. The Observatory is a part of the National Astronomy and Ionosphere Center, which is operated by Cornell University under a contract with the

20

National Science Foundation." She stopped, looking at him curiously.

"Go ahead."

"Well, Boo, it's only an idea of mine, not even a theory actually. But from somewhere I get the ridiculous notion that the Arecibo Observatory is related somehow with the mysterious goings-on in the Bermuda Triangle." Again she stopped, again looking at him curiously.

"So?"

"So, Boo-Boo, I told my superior at the Observatory, Dr. Bartlet, like in pears, and she promised to relay my foolish idea up the ladder to the proper authority."

"Maybe your idea is not so foolish. Two supertankers simply do not vanish into thin air."

"I wouldn't be too sure about that, Boo-Boo. Perhaps those two Syndicate gangsters in the Dainty Dish tonight aren't down here for frolic and fraus."

"Huh? What Syndicate gangsters? How would you recognize Syndicate gangsters?"

"I wouldn't. But Martha pointed these two out to me some time ago. They were in Arecibo where I live, and where Martha has a place also, and she pointed them out to me ... Let me make a point of saying this: I don't go to the Dainty Dish escorted, unescorted, when Martha is not there, or when she is. Do you read me?"

"I didn't ask. It's none of my business."

"I know you didn't ask, but it's a helluva lot of your business, Mr. Boo, because no man wants his woman to hang, to have hung, or to be going to hang around a filthy place that sells tickets to a pornographic sideshow, and until you pull the vanishing American bit on me again, you might as well get accustomed to having me under foot and to thinking of me as your woman, because *I am*. Why else do you think I'd take off all my clothes tonight and come prancing out there stark naked?"

"It's occurred to me. Why did you?"

"I was at the Dainty Dish tonight to meet a contact who turned out to be you. Dr. Bartlet said this cloak and dagger stuff always takes place in bordellos, sleazy flophouses, in places like the Dainty Dish and the like,

21

which is why she arranged for me to meet you there. I wasn't there for any other purpose and above all not to take my clothes off. When I arrived at the Dainty Dish for the purpose of meeting my contact, you, I had five or ten minutes to spare and went around back, entering through the rear door—the management never goes in back when Martha's act is about to begin—to have a few words with Martha. That's when I found her dressing room a wreck and Arnie-Dingus dead in his. Then I peeked through the curtain and saw you, then saw the two gangsters and feared they might shoot you, so I jerked off my clothes, got the orchids the management always buys for Martha, and came prancing out front like a goof, hoping to attract the gangsters' attention so you'd have a chance to get away, and you know the rest. Whew!" She grinned engagingly. "I can talk a blue streak, can't I?"

Bucher looked at her somewhat agog, not from her running dialogue or because so much had been taking place in the Dainty Dish, but because she had done it all by herself. And for him. And only for him.

"The hoods," he said. "Who did Martha tell you they were?"

"Luigi Nappo and his bodyguard."

Bucher shook his head; he knew a Big Jute Nappo but not a Luigi. And Big Jute, as far as he knew, had no relative named Luigi.

"You don't know him?" She was incredulous.

"Afraid not."

"Have you ever heard of Jute Nappo?"

"Hell, yes!" Big Jute was a *capo*, a hundred percent Syndicate and mean as a barrel of rattlesnakes just for the hell of it. "But Big Jute wasn't at the Dainty Dish tonight."

"Oh, darn it, I know that. But his kid brother Luigi was."

"Well, I be damn." Bucher frowned, remembering. "Which one was he?"

"Well of all things!" Kleyr said in amazement. "He was the gorilla you clobbered for grabbing me. Didn't you recognize him?"

22

"That was Big Jute Nappo's kid brother? I didn't even know Big Jute had a kid brother—else I'd have busted him harder. What about the bodyguard?"

"An elderly man. Neat dresser. But an odd name. Suds? No, not Suds. Surd! That's it!"

"Surd Gulgar?"

"That's it; then you do know him."

"Sure. Gulgar used to work for me sometimes, before I broke with the Syndicate. Gulgar's been Big Jute Nappo's bodyguard and flunky for years now. What could he be doing in Puerto Rico with his kid brother Luigi?"

"Martha said she heard a rumor. At the Dainty Dish. Luigi Nappo is down here in exile, in a manner of speaking, until his brother Jute can smooth over some trouble he caused in New York. Or was it Miami?"

Bucher studied her from the corner of his eye in no little wonder, experiencing a strange, heady elation from knowing she had gone to such extremes for his sake, to protect him when she had assumed him in danger. The fact that her assumption had been in error had absolutely nothing to do with it. She had thought him in danger and had thrown herself into the battle at his side without a word, without even considering the risk or consequences of failure; in a classic example of what psychology termed "ultimate devotion." Bucher was about to comment on this, when Kleyr pointed toward a dim glow of lights ahead in the distance.

"There," she said. "That's Aldea—Loiza Aldea. Soon we will be at the home of my cousins, and I will then have clothes to wear home to Arecibo."

Kleyr was mistaken in this. She did not get clothes from her cousins. Her cousins were not at home, which she and Bucher discovered after she coached him through a maze of side streets and alleyways in Arecibo.

"But I don't understand," she said, after calling from the cab of the van several times, in both Spanish and English, from where Bucher had stopped the vehicle close to the house in front of the door.

"Would you like for me to go knock?" he asked her.

"It would do no good." Kleyr was obviously puzzled.

"There is no one at home; I cannot understand why. They never leave the house by itself. I hope you don't object to me going nude."

"Silly woman."

"Because now I must wait till we reach my place in Arecibo." She indicated with a nod. "Drive that way to the dead-end and turn right. We will be at the beach in only minutes. It is not a balneario, not a public beach that is tended, but there are tables, an outdoor fireplace of stone, and it's clean."

"The day I get this freaky case cleared up, I'm starting a long vacation," Bucher mused as they pulled away from her cousins' house. "Could you help me survive a few months of frolicking from beach to beach here in Puerto Rico?"

"You try to frolic without me, buster, and I'll mow you down." Yet she eyed him as if she suspected he might be teasing. "When did you decide on a long vacation in Puerto Rico?"

"Well, I'd say it was about the same time I saw Mary Jo at the Dainty Dish tonight." Inexplicably the flushed, meaty face of Luigi Nappo popped into his mind on the heels of these words.

"Thank you, kind sir. I'm flattered, though not because you first saw me after all these years when I was doing the Mary Jo bit." She was silent for a moment, then clapped a palm over her mouth to stifle a rush of giggles. "Imagine a tooth enamel test each night."

"A what?"

"Don't tell me you've forgotten the tooth enamel test."

Bucher frowned in effort to recall, but failed, at last shaking his head. "You got me."

"You *have* forgotten. Oh, Boo." The way she said it made his lack of memory sound like a capital offense. "You remembered 'ecstasize' readily enough. And 'earthquake,' so ... You don't remember? It was about a week before we went up to the Catskills. Don't you remember the verbal holocaust over that little underground high school newspaper the students were turning out on the sly in the school printshop? Merciful heavens. I'll bet there are

24

plenty of parents in New York who still remember it well, after reading in the prestigious *Times* a verbatim account of a student group discussion on the question: 'Is oral sex harmful to tooth enamel?' "

"The *Times* reprinted that entire issue of the underground paper that ran the group discussion," Bucher cut in, remembering now, but also now thoughts of Big Jute Nappo had joined those of Luigi Nappo in his mind. Was it possible that the brothers Nappo could have swiped two supertankers? Big capers were right up Big Jute's alley, so to speak. "Think big" was the man's favorite expression, and the bigger the caper, the better Big Jute Nappo liked it. But where, Bucher demanded of himself, had Big Jute kept brother Luigi hidden all the punk's life? He could not remember Big Jute having a brother. Maybe White Hat would be able to dig up some facts on Luigi Nappo.

Bucher joined Kleyr as she was saying:

" . . . and doing all those things."

"All what things?"

"All *what* things?" Her perplexity was evident. "Well ..." Then, after half a minute: "All those things you taught me at that lodge in the Catskills, worm. That's *what* things."

From this last Bucher took his cue, now knowing the subject she pursued. "So what's wrong with the things I taught you at that lodge in the Catskills? You wanted to learn, and as I remember, and, believe me, I do remember, you were an exceptionally apt and avid pupil. Everybody does *those* things."

"In *public*? Before an *audience*? Would you take a tooth enamel test in public?"

"Oh. I see." Bucher realized she'd lost him somewhere along the line. Or he'd lost himself.

"Oh, I see, he says." She snapped her fingers in front of his face. "Hey, Boo. Come back. It's been a long time. Do you recall what 'tooth enamel test' means?"

"You included it in your collection of synonyms in the lexicon as 'oral sex' as I recall."

She addressed an imaginary throng of people, indicating

him with a gesture. "You see folks. It not only talks. Under certain conditions it can even remember."

"What did you say the real Mary Jo's real name is?" he asked.

"Boy, if you don't beat all," she said slowly, eyes on his face.

"Okay. I confess. I was thinking about the Nappo brothers too and missed part of what you said. What was it?"

"Nothing really. Mostly idle chatter. I said Martha must love her three children very much to take the tooth enamel test at the Dainty Dish every night. With Dingus."

"And what is her last name?"

"Andrews. Martha Andrews. Why?"

"I'm not sure. But she seems to hear a lot of Syndicate information. Does she hustle on the side? I've known goons who'd spill their guts to a broad in bed, but the DA couldn't get the broad to tell their names and addresses in court. Perhaps that's how she gets her Syndicate information."

"I don't know if she moonlights or not, Boo, but—there! There!" She pointed to a soft-surfaced side road. "It takes us to the beach. See?"

Bucher saw. The house of Kleyr's relatives was on the edge of town, and since leaving it, they had been traveling away from Aldea. Now, as Kleyr pointed, the lights of the van revealed a thick band of palm trees, and beyond the trees Bucher saw light reflect off the water-sheen of the surf.

"There are two outdoor picnic tables," Kleyr told him as they entered the palms. "An outdoor fireplace to cook on, and the swimming is superb. There. See those tables? That's the place."

She was out of the van and racing toward the water almost before the vehicle stopped at the end of one of the tables. And when Bucher switched off the lights, thick blackness imploded silently around him and the van, creating total invisibility until his eyes adjusted to the lesser light. Even after his eyes became accustomed to the

26

darkness Bucher remained in the cab of the Dodge, thinking.

Thinking of the Nappo brothers, and not sure he believed the gorilla he had busted at the Dainty Dish was Big Jute's kid brother. It was possible, but he wanted to know where kid brother had been all his life, and also wanted to know what kid brother and Surd Gulgar were doing in Puerto Rico. How Martha Andrews got her information about the Syndicate was another thing he wanted to know. And why was Dingus-Arnie whatever-his-name-was killed tonight? Why tonight? Why not last night? Or why not tomorrow night? And why had Martha Andrews' dressing room at the Dainty Dish been wrecked? "Looked as if it had been torn apart from somebody searching it," Kleyr had said, or words to that effect. And why, Bucher grimaced in distaste at the thought, was he trying to tie these shabby events and even shabbier people in with the vanishing of two multimillion dollar supertankers? "The trouble with you," Bucher told himself aloud, "is that you—"

"Bucher! You lazy ape! Don't sit there like a dullard! Come *on!*"

Bucher responded with alacrity to Kleyr's command, tossing all his garments into the rear of the van, except his T-shirt, in which he wrapped the Walther P-38. He had parked within a foot of the end of one of the heavy wooden tables and was forced to turn sideways to pass between the end and the side of the vehicle. When he neared the water, he placed the Walther a few feet above the high-wave mark and turned toward Kleyr Boriquen, who stood mid-thigh deep out in the surf watching him with enormous impatience.

Kleyr's heart, earlier, at the Dainty Dish, had begun doing ecstatic flip-flops the instant she had recognized Bucher and was still doing them. And all the years of self-denial she had imposed on herself, except for one instance the year before last when she had tried to substitute for him and failed miserably, were now focusing into ravenous feminine hungers too long thrust aside in favor of her work at the Observatory. But she was no longer thrusting them aside. They were to be appeased, to the ul-

27

timate degree, up to and far, far beyond the point of sur-
feit, and when Bucher left her this time, if he left her, this
time she would not resort to a rope, for she would have
his child to comfort her. At the thought of having
Bucher's child, she seized herself with both arms, hugging
herself deliciously. Eeeeyi! How sweet to be alive!

3

Without knowing it, as Bucher straightened from placing
his Walther on the sand, he was in much the same frame
of mind as Kleyr Boriquen. At least for the moment he
was free of high-tension strain from the pressure-cooker
life style Fate forced on him when he broke with the Syndicate. The immediate environment was doing its share to
promote his present mood also: the fat, silvery globe suspended in the heavens, stars remarkably sharp and clear,
the gentle caress of night breezes drifting off the tropical
waters to sift through the palms behind him—and the
vivacious, impulsive angel-come-to-earth in the form of
Kleyr Boriquen, who stood watching him from a few
yards out in the water. Bucher's laughter was good and
free; a happy reflection of joy from being fascinated and
spellbound by her fetching sparkle, by her spontaneous en-
thusiasm and zest for life, and by the utter and absolute
feminine femaleness of her.

Then Kleyr was hurrying toward him through the water.
Moonbeams danced off the springy play of her curls and
bathed the immaculate perfection of her nude body with
gossamer silver. And Bucher stood without moving, luxuriating in this moment of theirs, watching as she skipped
from the water across the few yards of sand to stop in
front of him a step away. Then Kleyr tilted her face a
fraction, and the moon revealed it to Bucher in greater
detail. He braced himself. The delightful mischief of the
saucy smile flirting with her ripe lips suggested he might become the object of some playful prank of hers.

"Hummm." Forefinger against one cheek, she surveyed

28

him in critical appraisal from crown to toe, merriment dancing in her limpid eyes. "Hummm, I'm not sure I don't prefer you naked to clothed, ape, in spite of all those scars. And you seem to have retained all your, ahem, parts, shall we say? since we hibernated at Hibbings Lodge in the Catskills." Slowly she circled him, still pretending to be doing her critical survey. "And I assume all your parts are in working order?" She came around to stand in front of him again. "Are they all in good working order, Boo?" For a second from between her lips a pink tongue peeked impudently at him in sly suggestion, and as mirth overcame her, Bucher began to suspect the reason behind her delightful charade.

Ignorant of her youth and innocence at the onset of their visit to the Hibbings Lodge, Bucher had been appalled, literally, by her vast lack of knowledge concerning the ways of man and maid. Yet she had perceived the enormity of his knowledge and insisted he teach her everything. He complied. He had taught her everything, and the results amazed him, for straightway she became the aggressor. Also a relentless practitioner. He also knew what was coming when her mirth subsided as surely as if he could read her mind. Nor was he mistaken.

She tiptoed, drew his head down to hers, hooked both arms about his neck and clung to him, electrified quivers shaking her body; and continuing to shake her until Bucher cradled her in his arms and waded into shoulder-deep water.

"Uncouth beast," she smiled at him after paddling about for some time.

"What's on your evil little mind, cherrybomb?" Bucher smiled.

"You know what's on my evil little mind, lout, so let's be about our obligations, huh?" She giggled impulsively. "Before this water turns to steam. Come on."

It was she who picked up the Walther when they emerged from the water, insisting impatiently: "Come on, Boo. It's *late!*"

It was not late in time as time was recorded by Bucher's chronograph when they entered the rear of the

29

van; the moon was still three hours short of its zenith when he reached for her and she whimpered wanly: "Madre de Dios, por favor-favor-favor," and for a while the time seemed suspended, like the moon in the heavens, suspended but not moving, suspended in a soundless vacuum except for an occasional cry of the "gnome of the forest" turtledove and the "coqui-coqui" of a tiny tree frog; soundless except for the whisper of waves purring on the beach and the softly sighing wind sifting through the palms; soundless except for the helpless and wild-strangled blind-clutching convulsive spasms heard from inside the van, heard repeatedly during the three hours the moon was reaching its zenith.

Bucher reached up with both hands, combed fingers through her silken tresses. "Happy?"

"So happy I'm terrified."

In the moonlight streaming through a window of the van, Bucher's face was outlined in sharp relief; with pursed lips, Kleyr pecked down to the tip of his nose. He drew her head down to rest against his chest.

"Comfortable?" he whispered.

"Mmmmmm."

"How can you be comfortable with your knees so tightly folded?"

"Mmmm, don't worry about me." She squirmed snugly.

"Satisfied?"

"Mmmm, but I'm catching my breath." She added primly: "One must pause to catch one's breath on occasion, mustn't one?" Then, in the tone of confession: "Boo? Are you ready to hate me, Boo?"

"I couldn't hate you if I tried, but if it'll make you feel any better, tell me about him."

She thrust upward to brace on both elbows, and stared down into his eyes in stern wonder. "How did you know it was a 'him'?"

"Because I know damn well it wasn't a 'her,' and the quality of your tone can only mean regret. But I don't, won't, and could never hate you, not for any cause imaginable, including a dozen men daily."

30

"Eeeeyi, Boo-Boo," she breathed against his mouth. "It is no wonder I can never love another. Well ..." Then silence. A long silence, but Bucher waited, his patience at last rewarded.

"Well," she began again, hesitantly, clasping his head between her palms, holding his eyes with hers. "Well ... you'd been gone for years, charging around all over the globe, saving the world with that silly old pistol of yours. Oh, yes, Boo, I've been reading of your derring-dos quite often; and there was another man, not long ago, a few months ago, Charles Everson, a tourist from Boston, Massachusetts. He was staying at a hotel in Arecibo,-where I live—my apartment is near my work—and, well, I saw right away he was going to flip over me, so I let him flip. But no matter how hard I tried I couldn't flip for him, not in any manner." Suddenly she gritted against his mouth: "Damn you—damn you, Boo, *damn* you; I needed you so." For a time she ceased to speak, just lay tight against him, breathing hard with emotion, at last continuing: "Anyway, he kept insisting that he move to my place, and so I finally let him." Again she was silent, for a minute or so, and Bucher was relieved to note laughter underlying her tone when she proceeded.

"Boo, medical science claims human involvement is ninety-nine and ninety-eight one-hundredths percent mental and the remaining two hundredths of one percent physical where sex is concerned; only two hundredths of one percent of human sex activity is physical. This I could never believe, nor accept, until I met Charles Everson, only where he was concerned, with me; it was zero percent, both mental and physical." A curiously baffled expression appeared in her eyes. "Just—zero. The fault was mine of course, or yours, damn you, but he was a complete zero. He did nothing, *could* do nothing at all for me. And he was huge, with broad shoulders, handsome as a movie star, wealthy, well mannered and courteous; my girl friends in Arecibo turned green with envy when he chose me, but he was a complete boudoir zero where I was concerned and he *knew* it. Knew it from the first. You know something, Boo? I thought there was something terribly

31

wrong with me—as there *was*, damn you—and that it might help my case if I could remember exactly how it was with you and me in the Catskills that time. So I tried. I honestly tried. But when all of a sudden I could no longer remember even your beloved-ugly dearest-ugly darling-ugly mug and what it looked like, I knew Charlie-boy had to go. The blow to his gigantic masculine ego was murder, Boo." Her silver-tinkly laughter rippled in the moonlight around them. "You see, Boo, he had a bigoted, narrow-minded and somehow inherently establishmentized evil outlook on sex, plus tons and tons of good old middle class do-gooder American holier-than-thou prudery, so I decided before he left to shake up his pruderized misconstrusions by suggesting a bit of bedroom Americana everyone but his tragic little type has long known as routinely normal. Of course, I couldn't say let's take the tooth enamel test; he wouldn't have known what I meant and besides tooth-enamel-test is from *our* private vocabulary, so I simply placed it on the line in unmistakable terms. He had convinced himself I was frigid, you see, so I said to him: "Charles, perhaps cunnilingus is the answer to my frigidity; perhaps that will break the ice."

Kleyr thrust herself upright in a frenzied paroxysm of mirth, small fists thumping Bucher's ribcage as she squealed with laughter.

"And do you know what that poor neuter-zero did?"

Bucher managed to separate her laughter-garbled words, though only just. After some time she simmered down a bit.

"He—he suggested I see a psychiatrist! It's *true*! He *did*! He thought I was some sort of depraved pervert. Well— I've mentioned Dr. Philbrick to you, haven't I? Dr. J. M. Philbrick? The retired psychiatrist who writes these huge tomes, some of which are being used in favor of Freud? He lives in Arecibo and I've known him all my life. He arrived within the hour, and when he finished explaining some of the facts of life to Charles, I thought Charles would faint with shock. It jarred him to the soles of his feet. And when Dr. Philbrick left, Charles hinted that he'd

32

like to stay for at least the rest of the week since he'd moved most of his stuff in the day before—"

"Two days only?"

"One night only, buddy-boy. By that time I was disgusted by the sight of him, but a hundred times more disgusted with myself—damn you, Boo!" Her open palms cracked smartly against his ribcage. "Can you imagine anything so incredibly—so incredibly dumb? ignorant? naive? *stupid?* Years ago you'd left me flat, simply walked out without looking back and never said a word or anything, yet I was utterly disgusted with myself because of that night with Charles because I had been *unfaithful to you!* I felt dirty, soiled, unclean. And all because—Oh!-Oh!-Oh!-Oh!"

Her eyes protruded oddly and she pitched forward, crumpling on his chest where she lay midst violent shudders that soon passed, and Bucher held her close until her breathing quieted, and then they slept. Bucher was the last to succumb and, two hours later, the last to awaken.

"Boo, darling. Wake up, darn it. I've been thinking."

"Yeah?" Bucher grinned, feeling good all over. "Don't tell me you feel guilty about being unfaithful to Charles Everson."

She bit his chin, clamped her knees hard against his sides, and tickled his ribs furiously with both hands until he captured her wrists.

"You barbarian," she stormed happily. "Another crack like that and I'll slap a noise out of you!" Then a bark of pain escaped her when she moved to the mattress beside him. "Oh, murder," she groaned, grimacing painfully. "See how you torture me, brute?" But her expression relaxed as she slowly straightened both legs, sighing luxuriously as the cozy warmth of relief flushed through them, replacing the discomfort.

"You were thinking . . . ?"

"Yes. What time is it now?"

Bucher checked the luminous dial of his chronograph. "A little past two."

"No later? Well, then, we have scads of time."

"For what?"

"Why don't we drive to my place in Arecibo for breakfast. Then when the day shift comes on, I'll show you the Observatory. It's only a short drive from town to the Observatory."

"I'll buy that." Bucher also wanted to reach a phone to call White Hat in hopes of learning why Luigi Nappo and Surd Gulgar were in Puerto Rico, among other things. "Can we make your place by dawn?" He scrambled out of the van, Kleyr emerging into the moonlight after him.

"Did you say by 'dawn'? We can make it in little more than an hour with no special effort. Don't forget Puerto Rico is only a hundred miles long; Arecibo is just down the coast from San Juan." She took him by the hand, towing him toward the water with an enigmatic little smile on her face. Bucher acquiesced without question, for they needed at the very least a quick dip, in view of Kleyr's insatiable appetite. Following a step behind in the moonlight, he grinned at recalling . . . Kleyr Boriquen fit into no classification familiar to him, so for the present "insatiable" would have to do.

They bathed in silence, and during this time Kleyr found herself unable not to look at Bucher, for she was only now beginning to realize fully the measure of change, of glorious, wonderful change that had entered her life only a few short hours before. As yet she was not certain as to what Bucher would be doing while here in Puerto Rico, but she knew whatever it was, she intended to make sure he succeeded. As yet she had no crystallized plan as to how she might help, but she knew she would do it, regardless. Then, quite shamelessly, she thought: Ayeee, por Dios, what a man is my Boo. What a ferociously lustful animal he is, so violently virile, yet tender as a new mother is he. Still silently, she maneuvered around close in front of him, holding him now with her eyes, impishly murmuring: "Aren't you the least bit exhausted, dear?"

"Never in a hundred years," he grinned, feeling better than before, suspecting nothing.

"Oh, how utterly delightful, dear," she purred against his lips. "I feared you might be too exhausted for any further husbandly responsibilities."

"Any further *what?*"

34

"Don't what *me*, worm." Her eyes sparkled with gay mischief. "You know *what*. Do I talk to you in terms of tooth enamel tests, or shall I have Dr. Philbrick explain the facts of life to you also?"

"No," Bucher chuckled. "I know the facts of life well enough, and you know I do, since I taught you." He shook his head in wonder. Why bother to try reclassifying her when she fit so perfectly into the category headed "insatiable appetite"? "Here and now?" he grinned. "In the water?"

"Of course not, lout. Civilized man has learned to eat at a table. Come on. There is a table at the van."

Seconds later they were on their way to the van, holding hands, walking fresh and free in the gossamer moonlight, when Bucher spoke softly:

"Listen."

Kleyr had heard nothing out of the ordinary, yet the tonal quality of the single word "listen" sent a quick shiver of terror through her naked body. She started to speak, but Bucher was racing for the van.

"B-Boo, what is it?" she whispered when she also reached the van, where he stood at the end of the vehicle, Walther in hand.

"I don't know for sure," he told her in a tight whisper. "Get inside and hand me my clothes."

Kleyr obeyed promptly, and Bucher jerked his clothes on but without ever taking his eyes off the dirt road leading to the blacktop. Someone was out there, on the blacktop, in a car. He had heard the strange vehicle as they were coming from the water, which in itself was not unusual, but the car had been approaching from the direction of Loiza Aldea and without lights, which made no sense. Even with the moon as bright as it was, only a fool or one bent on nefarious intent drove without lights. Then he heard the voices. Two of them. Two male voices. Moreover, the voices were much closer than the sound of the vehicle had been, which told Bucher the strangers had passed the dirt road turnoff leading from the blacktop to the beach where he and Kleyr now were, and were now much nearer the van in the palm trees, but to reach it must come on foot. Or else retrace their way and come

35

down the dirt road. Thus ran Bucher's thoughts. It did not once occur to him that the strangers might not know of his existence; were out for a lark the same as he and Kleyr. His mind did not work that way. And he was alive because it did not; a fact brought home with forceful conviction when he, and Kleyr, heard the two men talking clearly now.

"I tell you they ain't out here, Seeto," a coarse male voice rasped. "Like I told you a hundred times, she's nakeder'n hell, ain't got a stitch on because she left all her clothes in the rear of that joint—that Dainty Dish, and ain't no naked woman doing nothing until she got herself some clothes on. And damn well she can't get no clothes out here."

The voice that replied was thin and reedy and sarcastic. "You've had the jitters ever since we learned she's with that damn Butcher, Mack. You don't want to find the broad. We wouldn't be in this fix if you hadn't glommed onto the wrong one at the Dish. But orders are to hit this little Puerto Rican chick at all costs, and hit her we do, but first we find her. And we find her even if she's with a dozen Butchers, get it; I can use that quarter-million clams on the Butcher's head."

"Well if they're out here, then where the hell are they?" Mack demanded. "Show 'em to me. Otherwise I'm heading back to San Juan; there's plenty of places they can hide in San Juan without coming out here in the boondocks, dammit."

A small motor coughed to life, in rapid succession made noises of turning around, then headed back down the blacktop at quickly increasing speed. Bucher continued to listen long after the vehicle, a Volkswagen in his estimation, passed from hearing, and he wondered if the VW's color was a deep purple. From the inside of the van, Kleyr gulped in fear.

"B-Boo, they were discussing us. Why on earth would they want to kill m-me?"

"Don't worry about them," Bucher consoled her. "I'll take care of both the bums, only—Kleyr, why would the Syndicate have a contract out on you?"

36

"Y-You recognized them? By their voices?"

Bucher nodded, still listening. "Elmer 'Mack' McReady and Seeto Loyoka, two of Big Jute Nappo's sharks. You didn't answer my question. Why would the Syndicate have a contract out on you?"

"I don't know—merciful heavens!" A violent shudder seized her, the stark terror she felt reflected in her eyes as she cried Bucher's name. It took some doing, even with her trying to help, to get a couple of hefty jolts of raw rum down her throat, but between them they at last succeeded, half a pint of the rum spilling down her naked front in the process.

"You'll feel better soon as it takes hold," Bucher told her, returning the quart bottle to the box of foodstuffs in the van.

"I'm already feeling better." In an effort to prove her words she offered him a weak smile; but there was a firm set of her small jaw, and the fear was no longer in her eyes. "The shock," she said with a firm voice also, "the shock of suddenly discovering someone is trying to kill you was a bit much for me."

A smile touched Bucher's bleak visage. She had grit, enough grit to sand down a railroad track. But then he'd known that for years.

"The secret is: don't worry," he grinned at her, the moonlight not strong enough to reveal that his grin was a bit forced. "I'll take care of you. Can you drive?"

"Yes."

"You drive back to San Juan, then. That'll leave me free to take care of any baddies that show up along the way. I'll get us another car soon as we reach town. Unless you can get us beyond San Juan without entering the city. And to Arecibo?"

"I can. It's easy. We'll come out on Highway 2 at Vega Alta."

"Where is Vega Alta in respect to Dorodo Beach?"

"It's beyond Dorodo a good ways."

"Then let's move it."

Kleyr moved it, at times moved it as though she were the original speed demon, but never once was the big

Dodge van under anything but perfect control. As with everything else, Bucher noted, she did it to perfection. There was very little conversation between them during the trip. Even with the roundabout route it was little more than an hour after leaving the beach before the lights of Arecibo began swiftly approaching from dead ahead. Bucher, mind busy with a dozen matters at once, one of which was the defendability of her apartment, asked:

"What is your apartment? Upstairs? Downstairs? End apartment or what?"

"It's ground floor, a stone building with heavy wooden shutters on the windows against tropical storms. Why?"

Bucher ignored the inquiry and voiced a question that had been bugging him since they had overheard goons Seeto Loyoka and Mack McReady. There had to be some big and important reason for sonofabitch Big Jute Nappo to order a little 23-year-old woman hit at all costs.

"Kleyr, what do you do besides radio astronomy at the Arecibo Observatory?"

"Everything?"

"Right—everything."

"Well," she said slowly, thoughtfully, "I write some, about my work, about a branch of theoretical mathematics I'm interested in, I read scads, I piddle around in a little makeshift laboratory Dr. Bartlet, Dr. Philbrick, and I have, I take care of my house, I swim a lot and follow a jogging exercise program—and that's it. Anything wrong?"

"Yeah. Somewhere, only I don't see it yet."

"See what, Boo?"

"The reason for that hit contract on you. Big Jute Nappo is mean and vicious as a rabid tiger, but he's not stupid. He doesn't take unnecessary risks. So somewhere there's a solid reason behind his sharks chasing you. Who are your friends?"

"Dr. Bartlet, Dr. Phil—"

"No-no, who do you horse around with during your leisure time?"

"Boo, I do *not* 'horse' around, except with you, *only* with you—and despite our danger, if you want I'll stop this vehicle right now on the side of the road and we'll crawl

38

in back and horse around some more; you have not, as yet, taken the tooth enamel test. Without you, dear ape, my leisure time would be spent as I told you; writing, reading, studying—"

"Yeah, I'd forgotten that." This was true. He had forgotten that geniuses were simply not like other people.

"Forgotten what, dear?"

He told her.

"Oh, fiddlesticks!" But she was pleased. "I'm no different from any other young woman with my interests."

"That's what I said—the key word is 'interests'; no young woman except the blinding-genius type would dig your interests."

In spite of learning recently she was marked for death, she laughed happily. "I'm a female sex fiend."

"Yeah; ain't it wonderful?"

Her gaiety increased. "I go for tooth enamel tests, so don't think you're going to squirm out of the one I almost had back at the beach."

"I don't want to squirm out of it, dammit, but I do want to stay alive, and keep you alive, so we can run mucho tests in the future. What about that Mary Jo character?" Bucher could not erase the conviction that any woman who did what Mary Jo did at the Dainty Dish, in public, simply had to have a few kinks somewhere.

"What about her?"

"I asked that first, dammit. She may be a connection pointing to the reason for the contract on you."

"I don't see how. I never talk to her except occasionally when we meet on the beach."

"That's all?"

"How on earth could an association with Martha Andrews make someone want to kill me?"

"That's what I'm trying to find out."

"If it weren't for her three children—"

"You've seen these children?"

"No. They're in boarding school in Miami."

"So Martha says. But you have no proof she has any kids, have you? Besides her word?"

"I . . . well . . . But why on earth would she lie about

39

something that could make no difference to me one way or the other?"

"Why on earth would someone want to kill you?"

"Oh." Silence, until a giant Ronrico Rum sign hove into view up ahead, at an intersection, then, grimly: "No one is going to kill me, because that would kill my baby, and—"

"You're pregnant?" Bucher stared in surprise. Charles! That goddamn Charles Everson! He was the father! Kleyr had said her attempt at a—

"Well, I don't take the pill, worm."

"You're pregnant!" Bucher blurted again.

Kleyr's dazzling smile could have melted a heart of stone. "Yes, Boo. I'm pregnant."

"How far gone? How long have you been pregnant?"

"Mmmm, since about nine o'clock last night, wasn't it?" All her restraint collapsed at his expression. She literally shrieked with mirth; so heartily overcome by it was she that Bucher was forced to seize the steering wheel of the dangerously swaying van and right the vehicle—and by this time they had passed the Ronrico Rum sign and had to back up for the turnoff to Kleyr's place.

"Boo-Boo, if you could have seen the look on your face," she marveled at last. "You were thinking of Charles Everson, no?"

Bucher made no attempt to deny this; she had always been adept at knowing his unspoken thoughts on matters where she and he were concerned. Were she a stranger, it would have been alarming.

"There's my place, Boo." She pointed to a large single-story stone building on their right.

"Slow down," Bucher rasped, surprised at the sound of his tone. "Take it easy. There may be an ambush. Where do you park?"

"At the end of the house there. It's a double garage. With a heavy metal door and it can be fastened from the inside." They were within fifty yards of the house when Bucher spoke again.

"Stop, and stay here until I go forward and check the layout."

40

"Oh, heavens! My keys are in my car, and it's parked on a lot two blocks from the Dainty Dish. How will we get in?"

"No problem. But if shooting starts, head for the local police at top speed, okay?"

"Naked and all?" She wasn't scared because she wasn't serious enough for one scared. Bucher replied in kind.

"Yeah, naked and all—and watch those police-types turn green with envy when they see the stable I've got for my horse."

A thorough search of the grounds around the house disclosed nothing, and after a second time through the shrubbery close to the building, Bucher opened the garage doors and quickly stepped aside, free from any possible line of fire. But there was no fire, which brought a puzzled frown to his hard face. Apparently the two gunsels who came to the beach in search of Kleyr had either not thought of staking out her house or had had insufficient time to do so—yet. For a stakeout would come as a matter of course. And be maintained until Loyoka and McReady finished their grisly task—or failed in attempting to finish it.

"And they will fail." The cold savagery on Bucher's face would have caused Seeto Loyoka and Mack McReady to have second thoughts about their mission if they had seen it. "Else I won't be around to know they don't."

After Kleyr pulled the van into the garage, she dismounted and switched on a single electric bulb in the garage for light to enable Bucher to lock the garage doors securely.

"Watch poppa," he grinned at her. "See how I'm going to train our son." He turned toward the door opening from the garage into the house.

"What if it's a girl?" From her tone, Kleyr heartily approved of the subject.

"I hope it is a girl. We want nothing but the best, and the female of the species is far superior to the male."

Kleyr, who was looking around one of Bucher's bent shoulders as he worked on the automatic lock, leaned further around for a look at his face to determine if he teased. "What did you say, Boo?"

"I say women are far superior to men. Women don't start wars, cause famine, plagues; check history. I never met but one woman professional killer in the Syndicate and she was mentally deranged."

"How long have you known this? That women were superior?"

"Since I was old enough to reason—hell, any man who can see around his ego knows women are superior except for brute muscle. Getting him to admit it is another matter. Ah—there she is." He shoved the door open, felt for the light inside, and turned it on.

"Well, I never ..." Kleyr said in amazement at the facility with which he picked the lock. "That lock is one of the most expensive of its kind and—" Bucher caught her arm as she started past him.

"Me first," he told her. Kleyr gasped at sight of the cold savagery on his craggy face.

"Mercy." She gulped. "G-Go ahead then, B-Boo."

Bucher found no one hiding in the house in ambush either, and was openly amazed at the size of the place. "You call this an apartment?"

"It's habit." Kleyr headed for the shower. "I lived in an apartment in town so long I call this place an apartment also. You wanted to use the phone?" She paused, pointing to a door beside a door of a huge bedroom. "In there. My library-study. The phone is on the desk." She disappeared toward the bathroom.

Seated at Kleyr's neat desk a minute later, Bucher dialed his exclusive thirteen-digit White Hat number and waited, surveying the room with curious eyes, through a series of electronic clicks, pops, and related noises, until a quiet voice from several thousand miles away said: "Go ahead, please."

"This is the Iceman," Bucher replied, then proceeded to give a detailed account of his actions and related matters since arriving in Puerto Rico, including Kleyr's address and telephone number where he could be reached for the next few hours. Then he listened. And when he ceased to

42

listen, he returned the phone to its cradle and remained seated at Kleyr's desk, a silent scream of protest searing his brain from the things he had heard, suddenly feeling the clammy presence of Death in the house.

"Why?" he demanded of the four book-lined walls surrounding him. What in the name of all that was holy could a little half-pint angel like Kleyr have done, or be involved in, that made her death an "irrevocable imperative" worth five million dollars? Who had issued such a fiendish order and placed the five million in escrow with the Syndicate to pay for the cursed order being executed?

Almost desperately he studied the face of his chronograph—and the painfully tight knot of tension in his chest began to loosen when he saw the time. Always before he had preferred to work alone no matter how grave the risk, but not this time, for the risk was not his. Hence the relaxing of tension when he realized the help White Hat was sending in a supersonic jet already had plenty of time to have landed at San Juan. Given anything like a chance, any goddamn kind of chance, brother, and he'd ram that "irrevocable imperative" up somebody's backside. Yet what could anyone, any human being on the face of the earth, have done that made his death worth five million dollars? He knew torpedo crews who would fight for a chance to kill the president for five million dollars—and throw in half of Congress as a goodwill gesture to bind the bargain.

Kleyr's desk was of dark, heavy wood, a large desk, and toward the right corner opposite where Bucher sat, two black marble bookends held upright a dozen volumes, all of which appeared well used. Bucher was about to rise from the desk when the author's name of one of the books caught his eye, and he plucked it from the others with sudden, enormous curiosity. She had told him she spent a good bit of time writing, though he had never heard her mention any books of hers that had been published.

"Jesus Christ," he muttered, staring at the title: *Boriquen's Sylurgics* by K. M. Boriquen. "It sure won't ever make a best seller list in Idiotville—or my neighborhood

43

either, for that matter." Then he replaced the volume quickly. Time wasted. Right now he must barricade the house by every possible means.

4

Half an hour later the windows were sealed securely from the inside by the heavy storm shutters and covered with blankets to prevent inside light from shining out, and all the doors were barricaded with the heavier, more solid pieces of furniture. There was no cellar to worry about; therefore all that could be done had been done—except to turn out all lights except tiny penny-watt night lights in sockets near the floor in the living and bedroom. These preparations completed, Bucher took a fast shower to wash off the salt water stickiness of their frolic at the beach, and when he returned to the main room, Kleyr handed him a tall, frosted drink.

As yet Bucher had not told her of the "irrevocable imperative" order for her death, the numerous teams of sharks prowling Puerto Rico in search of her or the five million dollars that went to the bastards who burned him and got to her. He did not want to tell her until the last minute; until he had no choice, or until the promised help from White Hat arrived.

The feeble output of the night light was just barely sufficient for them to see each other as they sat on the sofa in the living room, sipping their drinks—and Bucher did not have to tell Kleyr anything for her to know something was terribly amiss, something of greater fear-causing magnitude than the knowledge that two killers were searching for her. Happily, now that she had adjusted to this knowledge, she no longer felt fear, had felt no fear some time before their arrival here at the house. With Bucher's experience, from things he had told her of himself and from things she had read, if he could not neutralize anyone who came to harm her, then there was no hope anyway, so

44

why be afraid? She shifted hands with her drink and scooted closer to where he sat.

"Hey, Boo-Boo," she whispered close to his ear. "Do you tell momma about it or must I guess?"

"No problem," he said lightly.

"Then why all the worry? And the barricades?"

"No problem until someone comes; until the wrong type of cowboys cut us off at the pass."

"Then you're expecting some good cowboys maybe?"

"Right."

After some moments she captured his chin in one small hand and turned his head toward her. "Boo, is it true that a man wants his woman to be a puritan in public but a versatile and aggressive prostitute in private with him?"

Bucher could not hold back his laughter at this, nor did he want to, for it relieved the tensions that had begun rebuilding. Also, Kleyr's abrupt change of subject was an overt move to divert his worried thoughts into lighter channels. Which, in reality, was the sensible course. The enemy could not enter without their knowledge, so the sensible thing to do was to make the best of a tight situation until either friend or foe arrived.

"You're about as subtle as a ten-ton truck," Bucher laughed, knowing full well what she had in mind.

"I'm not trying to be subtle, nut. I'm trying to get myself made love to. What are my chances?"

"A hundred percent."

"Wow, so prove it." She jumped to her feet, pulling him after her. "Come on into the bedroom and discover what a versatile and aggressive prostitute you have on your hands."

At the door of the huge bedroom, Bucher paused, thinking he heard the sounds of helicopters, and at that instant the extension phone at the head of the bed peeled stridently in the silence. Bucher dashed forward and seized the instrument. A faint radiomagnetic inflection coming over the earpiece told him the caller spoke over a radio phone unit.

"Yes?" Bucher said.

"One-two-three-four-one." The code numbers identified and at the same time confirmed the caller to be White

45

Hat's director Sam White, for the numbers were spoken in a long-dead dialect of the ancient Osco-Umbrians. Massive relief flooded Bucher's big frame; his hand holding the phone trembled with it.

"Is this the cold storage plant of Universal?" The director's voice continued, the words "cold storage" giving Bucher his cue.

"This is Universal's cold storage manager," Bucher replied, also in the dead Osco-Umbrian dialect. "But our systems are gravely overloaded. The Iceman needs all the help he can get."

"Inform the Iceman five airborne carloads are arriving momentarily to alleviate the situation."

Bucher could hear the covey of five swiftly approaching helicopters as he put down the phone, and when he looked across the dim bedroom to Kleyr regarding him in wide-eyed wonder, his already massive relief overcame him.

"We better get some clothes on," Bucher finally said. "Unless you'd rather be introduced nude to some friends of mine."

"Oh, darn!" she replied in pretended great disappointment, glancing in the direction of the bedroom. "I'd rather be reintroduced to you, in there, with both of us nude." Now they stood in the semigloom of the kitchen, scant inches apart, and Bucher could feel a fierce animal heat wafting upward from her small body in determined, aggressive waves. "Don't you want to see your friends turn green with envy when they see where you stable your horse?"

"Get dressed, wench, and get prudish." He smacked her bottom lightly. "The rules are: prude in public and *puta* in private, and for *you* that means in private *only* with *me*."

"Ayeeee," she said over her shoulder on the way to her dressing room, joined to the bedroom by a connecting door. "Now the beautiful life-loving butterfly returns to being a dull and unbecoming caterpillar again. But not a day longer, not an hour or minute longer, than necessary."

Bucher was not to understand what she meant by the butterfly returning to the caterpillar until after he dressed, switched the lights on, and removed the barricading furni-

46

ture from the front door to let White Hat's director, alone, enter. At that same instant Kleyr also entered the main room, and at sight of her Bucher received the distinct sensation of his jaw sagging in surprise. Her bouncy, springy wealth of glossy dark curls was drawn back severely into a tight bun on the nape of her neck, and the cut of her garments, the plain white high-necked, long-sleeved blouse and straight off-gray skirt, was equally painfully severe and quite effectively camouflaged the tantilizing swell of hip and the outward and slightly up-jutting thrust of plump breasts. The thick-soled leather oxfords adorning her dainty feet were the same dull gray of her skirt. But there was more, and at which Bucher felt as if he boggled anew.

Her dazzling beauty was woefully cramped by an enormous pair of horn-rimmed spectacles, which, oddly, reminded Bucher of two one-eyed owls peering simultaneously through glass portholes. Also, the normal, delightful blush of vigorous health of her cheeks was now greatly diminished by overmuch makeup, and to complete the picture an inexpensive but functional ballpoint pen was thrust into her tight hairdo above one ear, and in her hands she carried a small book snugged beneath her breasts. She wore no jewelry of any sort. Not even a watch. Possibly because of the virtually unbelievable contrast between the image she now projected and the vivacious, sparkling, and mischievous nymph Bucher knew her to be, to himself he acknowledged that never before had he beheld, in her present likeness, such an authentic portrayal of the dowdy and juiceless classic character of Miss Puritan Pure Prunella Prude.

"God's very eyeballs!" Bucher let out in surprise; at which Kleyr's midriff region bucked with violent laughter, though the studious, faintly inquisitive expression of her face altered not a whit.

"Yes?" Kleyr turned large eyes on Bucher in obvious request for an introduction to the newcomer, as Bucher closed and rebolted the door.

"This is, uh, a friend of mine." Bucher made vague gestures. "Ms. Boriquen, uh, Sam White."

"Ah, Dr. Boriquen." White Hat's director took Kleyr's hand, and Bucher watched in silent nonbelief as the older man bent forward, kissing it. Sam White continued: "What a delightful privilege to meet in person the world-renowned Dr. Kleyr Maria Boriquen. This moment will occupy a foremost place in my memoirs, believe me."

Kleyr's distant quarter-smile and brief nod accepted this small accolade as her just due. "Perhaps you can explain the why of this untoward, unseemly furor, Mr. White."

"Believe me, Dr. Boriquen, it is neither untoward nor unseemly." The director looked at Bucher. "How much have you told her?"

"She knows there's a contract out on her and that Seeto Loyoka and Mack McReady are trying to find her. She doesn't know about the other torpedoes and the amount of the hit-price." Bucher was now recovered from surprise, though thinking of Kleyr as *Doctor* Boriquen would take a bit of getting used to.

"I see." Sam White dry-washed his hands thoughtfully. "Then, best we acquaint the young lady with the facts of the matter forthwith. But first I have a confession to make to both of you, and perhaps especially to you, Mr. Bucher, all things considered. May we sit, Dr. Boriquen?"

Kleyr and the director sat on the couch; Bucher drew an overstuffed chair in better position to see them both as they talked, none speaking till this was done. Then it was Sam White.

"Dr. Boriquen, the information that you think Arecibo Observatory in some way is linked to the vanishing of the supertankers was forwarded to my office, and it was a veritable godsend." He looked at Bucher. "I told you I wanted you to come to Puerto Rico on the supertanker thing because you're a catalyst, that whenever you're around things happen; that was only partly true. I ask you both to forgive me what might appear to be my poor conduct toward the two of you when I tell you my real reason, Mr. Bucher, was in the hope that you and Dr. Boriquen might reestablish the friendship you had before."

"Friendship where?" Kleyr asked promptly.

"In Ithaca, where you graduated, and . . ."

"And where?" Bucher's tone had a frozen ring to it.

Hastily the director said: "You were *not* spied on during your stay at Hibbings Summer Lodge in the Catskill Mountains, Mr. Bucher. The information that you and Dr. Boriquen knew each other came to light during the mandatory routine security check run on Dr. Boriquen, because Arecibo Observatory is partially funded by government money, and when I reviewed the results of the check recently and learned she attempted suicide when you—" Abruptly Sam White ceased, looked from Kleyr, who sat wide-eyed with fingers covering her lips, to Bucher, who stared at her in surprise. In an apologetic tone the director said, after a pregnant pause, "Well, there goes my big foot in my mouth again."

"No-no-no," Kleyr said, looking at Bucher. "Don't apologize, Mr. White. Boo, is this man your friend—a real friend?"

Bucher only nodded, too shaken at the moment by the knowledge that he had been responsible for Kleyr's attempted suicide.

"Then if he's your good friend, he is also my good friend, and good friends don't snitch on good friends to bowl-bellied Congressmen, so . . ." Off came her glasses, then she unsnapped the hairclasp at the nape of her neck, shook her head vigorously, and her wealth of curls sprang to life at once. "There's no further need for me to continue this egghead bookworm image with you, Mr. White." By way of explanation, she added: "You'd be astonished how quickly dimwitted politicians cut appropriations for scientific research if female scientists fail to measure up to their stupid misconceptions." Then she said to the dumbfounded director: "I hope you don't mind."

"No," he managed with a startled laugh. "I certainly don't. In truth I find it a definite improvement." He continued before either she or Bucher could speak. "Mr. Bucher, I was unaware that you did not know of Dr. Boriquen's attempted suicide when you left her at the lodge in the Catskills eight years ago, but—"

"But now he does know, and it's all over and done with," Kleyr cut in. "So suppose we proceed directly to the business at hand, which, like it or not, seems to be me. I'd like to know why, Mr. White."

"Because someone gave the Syndicate's Big Jute Nappo a five million dollar kill contract on you, Dr. Boriquen, and at this minute ten teams of Nappo's killers, ten that we know of, are prowling Puerto Rico in search of you. We have no reason to believe there won't be more of these killer-teams in Puerto Rico soon. Mr. Bucher, explain what 'irrevocable imperative' means in Syndicate jargon, please."

"The five million dollars is now in escrow, Kleyr, and Big Jute Nappo, in accepting the contract on you also accepted an 'irrevocable imperative' to fulfill the contract, and if he fails to fill the contract, if his men do not kill you, then the five million in escrow goes to the one who kills Big Jute."

"Merciful heavens," Kleyr said quietly. "Are these human beings we're talking about? But why me? Why am I worth five million dollars dead?"

"Dr. Boriquen, while you were at Cornell you were invited to witness an experiment at the Boston Navy Yard, were you not?"

"Why, yes, I was. The Boston Experiment, as it was called. Four scientists who'd done work in the field of electromagnetism were invited to observe the experiment and later render an opinion of its feasibility. I was—"

"The other three are dead, Dr. Boriquen. Murdered."

Kleyr's eyes searched Bucher's face before she looked back to the director. "But why?"

"Insurance, we think. Not insurance as you understand the definition, Doctor, but insurance against them disclosing what they had observed during the Boston Experiment and the possible consequences of that experiment."

"But . . ." Clearly Kleyr was confused. "But all four of us rendered an opinion."

"Correct," the director agreed. "Which tells me that the people who had the three other scientists killed did not know, at the time the killings took place, that you were the only one of the scientists to witness the experiment who

50

saw it as a step toward proving Einstein's Unified Field Theory."

"But the essentials of my paper on the Boston Experiment were really published almost a year before the experiment was conducted. My *Sylurgics*—"

The director interrupted with an apologetic laugh. "Dr. Boriquen, Albert Einstein, or Poincaré, or Voigt may have understood your sylurgics, and we have two mathematicians who are certain they understand most of it, but that's about as far as we've been able to get."

"Am I to be left behind in this conversation?" Bucher wondered aloud.

"You most certainly are not, darling," Kleyr stated with force.

"Then please define *Boriquen's Sylurgics*, if you will," Bucher grinned, largely at the director's quick double take of him from Kleyr's calling him darling. "I saw a volume on your desk when I used the phone earlier."

"Bravo," Kleyr smiled. "That you weren't frightened away by it, I mean; since some men dislike intelligent woman. Oh, yes, I know you aren't one of them, but bravo nevertheless. Sylurgics Boo, is the word I compounded from a group of ancient Latin words as a name for my theories concerning Fourth-Dimension mathematical probabilities."

"Are these theories of yours related to the single-entity concept of time-space and matter-energy transmutable under identical conditions of electromagnetic provocation?" Bucher asked.

Kleyr's face lit with delighted approval and the director expressed his surprise with a less esoteric "By god!" which was followed at once by: "Your record doesn't make any mention of your acquaintance with Einstein's Theory of Relativity, Mr. Bucher."

"That isn't Einstein's Theory of Relativity," Bucher told him. "But his Unified Field Theory."

"By god!" the director said again. "I may not be quite as astute as your former superior despite the similarity of names, Mr. Bucher—do you understand these things? The ones I'm attempting to discuss with Dr. Boriquen?"

"Not really," Bucher laughed. "Though I did read a book once upon a time."

"Then you take the ball right now, young man. You've got the play, but I must warn you that knowledge of the Boston Experiment is intellectual nitroglycerin in more ways than one."

"At the moment I'm far more interested in keeping Dr. Boriquen in her present state of health than in the Boston Experiment," Bucher said. "What have we got outside?"

"Twenty-five of our own men, which include the five pilots, and Dr. J. Joiner Mull, head of the Cambridge Institute of Electro-Dynamics, and who supervised the Boston Experiment, by the way, and Lyle Hardiman, Dr. Mull's nephew and bodyguard."

"Do we have access to the National Guard armories here in Puerto Rico?"

"We have."

"Would you please bring me paper and a pen, Princess?" Kleyr was on her way by the time he finished the question.

"Mr. Bucher," the director said quietly the moment she left the room, his tone apologetic, "I couldn't miss her 'darling' in addressing you a bit back. And I could mash my tongue with a hammer for tattling about that suicide thing."

Bucher laughed good-naturedly to relieve the director's embarrassment for feeling privy to unwarranted knowledge. "It makes me about the luckiest man alive, I guess."

"There's no guessing about it. But doesn't her intelligence keep you on alert? I'd be a nervous wreck in a week. Did you know her IQ is 200 and—" He cut off the instant they heard Kleyr returning.

"Will this do?" She handed him several sheets of yellow foolscap and the ballpoint taken earlier from her hair.

"Perfect." In rough symbols Bucher quickly drew the house they occupied and the surrounding grounds as he recalled them from his cursory survey during their approach and his search of the grounds earlier in the evening. "Kleyr, that other stone building seventy or eighty yards up the street, the one next door. Who lives there?"

"No one. It belongs to me also. We use it for that lab I told you about."

"Good. Things are looking up already." He drew a circle around the symbol for the house they were in. "Start at ten feet from the building and in all directions for a distance of twenty-five yards I want one Bouncing Betty antipersonnel mine each hundred square feet of space— except for the street out front and the cement walkway leading from the street to the front door here. And tie each four mines together with trip wires. Just beyond the perimeter of the outer mines I want a three-tier spread of accordion barbed wire; that's three on the bottom, two on the middle, and a single roll on top, and I want it electrified to maximum voltage. What are our people armed with besides sidearms?"

"Tommyguns."

"Then from the armories—" He looked at Kleyr. "Does Arecibo have a National Guard armory?"

"A small one, yes. The main one is in San Juan."

"Get half a dozen .50 caliber machine guns with both tracer and armor-piercing ammunition, all you can haul; at least four of the 90mm recoilless rifles, and all you can, twenty if possible, of those antijet one-man rocket launchers—" Bucher snapped his fingers in irritation, trying to remember the weapon's name. "The launchers that fire the projectiles straight into a jet's flame tubes. The rockets infrared guidance system that zeros in on the flame and bingo."

"The Minuteman," the director said. "At least that's what they're called unofficially."

"Good enough. Just so *we* know what we're talking about. I also want an armored car. The fastest you can find in a hurry, but the one with the heaviest armor also. A troop carrier won't do, unless it can be closed. A light tank will be best." Bucher paused to watch the director scribbling hurriedly. "Am I going too fast for you?"

"So far no. What else?"

"Floodlights. Big ones. Both the individual portables and the stationary type, for the corners of the buildings and anywhere on the eaves necessary. Circle this building with

53

two lines of the large portables. One line shining over the grounds of the house through the barbed wire, the second line shining away from the barbed wire. Got it?"

"Got it."

"These men of ours you brought with you," Bucher asked slowly, "how would they stack up in a man-to-man kill-quick-or-die blood-gutsy against Big Jute Nappo's killer sharks?"

"Well . . ." The director sat motionless, staring at but not seeing the floor, thinking hard. "Their kill-quick-or-die training, as you so aptly term it, was taught according to that course you helped outline. They're not as fast as you with a pistol, and they miss sometimes, but they're fast and they're good. If they can't outdo Nappo's killers, it's time we folded our tents and silently crept away. What's on your mind?"

"Can they identify Nappo's people?"

"Each man has a photo and a thumbnail biography of every known Nappo man, including Nappo's brother Luigi and Nappo himself. They can identify them all right."

"Send four teams of two men each into San Juan gunning for Big Jute's men, all except brother Luigi and Surd Gulgar, with orders to shoot first and talk second. Only wait until after the defenses for this house are up and working. Now, how did Big Jute Nappo manage to conceal the fact that he had a kid brother for all these years?"

"He kept brother Luigi in school, Harvard yet, under an alias, Oliver Dillingsworth, until recently. Luigi it seems is a brain of sorts. Far above Syndicate average, as we got it."

"And why is he here in Puerto Rico?"

"Luigi is also a sadist. Real gone. He's down here until Big Jute can smooth over a couple of murders Luigi committed for the fun of it."

"Oh, please," Kleyr said in hushed tones.

"Sorry, Doctor," the director said kindly. "But it's our lot, your husband's and mine, to encounter more than our share of humanity's depraved. I'll try to remember." At

54

his mention of "husband," Kleyr gave Bucher a "Hear! Hear!" look and laughed pleasantly, saying:

"That's kind of you, Mr. White, but it really isn't necessary. In time I'll grow accustomed to it."

"How long will it take you and our people to finish forting up this place?" Bucher asked.

"Three hours at the most. Less if we're lucky. You're remaining inside here? With Dr. Boriquen?"

"Constantly. Do we have anything on a woman named Martha Andrews?" Bucher looked at Kleyr. "You don't recall Arnie's last name?"

"I'm not sure I ever heard it."

"Martha Andrews?" The director frowned. "Here in Puerto Rico?"

As delicately as possible Bucher told the older man of Mary Jo/Martha.

"I remember now," the director said slowly. "Wasn't she mentioned in your briefing prior to coming here to Puerto Rico?"

"Only as Mary Jo, and of course that's a house name. When I phoned from here a while ago and learned you had already left New York for Puerto Rico, I asked for a rundown on her and also on the dead Arnie."

"Any idea who killed him? And why?"

"I suspect Seeto Loyoka and Mack McReady, and they're probably driving a deep purple VW Bug." Bucher thought in silence for a moment, then continued. "Listen to this and try it on for size." He grinned at Kleyr. "You too, Missy Doktari. Lend your genius to the peasantry a moment."

Kleyr smiled, poking a feisty tongue at him through the smile, and White Hat's director shook his head in no small amazement that she could remain calm with a huge pod of tiger sharks seeking her blood. Bucher continued:

"Under his flint-hard Syndicate exterior, Big Jute Nappo is as superstitious as they come; oh yes, even to seeking council from chicken entrails, and believe you me, before Big Jute Nappo accepted a kill contract under conditions of the irrevocable imperative, on anybody, and especially one for five million dollars, Big Jute consulted a lot of

55

chicken guts. So let's do this. Whenever our people rub any of his, they hide the bodies so they can't be found at least for a few days. Question: What would a superstitious killer of Big Jute's ilk do if his gunsels began disappearing without a trace?"

Kleyr replied at once. "He would conclude that some person after the five million dollars considered killing him much less risk than killing me."

"Right," Bucher told her, the director nodding. "And then what does Big Jute do?"

"He decides to correct matters by taking them under his personal supervision. By coming to Puerto Rico and filling the contract on me himself."

"Which is exactly what Mr. Bucher wants," the director told her, looking back at Bucher: "Isn't that right?"

"Right. We isolate Big Jute down here in Puerto Rico, cut him off from all help and all hope of help, and then he'll tell me who placed that five million dollars in escrow. Or else."

"Or else?" Kleyr asked quietly.

"Or else I burn the bastard."

"But what if he tells you who placed the five million in escrow?" Kleyr asked.

White Hat's director sat eyeing the two younger people with considerable interest and satisfaction, nodding approval to Bucher's commentary.

"Then I take a chance," Bucher growled. "I grant the son of a bitch a final prayer."

Bucher's impatient gesture dismissed the subject as he spoke to Kleyr. "Does that place of yours up the street have a phone?"

"Yes."

To the older man, Bucher continued: "Call me on the phone to notify me when anyone, such as you, comes to the front door there. That front door will be the only entrance and exit used. Don't let anyone get near that door without a phone-alert unless you want him shot. Okay? And nobody enters that door, even after a phone-alert, except by my personal permission. Not Dr. Boriquen's. Only mine. Otherwise somebody gets hurt. Make sure this is un-

56

derstood outside. I'd hate like hell to rub any of our own people. Now, what are this J. Joiner character and his bodyguard doing here in the first place? Unless they're our people."

"They aren't. Dr. Mull wants to discuss your sylurgics with you, Dr. Boriquen."

"Keep him outside," Bucher said flatly. "His bodyguard too."

"Boo, Dr. J. Joiner Mull is a pioneer in electromagnetism as we understand it today and one of the greatest names in the world's science community, so—"

"Fine, splendid, fantastic, but let J. Joiner play with his electromagnetics and whatever outside for the time being."

"It's your ball game, Mr. Bucher," the other man said as he rose to his feet, obviously pleased with Bucher's precautionary measures. He eyed Kleyr significantly. "You've got the most to lose personally if they get her, so you call the shots as you see them until we get this rat race cleared away." He turned toward the door.

"What about the missing supertankers?" Bucher asked.

The director stopped at the door, turned to address Kleyr: "Dr. Boriquen, I have the authority to release you from that oath of secrecy you signed and swore to before participating in the Boston Experiment, and this I now do insofar as Mr. Bucher is concerned. Explain the experiment to him, will you please? Dr. Mull claims that if we ever discover how to perfect the Boston Experiment, the same principles can be applied to supertankers. Or anything else, for that matter."

"Of course, Mr. White. I'll be glad to explain to Boo. Sir, you say Dr. Mull came all the way to Puerto Rico just to discuss my sylurgics with me?"

"Yes. That's my understanding."

"Then please tender my compliments to Dr. Mull, and tell him I'll see him some time later today—"

"Just tender her compliments," Bucher cut in. "And let it go at that for now." He followed the director to the door. "Mull and his bodyguard stand muster to me before he gets inside the house. Why the bodyguard anyway?"

"When he learned the three scientists who attended the

57

Boston Experiment with Dr. Boriquen had been recently murdered, Mull felt he needed a bodyguard. And his nephew is a pro—of sorts. Chief of Security at the Cambridge Institute of Electro-Dynamics."

"And this nephew's name?"

"Lyle Hardiman."

"Just one other question. I come down here to search for vanished supertankers, but a switch has been made—to protecting Dr. Boriquen—a switch you obviously knew would be made even before I left New York. How did you know?"

"First there are the three murdered scientists who witnessed the Boston Experiment with Dr. Boriquen. These, in my book, said she would either be killed also, or else kidnapped and brainwashed of all she knows. You see, Mr. Bucher, recently we discovered that certain foreign countries have suddenly evinced considerable interest in the results and subsequent analysis of the Boston Experiment. Somebody, somehow, triggered that interest, possibly with plans of selling information related to it to some foreign country. And if we let our scientists get kidnapped, brainwashed, killed and the like without going to their aid or punishing their killers, we'll be cutting our own collective throat, for soon we wouldn't have any scientists, or those we did have would keep their findings to themselves. I didn't mention any of this to you before you left New York because I feared you might not come from knowing in advance you'd be meeting Dr. Boriquen. Then between six and seven this evening one of our people got word of the 'irrevocable imperative' contract for five million on Dr. Boriquen, and we were on our way to Puerto Rico within thirty minutes."

Bucher nodded, waited until the director departed, then closed the door, locked it, and braced a wooden kitchen chair under the knob.

"*Doctor* Kleyr Maria Boriquen," he grinned, turning toward Kleyr. "You might have dropped a hint. That 'doctor' bit is real heavy."

"Oh, Boo! What difference does *that* make? Between us?"

Her de-emphasizing the importance of her title strengthened a suspicion of Bucher's regarding it and her superior intelligence. He walked to where she stood unbuttoning her blouse, still grinning.

"Don't ever feel guilty or be self-conscious because you're more intelligent than others, Kleyr . . ."

"Does it show that much?"

". . . also don't ever denigrate yourself to others. There are plenty of bastards in the world ready and anxious to do it for you."

"Boo, you call yourself only an itinerant gunfighter, and yet you come up with some of the most profound observations at the most unexpected times. But I don't play myself down to you. I have done it to some; to some I've been doing it quite some time, but I never have to you. Not ever. I couldn't. The price would be sincerity. And if two people such as we don't have sincerity, we have nothing, for sincerity is the foundation of all lasting human relationships." She turned her back to him. "Undo me please; the buttons are in back on this blouse. It's one husbandly function you can do standing up."

"Before we get to husband and wife functions—what's with the Boston Experiment?"

"All right. But come on. I can tell you in bed as easily as anywhere else. Try to keep an open mind, though. I don't want you to think me a witch.

"The Boston Experiment was a joint effort of the navy and the Cambridge Institute of Electro-Dynamics, and conducted by Dr. J. Joiner Mull, to use the degausser-type alternating and direct flow magnetism generators to protect metal ships at sea from magnetic mines in time of war. The vessel used in the experiment, an obsolete destroyer, was located out in the water a hundred feet from the pier where we observers stood. Twelve minutes after the power of the magnetism generators was turned on, a thin electric blue haze began to appear around the vessel, the haze at first extending only a few feet past the limits of the ship. But as the magnetic force continued to build the blue haze became more pronounced and extended gradually to approximately seventy feet beyond the destroyer in all directions. Abruptly the blue haze faded, almost as though the current had been switched off, and the entire vessel was as transparent as a window pane, almost invisible. After a minute the haze reappeared, but gradually dissipated within the following quarter of an hour, and when it was gone completely, the ship was back to normal. No one, including Dr. Mull, knew what had happened to cause the ship to almost disappear, and since I was very young at the time, nobody bothered to ask me, and I did not venture any opinion. Not until later, in my written analysis, which set forth my conclusions regarding the experiment also. The essentials of my report were largely based on my *Sylurgics,* which had been published some months previously."

"The essentials of your analysis on the Boston Experiment were already published months before the experiment took place?" This, to Bucher, somehow smacked of locking the barn door after the horse has been stolen.

"The essentials, yes, but *only* the essentials and the essentials as I, only, saw them. As I told you, sylurgics are my theories of Fourth-Dimension mathematical probabilities, but they are *also* a complete system for compounding theoretical formulas of Fourth-Dimension mathematical probabilities. One has enormous latitude between the two."

"Yeah," Bucher replied. "One does, doesn't one?" Christ, he thought wryly, perhaps he should have learned the multiplication tables or long division or something.

Kleyr removed her heavy shoes and her hose and sat on the edge of the bed, frowning. Bucher, already undressed and on the bed, was half afraid to speak further. However, when Kleyr continued to sit there frowning, he urged her to do so.

"Go ahead and say it." He drew her down beside him, her head on his chest. "What made the destroyer transparent as a window pane?"

"Something happened to the magnetism generators. At the time no one knew, and they never did learn the truth. I suspected what had happened and learned later that I was correct. The vessel was almost transmuted into the Fourth Dimension. I reproduced the same effects here in

60

my lab by using the same type degaussers plus one phased in such a way it produced an effect similar to that of a powerful condenser charging and discharging large bolts of magnetic force."

"Did Dr. Mull never discover what happened to make the destroyer transparent?"

"No, not to my knowledge. To my knowledge no one has. However, I've reproduced the same effect but on a much smaller scale. I use a five-foot oxygen cylinder with the ends cut off. I built the generators myself, very small but very powerful ones." She laughed softly. "Boo, what I'm telling you is not for general publication. In fact, it's for no one but you. But don't think me loony. You don't, do you?"

"You know better than that. I just need a minute to get my breath. I'd like to see the experiment some time. What'd happen if the results of your experiment were made public? Became general knowledge?"

"Why—with a little bit of effort and know-how almost any person could transmute whatever he liked into the Fourth Dimension. Remember the atomic bomb and how secret it was at first. With a bit of the right kind of knowledge now, however, one can almost be produced in the ordinary home kitchen. Such as this place here."

"Who knows about all this except you?"

"You."

"Just now? Just like that?"

"Just now. Just like that."

"Why me?"

"Because you're you, nut."

"Yeah, I'll be a lot of damn help. I don't even understand half of what you say."

"I don't need help from someone who understands all about what I've told you."

"How come?"

"I'd get a biased opinion."

"And from me also, only biased with ignorance."

"Oh, shush."

"Kleyr, tell me. Is this stuff of value? The things you've just told me about the Fourth Dimension?"

61

"That depends somewhat on how the information is put to use. Value how, specifically?"

"Fame, money, power, and such."

"Yes. The works. But especially power. With a little imagination one could use the knowledge and, in time, rule the world I suppose, incredible as it seems."

Bucher released a long breath of thanksgiving. "By god, *that's* the reason behind the kill-contract on you! Now we know."

"What's the reason?"

Bucher was silent half a minute, then spoke as if thinking aloud. "Someone—or several—a scientist probably; no, almost certainly a scientist and a good one. But not good enough to master your sylurgics and not good enough to reproduce the Boston Experiment with the same results you get ... but he *knows it can be done,* and knows you have done it, knows without proof you've done it, and he wants the information from you, the information that would enable him to reproduce the Fouth Dimension aspects of the experiment, because without this added knowledge he is stuck solid and can't budge. So— *post hoc ergo propter hoc;* because of this, therefore this; hummm, by god. So this joker places a five million dollar 'irrevocable imperative' kill-contract on you, hoping to frighten you to Kingdom Come, then offers to withdraw the contract on you, providing you give him the information he wants. And when you agree to this, our friend withdraws the contract and you are no longer in danger, but because of the irrevocable imperative understanding of the matter, Big Jute Nappo gets the axe. And the five million price tag tells us our renegade scientist friend has money, plenty of money, enough money so that he can toss away five million without a grimace." Bucher sighed in relief. "And that takes care of that!"

"What takes care of what, darling?"

"When the bum contacts you—call him Mister X for now—when Mister X contacts you for the information or formula he wants, give it to him. Then you're no longer in danger."

5

Bucher lay there motionless on his back luxuriating in the conviction that danger no longer threatened Kleyr; and Kleyr lay alongside him, one immaculate thigh across his loins, head on his chest listening to the measured rhythms of his heart, and searched diligently among her troubled thoughts for the right words to express it, to tell him the truth as she saw it, understood it, words that would not only present her side of the question but would also make him see the matter from her point of view. When she at last concluded there were no "right" words except those related directly to the straightforward truth, she inhaled deeply, in the manner of a child about to undertake an unpleasant task, exhaled, and said:

"No."

Bucher snuggled her closer against him. "No what?"

"When Mister X contacts me for the information he wants to complete his mad scheme, no, I don't give him the information."

A person less rawhide tough than Bucher might have, and justifiably so, reacted with an emotional display, but not he. Due to his pressure-cooker life style his emotions were inured against spontaneous upheaval. Therefore, all he said in reply was:

"Why not?"

"Because of the terrible responsibility. After the last great war, World War II—I wasn't born then but I read the account later—an account written by a colleague told of Einstein's terrible guilt feelings and anguish from learning some of his work had furnished the foundation from which other scientists had constructed the first atomic bomb that killed so many thousands of innocent people. And also placed in the hands of man the ultimate destructive force with which he can easily annihilate himself. I don't have the courage, Boo."

"Is it that dangerous, then?"

"In itself, no. But it can be made to become dangerous with very little effort. It's a matter of technique, really. Not as a destructive force, per se, but it could be developed into one very easily. On a tiny scale, as an example, let's take a political race. Instead of besting your opponent at the polls, you simply transfer him into another dimension before election day. Nor does it take a lot of imagination to see how whole cities could be made to vanish . . . It's terrifying."

"This is why you've kept mum about all this?"

"Yes."

"And your story about Arecibo Observatory somehow being mixed with the missing supertankers a ruse?"

"Well—I don't think they vanished the same way that destroyer did, or almost did, in the Boston Experiment, if that's what you mean. But . . . This sounds very silly and immature, but I say it anyway; I said the information about the Observatory being related to the missing supertankers because of a premonition of impending disaster. No, not premonition. It was more precognition. For days I had been aware of, well, as if someone or something had been watching me. Perhaps it was all nerves, though I'm glad I did it. And to answer your question again, yes, yes, that's why I kept quiet about the nature and success of my experiment. It's also why I can't give Mister X the information he wants whenever he contacts us. Are you sure your assumptions in this direction are correct? Are you sure the kill contract as you call it, are you sure it's all part of a scheme to frighten the necessary information out of me?"

"I'm not positive. I have no proof. But I can't see it any other way." A frightening chill crept over Bucher's long body. God's very toenails! Her knowledge in the wrong hands could turn the world upside down. Or any cockeyed way the maniac wanted to turn it.

"You're angry with me for being so stubborn, aren't you?" She raised herself up to lie braced against an elbow in order to look at him.

"Don't be silly," he told her. "You know I'm not. Why should I be? But you've got guts."

"You really think so?" It obviously pleased her to know he thought her courageous, and she squirmed around to brace on both elbows, facing him squarely. "Perhaps you can think of a way to discover the person's identity when he contacts me."

"I doubt it." Bucher frowned in thought. "Like a ransom pickup in a kidnap, he'll arrange things for his own protection." He looked at her quickly, prompted by instinct, knowing she was far ahead of him. "What's on your mind?"

"I can include a factor among the information I give him that he will have to disprove himself in order to know it's a hoax. For example, in the formula I can include a combination of rare metals he must use as essential to the experiment's success. These are metals such as holmium, erbium, thulium—there are several others—usually of an atomic count between fifty-eight and seventy-one, and all exceedingly rare. In the time it takes him to locate these metals in sufficient quantity, then discover also that the formula I have given him is false, perhaps your friends outside will have had time to ascertain his identity by then."

Bucher pondered her proposal; it was clever, damn clever, and in the silence filling the bedroom, they both could hear the continued noises pursuant to Bucher's instructions in defending the house and grounds. At last he spoke, but slowly, feeling his way, putting himself in the place of their mysterious antagonist. "If Mister X knows enough about your work to be convinced you have perfected the Fourth Dimension thing, why won't he know these rare metals aren't necessary?"

"Yes," Kleyr said softly after a time. "I see. I should have thought of that myself. Then there's nothing we can do until Mister X contacts us, is there?"

"As I see it—no."

Kleyr relaxed beside him again, head on his shoulder once more, and in the stillness of the house, before long Kleyr dozed, while Bucher wondered why he and Kleyr had found no ambush waiting for them when they arrived from Loiza Aldea. This same annoying question had continued to nag at him from the perimeter of his consciousness, like a blurred image barely within range of peripheral vision.

That there had been no ambush waiting made no sense. Even in view of his belief that the five million dollar contract on Kleyr was primarily intended to induce her complete cooperation rather than to assure her death, it still made no sense, unless—!

Bucher's start awakened Kleyr, but before she could move or make a sound Bucher's hand was over her mouth, a warning frown on his face. Suddenly, the answer to the annoying question had come to Bucher. He made sounds of one turning restlessly in sleep, then his lips against Kleyr's ear, he whispered to her:

"Keep pretending to be asleep, but point out to me the most likely places a microphone could be hidden. Mister X made a mistake in not having at least a token ambush waiting when we arrived. But he wants us to remain here, in this house, because it's bugged."

Bucher was three minutes over an hour finding the small, transistorized battery-powered ultra-short wave broadcasting unit in the hollow metal curtain rod over a bedroom window; after which, finding the others, one in a similar location in each room of the house, was simple. However, he did not disturb any of these electronic bugs until after he returned to the small pantry off the kitchen and stepped up in a chair to bring his eyes two or three inches above the edge of the foot-square wooden box on the top shelf. Coolly, calmly, he detached the two fine copper wires connecting the dry-cell batteries to the solenoid radio-controlled switch wired to the length of primer cord—the all of which was the trigger mechanism for the twenty-five pounds of 4-C high explosive in the wooden box—and removed it. Only then did he collect all the electronic eavesdropping gadgets from the curtain rods and immerse each, meticulously, in the commode. After this he spoke to Kleyr, who for some time had been padding behind him on silent feet.

66

"Get dressed," he told her quietly, going for his own garments in a bedroom chair. "We've moving."

It was not necessary that he say this twice, nor give any further explanation, because Kleyr had been with him when he discovered the crude radio-controlled bomb in the pantry, and her complexion had swiftly faded to the ashen hue of death when she recognized the powerful plastic explosive that the bomb was made of.

"Will we be returning soon?" was all she said.

"Why?"

She indicated a gray metal four-drawer file cabinet through the open door of her library-cum-office.

"Valuable?" Bucher asked.

She nodded. "Very."

"White can take care of it until we return. Hurry."

When they left through the front door some minutes later, it was almost dawn. Bucher counted only two of the five helicopters.

"The others are at the National Guard armory in San Juan," White Hat's director said in reply to Bucher's query concerning the missing aircraft. Then he listened carefully to Bucher's account of finding the bugs and the bomb, not speaking until Bucher finished, then:

"Twenty-five pounds of C-4—that's enough to level this entire neighborhood." He tugged at an earlobe. "As for the nine little eavesdropping gadgets—quite sophisticated in a way. They explain the special tape recorder we found in the floor of that building you use as a laboratory, Dr. Boriquen. A couple of the men were doing a routine bug-check of the place and discovered it."

"In my lab?" Kleyr was aghast. "But ... I ... Who ...?"

"Who has access to the lab besides you, Dr. Boriquen?" the director asked.

A startled expression overspread her lovely features. "Why—Dr. Samantha Bartlet and Dr. Philbrick. I—we have—they come and go as they please. Each of us has a key. I ..." Her voice trailed off in an agony of confusion as her eyes, pleading for assurance that her colleagues were innocent, found Bucher's. "Surely not Sam and Dr. Phil," she said at last.

"We'll soon find out." This was the only assurance Bucher could give her, knowing White Hat would launch an in-depth background check on each of the doctors immediately. Already the director was talking to one of his men several paces from where Bucher and Kleyr stood. When the director returned, Bucher asked: "Where are Dr. J. Joiner Mull and his bodyguard Lyle Hardiman?"

"At the Mir Hotel in Arecibo. Mull got real miffed when I told him he couldn't see Dr. Boriquen until you said so. The old geezer's got a hair-trigger temper anyway and was already about ready to explode because his nosy bodyguard kept snooping about and blundered onto a security file I have on both him and Dr. Mull." The director laughed shortly. "I brought them along in case you wanted to see them yourself, Mr. Bucher." He looked at Kleyr. "In a case of this magnitude, Dr. Boriquin, we trust nobody but our own people. As for your two friends, Dr. Bartlet and Dr. Philbrick, I'll give them the benefit of every doubt, should there be any doubts, but if they're guilty, then they walk the plank. I'm sorry. In that nearest 'copter, Mr. Bucher, you'll find Mull's and Hardiman's files in that leather case behind the pilot's seat."

Kleyr followed a step behind Bucher as he made his way to the big heavy duty CH-47 Chinook helicopter. Under ordinary circumstances Bucher could not have cared less about the backgrounds of Dr. J. Joiner Mull and his nephew Lyle Hardiman, but circumstances were not ordinary. Kleyr's life was at stake. To Bucher this made all the difference in the world. He had no way of knowing whether Mull or Hardiman or both were not involved in some way with Mister X. In fact, Bucher was far from satisfied with Mull's reason for coming to Puerto Rico at this particular moment. According to the director Mull wanted to discuss Kleyr's sylurgics with her, but why now? Why not last week or last month or last year? Why was Mull's need to talk with Kleyr suddenly so damned urgent? Because of these unanswered questions, among others, Bucher was anxious to learn something about both

68

Dr. J. Joiner Mull and his nephew-bodyguard Lyle Hardiman, and to see what they looked like from their photographs.

The first of the two folders Bucher took from the leather case behind the pilot's seat in the Chinook was that of Dr. J. Joiner Mull, president and major stockholder of the Cambridge Institute of Electro-Dynamics, which Bucher had theretofore assumed to be some sort of institution of learning, not the highly sophisticated laboratories operating on both private and government grants and dedicated to the study of phenomena.

"Phenomena?" Bucher growled in surprise. "What in hell is *that* supposed to mean?" He looked at Kleyr, who sat beside him studying the file under the narrow beam of Bucher's pen-flash.

"I'm not sure, Boo," Kleyr said, frowning. "It's rather hush-hush in a way. The goings-on at the Institute I mean. Or so I gather from the rumors that filter down the pipeline from time to time. I think in this particular case the word 'phenomena' means such things as the Bermuda Triangle, UFOs—flying saucers—and conducting theoretical experiments on such subjects from time to time. Is it important?"

"It could be, but . . ." Bucher focused his attention once more on Mull's file, and was not surprised to learn the man had top-secret security clearance direct from the Pentagon. That figured. With the Cambridge Institute dedicated to the study of such phenomena as the Bermuda Triangle and UFOs, the Pentagon would naturally have an interest in Dr. Mull and whether the man was trustworthy.

"Boo, shine the light back on his photo."

The photo was passport-size and showed the kindly, benign face of an elderly man, topped by a thatch of unruly snow white hair. Kleyr studied the photograph for some time in silence, at last saying:

"Yes, it's Dr. Mull. He looks exactly as he did the day of the Boston Experiment. He hasn't changed one iota."

Bucher's gaze returned to the top page of Mull's file, which dated the photo as having been taken only three months ago. "You're sure about that?" he asked Kleyr.

"About the photo being of Dr. Mull?"

"About his not having changed one iota since the day of the Boston Experiment." The file gave Mull's present age as sixty-one, which would have made him fifty-three when the Experiment was conducted—and according to Bucher's reckoning, goddammit, a man that old should evince some sign of change in eight years.

"No." Kleyr shook her curls briefly. "He looks exactly as I remember him."

Bucher made no further comment on the man's appearance, instead scanning the remainder of the file quickly. He had not expected to find anything incriminating in the material, indeed would have been surprised had he done so; his perusal of the man's file was for the purpose of obtaining a statistical image of Mull for later reference if necessary. In fact, he found little in the file except what he expected to find: Mull had an arm-long list of degrees, both earned and honorary, behind his name, with the report at no time even so much as hinting at animadversion—which in itself was sufficient to arouse Bucher's suspicions. Nevertheless, he still said nothing. He folded the file and returned it to the leather case as he had found it, then opened the one bearing the name "Lyle Hardiman," at sight of whose photograph, also a passport-type picture, Kleyr Boriquen gasped sharply in surprise. Bucher looked at her quickly.

"What is it, Kleyr?"

At first she pointed, a small finger touching the photograph, then looked at Bucher in alarm. "That's Charles, Boo. The man I told you about? Charles Everson."

"You're sure?" He studied the photo, recalling her description of Charles Everson being as 'handsome as a movie star' and nodded. Hardiman, or Everson, or whatever the bastard's name was, was indeed handsome. Damn handsome. Almost pretty, actually. With meticulous care Bucher read the entire file, twice, and as with Dr. Mull, found in it nothing questionable. According to the information in the file, shortly after graduating from Yale, Lyle Hardiman had gone to work in Security for his maternal uncle, Dr. J. Joiner Mull, at the Cambridge Institute

70

of Electro-Dynamics, and that was that. Hardiman was neither married nor engaged and lived at the home of his uncle in Boston.

"Check these vital statistics," Bucher told Kleyr, pointing to the section of the file describing Hardiman. "Do they tally with the description of Everson as you remember it?"

"Yes." Kleyr's voice held an odd tremor. "Oh, Boo! I hope I don't have to meet that—him—Charles again. Ever!" The words prompted a question Bucher did not relish asking, but knew he must.

"Why not?"

"Why not? You can ask me that?"

"Only because it's necessary, Kleyr," he told her gently.

A time or two she opened her mouth, abruptly, to speak but did not speak, and the growing indignation in her eyes gradually dissolved. She then spoke in a small, patient voice.

"Well, Boo, I told you how disgusted with myself I felt because of that silliness with Charles, how I felt I'd been untrue to you and all, and—well—just the prospect of meeting him again makes me feel like an unfaithful wife about to be confronted with an old flame in the presence of her husband." She proffered a shaky little smile. "Perhaps I'm a bit old-fashioned, but darn it I can't help it."

No sign of Bucher's enormous relief was evident from his expression as he once again focused his attention on Hardiman's file. But the attention was only pretense. To conceal the relief. A moment ago, at Kleyr's expressed reluctance to meet Hardiman-Everson face to face ever again, it had occurred to Bucher that perhaps she had not told him everything about her tawdry one-night mini-affair with the man. Therefore, now, in the light of her explanation for this reluctance, Bucher's relief was enormous.

"Don't worry about the joker, whatever his name is." Bucher closed the file and replaced it in the leather case alongside that of Dr. J. Joiner Mull. "I'll take care of him if he becomes a problem, which he already has become insofar as the name Charles Everson is concerned."

"Mr. Bucher?" White Hat's director appeared in the

dawn light showing through the craft's cargo port—and a tiny voice in the hinterland of Bucher's mind told him Hardiman-Everson had acquired the upperhand. "Could I speak privately with you? Will you excuse us a moment, Dr. Boriquen? This'll only take a moment."

"Is it about Lyle Hardiman-Charles Everson?" Bucher asked. He wanted no information of this Puerto Rican affair that was related to Kleyr kept secret from her, no matter how trivial or remote.

The director nodded with a quick glance in Kleyr's direction. "Yes, it's about Hardiman, uh—"

"I've told Bucher all I know of the man, Mr. White," Kleyr said, slipping an arm through Bucher's. "Including the fact that he's a zero in bed, so there's nothing you can say of the man in my presence that would embarrass me."

The director nodded enthusiastically in approval, his admiration of Kleyr Boriquen quite evident on his seamed face.

"Thank you, Dr. Boriquen. I have a number of reservations about the man myself—" He paused, cleared his throat, looking at both as he continued.

"On the flight down here Hardiman told a couple of my men of a vacation affair he had engaged in with you while using the alias 'Charles Everson,' as he put it, 'just for kicks' as romantic embellishment. I wanted Mr. Bucher to know of this, and he would have told you of course that we know of it also, in order that it might not become an unexpected source of embarrassment."

"What kind of reservations about Hardiman?" Bucher asked. "And why?"

"Well . . ." The director tugged at an earlobe. "Because of his file. Nobody is that Simon Pure. We didn't compile the information in it, by the way, nor in Dr. Mull's either for that matter, but borrowed it from another agency. The whole thing smells to me like a sanitized, deodorized press release. It's unrealistic."

"Then his name is really Hardiman? Lyle Hardiman?"

"So far as I know right now. Our people in Massachusetts are already constructing a more realistic profile on the man; we'll know something within a few hours. Uh, Mr. Bucher?"

"Yes?"

"Dr. Mull has powerful influence in the higher echelons of the government—"

"So you want me to lay off nephew Lyle?" Bucher demanded, his frozen, brittle tone eliciting Kleyr's small spontaneous gasp of mingled apprehension and glad surprise.

"No-no." The director held up both hands, chuckling. "I merely want to suggest that you comport yourself with your customary diplomacy and integrity should this Lyle Hardiman's conduct toward Dr. Boriquen here prove, ah, offensive. Do you read me?"

Bucher himself chuckled, suddenly understanding. "I read you."

"Well, I don't," Kleyr announced emphatically, looking a question at Bucher. He explained:

"If friend Hardiman pushes me for a blood-gutsy hassle over the favors of Femme Fatale Boriquen, I make certain our set-to takes place in front of witnesses. That's the diplomacy. And leaving enough of him in one piece so the hospital can recognize him as a human they're signing in; that's the integrity. Sort of."

Kleyr simply looked at him, too amazed to comment, thinking: "Dear God above. What kind of world is it I've fallen into?"

"Hardiman is a mean pusher, Mr. Bucher," the director said quietly. "A big mean pusher. I doubt you'll have any trouble finding witnesses. Not after he learns of your relationship with the doctor here." His enigmatic sidelong look puzzled Bucher until the director added: "Which should be right about now."

"Hardiman is here?" Bucher asked in surprise.

The director nodded. "He blustered and pawed the ground threateningly when I informed him and Dr. Mull earlier that you were forbidding everyone to see Dr. Boriquen for the time being; and three or four minutes before I came to talk to you he showed up, walked from the Mir Hotel in Arecibo, where he left Dr. Mull. Claims he intends to see Dr. Boriquen now, regardless. As I said, I let him know, through one of our men, and tactfully of course, how matters stood between you and Dr. Bori—"

"Sam," Kleyr interrupted earnestly. "Could you not call me Kleyr, please?"

"Eh? Er—right, Doctor—er, Kleyr." In the dawn light his seamed face reflected a broad smile of appreciation. "Thank you."

"So you arranged to have one of our people tell Hardiman about Kleyr and me? And now Hardiman is chomping at the bit?" Bucher stood and gave Kleyr a hand up. "So what's keeping the bastard?"

"He thinks you and D . . . Kleyr are still in the house, where I have a team of our best bug-hunters taking the place apart for more eavesdropping gear and explosives, by the way. I didn't tell Hardiman that you and Kleyr were here, in the Chinook."

"Then let's enlighten the bastard," Bucher snarled softly.

"Boo—" Kleyr looked quickly from him to Sam White, then back to Bucher again. "Boo, you be careful, do you hear?"

Bucher grinned at the director and moved toward the door of the helicopter. "The honeymoon is hardly begun, and she's sounding like a wife already."

Kleyr rushed at him in a flurry of action, reminiscent of a bantam hen's charge in defense of her chicks—but the fear for Bucher's safety in her eyes destroyed the image. "Boo." She seized his arm and clung fast. "As Sam told you, Cha—Hardiman is mean. It's an inveterate part of his nature. And when crossed or thwarted, he can be vicious. Terribly vicious."

"I didn't ask before," Bucher said quietly, "because I knew that had I needed to know you would have told me, but things have changed. So now I'm asking. What happened when you threw Hardiman out that time? What did he do when you told him to leave?" A long moment of silence passed before Kleyr answered.

"He beat me."

San White nodded vigorously in confirmation, adding in a voice thick with revulsion: "He beat her brutally, ac-

74

cording to the information in our files. Fractured jaw, three busted ribs, left arm wrenched out of its socket, deliberately, I might add. Am I right, Kleyr?"

"You knew about this and kept it from me?" Bucher demanded, his face bleak.

"Yes. I knew about it. But I figured Kleyr would tell you in her own good time if she wanted you to know—but this was before I knew Charles Everson and Lyle Hardiman were the same man. As I said, this I didn't learn until a few minutes ago."

"What purpose would have been served if I had told you before we discovered Everson and Hardiman are the same person, Boo?" Kleyr released Bucher's arm but did not move otherwise. "But now that we do know, and you know he beat me . . ." Her Latin shrug was barely perceptible. "From their initial diagnosis the doctors at the hospital in San Juan doubted that I would ever walk again."

Bucher kissed her lightly, quickly, and dismounted from the Chinook without another word, and sauntered leisurely toward the remaining helicopter the director had not dispatched to San Juan, noting the protective measures thus far in operation as he did so. At each end of the four corners of Kleyr's large stone house stood a White Hat agent armed with a 9mm submachine gun the organization had recently developed for its own use. Two additional agents were inside the house searching for other electronic eavesdropping devices and other explosive mechanisms that he might have overlooked, with the two remaining agents at the second helicopter. With these two also was Lyle Hardiman, talking earnestly with one of the agents, his back toward Bucher and ignorant of Bucher's approach.

Some minutes before dawn had broken and now the opulent splendor of the new day poured across the island paradise of Puerto Rico, as only dawn in Puerto Rico can do, yet Bucher was unaware of this blessing of nature. His thoughts at the moment were weighing, judging, discarding pros and cons of current circumstances as he understood them, in an effort to discover some link between Lyle Hardiman's deceiving Kleyr several months before by

75

using the name "Charles Everson," and the present threat to Kleyr's life. He found none. Even so, another evaluation of Hardiman as a threat might disclose something to support an entirely different conclusion once the information contained in White Hat's own background check of the man arrived from Massachusetts later in the day. Regardless, Bucher swore to himself grimly, no goddamn background investigation conducted by any authority could alter events and protect Hardiman from circumstances about to overtake and befall the man as a result of the beating he had given Kleyr. In order to concentrate solely on the immediate task at hand, Bucher consciously cleared his mind by forcing from his thoughts all else but Lyle Hardiman and the brutal beating the man had given Kleyr. This Bucher accomplished as he drew near the second helicopter.

"Good morning, sir," said the White Hat agent not talking to Lyle Hardiman, as Bucher walked up. "Beautiful day, Mr. Bucher."

At the sound of Bucher's name, Hardiman spun from the helicopter like an oversized puppet manipulated by tight strings, an unwholesome smirk on his handsome face. He wore slacks and a short-sleeved sport shirt, and was easily as tall as Bucher without the crepe sole loafers he wore. To Bucher these things were superfluous, without moment, and he gave them no notice. But he did not ignore Hardiman's deep chest and wide shoulders, nor the long and heavily muscled arms.

From the Chinook Bucher had just left, Kleyr stared in wide-eyed apprehension toward the other craft and the four men near it, and swallowed hard in an effort to keep her voice steady.

"Sam, will he be all right? He will be all right, won't he, Sam?"

Sam White chuckled amicably. "If I'd thought otherwise, I'd've sent Hardiman packing when the bugger arrived from Arecibo a while ago. I'll tell you, lass. I've no liking for Lyle Hardiman. None whatever. As for Mr. Bucher being all right, why, keep watching, lass."

Kleyr obeyed, watching with all her power. Yet for all

her concentrated attention, she was not able to hear what Hardiman said when the man suddenly whirled from the helicopter to face Bucher. The next instant she was dashing toward the other craft as fast as she could run, and reached it just in time to hear Lyle Hardiman say to Bucher:

"So what if I slapped her around a little? She's *my* woman, and no ex-underworld creep is about to change that!"

"Perhaps you'd like to make a little bet on that, ol' buddy-roo," Bucher said easily.

"Why, big-old mean-old underworld dropout? You got two dimes to rub together?"

Deftly Bucher's left hand fingered in under the front of his buttoned shirt at waist level, and half a minute later pulled his money belt into view and tossed it toward the two young White Hat agents watching from a few feet to one side. "You fellows hold the stakes," he told them, then to Hardiman said: "There's twenty thousand dollars in that belt in hundred dollar bills, give or take a hundred or two. I'll give you two-to-one she's not your woman, but if you can prove she is, I'll give you two-to-one you can't take her. Put your money where your big mouth is, punk."

Hardiman, briefly put, was staggered by Bucher's response, which grievously upstaged him, stole his thunder. He shifted his attention to Kleyr as she arrived on the scene. And licked his lips in the anticipatory manner of a cougar about to pounce on a young and tender lamb—for Lyle Hardiman was obsessed by the psychotic fixation that women became hopelessly enamored with him once he "slapped 'em around a little," as he termed such vicious beatings as he had given Kleyr, albeit this particular beating was his reaction to her total rejection of him as a man. No such rejection had ever happened to him before. It had delivered a stunning clout to his grotesque masculine ego. Nevertheless, in the succeeding months this grotesque ego, in conjunction with his psychotic fixation, had convinced him Kleyr's rejection was only another exceptionally artful and cunning feminine wile, one that stated the absolute reverse of her true feelings of the undying

77

love and devotion she bore him. With such logic damn fools are daily endowed.

"Hiya, babe," Hardiman chortled when his eyes met Kleyr's. "Have you come to watch your ol' Big Daddy take this underworld dropout apart?" Beaming, misconstruing her shudder of loathing for him as a shiver of ecstatic joy in contemplation of their reunion, he started toward Kleyr—but the barely perceptible awkwardness in his stride caused by his right arm carried tight against his body did not escape Bucher's notice. Nor did the flick-open switchblade knife in Hardiman's right hand escape Bucher's cold eyes.

Inexplicably, in a flash of intelligence, Bucher saw his and Hardiman's caperings as ridiculous, and had a tremendous urge to terminate them as quickly as possible. After all, numerous other matters in immediate demand for his attention were far more important than keelhauling any one simple-minded egomaniac sonofabitch named Hardiman—who obviously intended to feint quickly sideways from his path to Kleyr and, with the flick-open switchblade in his right, attack by surprise.

This Hardiman did, and his attack was loaded with surprise—for Hardiman himself.

He was at first surprised at experiencing sensations of a chicken getting its neck wrung; during which time he was whirled, yanked, and twisted so that he wound up held fast in Bucher's vise-grip, locked on his knife hand high between his shoulder blades, with him in a half squat gaping stupidly upward in greater surprise and instant terror, watching Bucher's fist, armored by brass knucks, descending toward his unprotected face like the armored mace of eternal doom. The mace struck, embossing his terrified surprise with the crunch of crumbling jawbone—*his* jawbone! Those were *his* teeth blasted from their sockets by the roots, *his* teeth spewing from his mouth like corn from a sheller. Behind his bulging eyeballs rapid, successive explosions of white-hot flame in unison with the rapid rise and fall of the armored mace seared across his brain in blinding agonies not to be endured in silence, and in the fading seconds before entering total hysteria, he puzzled

78

feebly how he could have wandered into a threshing machining uniquely equipped with sledgehammers.

Then Lyle Hardiman commenced to scream in mindless hysteria, continued to scream in long, guttural, gut-straining blasts, was still screaming when White Hat's director instructed one of the agents watching the fight at the helicopter to guide Hardiman back toward the center of town and the Mir Hotel.

Kleyr Boriquen stood with wide eyes on Bucher, stood without moving, transfixed, recalling certain particulars she had read pertaining to terrible incidents involving him, incidents in which it seemed at the time as if his survival had been accomplished only by a miracle. Only now she realized there had been no miracle. Neither then nor now. Only the protective instincts of a jungle cat, reflexes so incredibly quick they deceived the eye. And a powerful determination to survive. "Gracias mi Dios!" she whispered in heartfelt gratitude, watching Bucher stuff his shirt back inside his trousers after buckling the moneybelt about his waist once again.

The two bug-hunter agents who had been going over Kleyr's house for additional eavesdropping devices and additional bombs emerged from the building loaded with electronic detection gear and approached White Hat's director.

"The house is clean," the agent in the lead told the older man. "The house is now clean as a hound's tooth, and I'll stake my life on it."

"You may be called upon to do exactly that before this shenanigan is over with," the director replied, laughing shortly. "So I hope you're right." He turned toward Bucher with an expression not unlike that of the cat that had stolen the cream. "It's a marvelous thing when one single incident benefits all concerned, Mr. Bucher."

"Such as?" Bucher replied, tightening his belt.

"Such as your chastisement of Hardiman just now. You and Kleyr benefited by paying Hardiman a debt long overdue him, my men and I benefited by watching a seasoned professional at work, and of course Hardiman himself was tremendously benefited in that he is never likely to lay another hand on Kleyr again and incur the possibility of your further wrath, so I'd say it is indeed a marvelous thing."

Bucher merely nodded, looking at the other. The director had earlier admitted to a dislike of Hardiman, but until this moment Bucher had discerned no inkling as to the depths nor the intensity of that dislike.

"H-How did you know about his knife, Boo?" Kleyr asked, voice a bit trembly with relief.

"From the way he walked in trying to conceal it," Bucher smiled at her. He turned to the agent who had told the director that Kleyr's house contained no additional snooping devices or bombs. "If you're not positive about the investigation of the place, then we may all wind up dead," Bucher said to the man.

"I *am* positive," the man insisted stubbornly as the sounds of approaching helicopters reached them from the direction of San Juan. "As I said, I'll stake my life on it. That house is clean!"

"Come on." Bucher extended a hand to Kleyr. "We won't be moving after all. Let's go back inside."

"What made you suspect that there were listening devices, Mr. Bucher?" White Hat's director asked.

"Because there was no ambush, not even a token ambush, waiting for us here when Kleyr and I arrived last night." Bucher continued, without mentioning Kleyr's Fourth Dimension experiment, explaining his theory that the mysterious Mister X was using the five million dollar hit-contract in an effort to frighten Kleyr into divulging to him certain very dangerous scientific information she had discovered. "This information is a mathematical formula for designing a type of motor that receives its fuel from the oxygen in the air around it," Bucher lied boldly, recalling on the spur of the moment having read recently that the Soviet Union had developed just such an engine. "But Dr. Boriquen is not going to knuckle under," he continued. "A fool can see how such an engine, multiplied by a million or so, could soon consume all the oxygen in the earth's atmosphere; and that's that." He motioned to Kleyr with his head. "Come on. Let's go back inside."

"You're a number one first-class liar, Mr. Bucher," White Hat's director chuckled a couple of minutes later, after he had followed Kleyr and Bucher back inside the house. "And not a one of those listening out there except me knows it—I refer to your yarn about the oxygen-powered motor. And I wouldn't have known you were putting up a smokescreen had I forgotten you and I discussed the same subject some months ago—when you told me of reading the Russians had developed such a motor. Remember?"

"Yeah," Bucher said, suddenly remembering and saying nothing else. Kleyr, on her way to the kitchen, had stopped in the doorway and stood looking at him, in the depths of her eyes the question of whether he would disclose her success in having reproduced the Boston Experiment, but with phenomenal results. With a mild start of surprise she realized that her not being absolutely positive Bucher would never betray the confidence she had placed in him was not merely small-minded on her part but suggestive of evil, and she turned from the two men seated in the main room, and proceeded to the kitchen, her face burning with shame.

"And when I checked with our people," the director continued, "I learned that we developed such a motor right after World War II. So I'm wondering what this Mister X of yours is really after. Do you know, Mr. Bucher?"

"Not exactly, and I don't intend to pry the information from Kleyr." Bucher used the same parallel Kleyr had used with him earlier. "After Hiroshima and Nagasaki I understand Einstein very much regretted having made known work of his that made it possible for others to produce the atom bomb."

For a long time the only sounds inside the house were those made by Kleyr in the kitchen as she went about preparing breakfast for herself and the two men, until at last the director asked in wonder: "Is it that big?"

"Bigger," Bucher told him. "It's like exploding the atomic bomb over, let's say for example, New York, but with only the people who exploded the bomb and the people of New York aware that the bomb had been exploded."

Again a long silence ensued, with each tick of passing time the director's seamed face gradually growing more incredulous, until at last he could manage no more than a flimsy: "My god!" and continued to stare at Bucher, believing, yet wanting reassurance. But Bucher shook his head.

"I don't have it to give," he said. "The only way I can keep it from frightening me is to not think of it."

"My god," the director said again, speaking as if to himself. "Would Kleyr tell me? If I asked her would she tell me what she told you?"

"That's entirely up to her, though I hope she wouldn't. I'm beginning to wish she hadn't told me."

"Then I let it pass," the older man said with evident relief. "At least for now. If it's of import equal to the atomic bomb, I won't ask her until it's a have-to case—and then I hope she refuses. I know it has to do with the Boston Experiment, and for right now that's enough."

The director declined Kleyr's invitation to breakfast with her and Bucher, which puzzled her no little until after the man left and Bucher explained what they had just been discussing.

"You mean the subject destroyed his appetite?"

"That's what I suspect," Bucher chuckled. "You'll admit he did look a bit greenish about the gills when he left."

"I didn't notice," Kleyr said, seating herself across the table. "I confess to being too busy gloating over what you did to Hardiman to notice." And at the quick look he gave her, she continued: "Yes! I gloated, I gloat, and I will gloat in the future until the day I die." She shuddered. "If you could have seen the evil joy in his eyes when he was wringing my arm out of its socket—" She stopped, staring at Bucher defensively. "Well, I don't *care*, Boo! I'm only human! I don't care if it isn't ladylike because I enjoyed watching you beat the stuffing out of him! You know something, Boo? I'd enjoy it again! Do you underst—!"

"Hey-hey!" Bucher held up both palms, laughing.

"What's all this about? No one is condemning you for being human."

She pouted fetchingly. "But you looked at me as if I'd been pulling little rabbits' heads off."

"To me it couldn't mea—"

The phone interrupted and Bucher shook his head to Kleyr, rising to his feet himself to answer it, Kleyr remaining at table, though with her breakfast getting little more than scant and indifferent attention as she listened to Bucher talking in hushed monosyllables in the other room. When Bucher returned at last to the table, he offered no comment regarding the call, even though Kleyr sat regarding him expectantly. He persevered stubbornly, artfully sidestepping the openings she afforded him by resuming the conversation toward the close of the meal. Thus it was that they were drinking a second cup of coffee when Kleyr became very still, eyes holding him steadily, for it had just occurred to her that Bucher's stubbornness was all for her benefit, that the telephone call concerned her and had brought bad news from which he was trying to protect her, at least until a more appropriate moment.

"That is it, is it not?" she asked after explaining her conclusion and the reason for it. "The phone call was about me and carried bad news, no?"

"It did," Bucher said, pushing his plate back.

"Then tell me, Boo. I have a right to know."

"I'm not disputing your right, Kleyr. I'm trying to find the right words. Your cousins in Loiza Aldea? You told me their names last night—"

"Rachel and Nora Cordova?" Color drained from her face, and she continued but her tone was unnatural. "Something has happened to Rachel and Nora?"

Bucher nodded, wishing desperately there was some other and less distasteful way of doing the chore. "I know now why they didn't come to the door last night when we went to visit them to borrow some clothes for you."

"You know why—?" Kleyr whispered in dread.

"The same as that Arnie-Dingus character you found in his dressing room at the Dainty Dish last night." According to White Hat's director's account of the double

83

murder over the phone, the two old-maid sisters, Rachel and Nora Cordova, had been found in their home bound to chairs and gagged, their throats cut. Kleyr's blanched countenance resembled the face of a corpse as the information gradually transformed the soft planes and curves of it slowly into a mask of grief.

"T-They were very dear to me," she managed to say before the tears started, and she rose hastily, leaving the room.

Bucher did not follow her into the bedroom, albeit he felt the inclination to do so, for none knew better than he that there are times in a person's life when one must be left alone. Moreover, he needed a few moments alone himself. To think. From the onset of this crazy caper he had recognized that the mysterious Mister X had done considerable research into Kleyr's background, living habits, family, and such, and the senseless butchery of the two old-maid cousins in Loiza Aldea last night was all too graphic emphasis of this, but he had not imagined the man would go so far before contacting Kleyr. And since he had, what did the bastard have in mind for reserves, as a clincher, or persuader, should Kleyr hesitate in giving him the information he would demand? Obviously the man was mentally unbalanced—and not in the general sense that all desperate criminals are unbalanced, either.

"I've got a damn strong feeling I'm doing nothing but spinning my wheels," Bucher said aloud to his half-empty coffee cup as he rose from the table and went to a front window to watch the activity outside. The three helicopters dispatched to San Juan some time previously for the munitions and other items Bucher had requested had returned from their trip now, and at present the entire crew outside was very busy setting up the defenses he had outlined. Oddly, Bucher wondered if the precautions to defend Kleyr were enough; if they would be at all effective in saving her when Mister X made his big play. Somehow he was beginning to doubt they would. He was also beginning to doubt the feasibility of his overall plan, which called for him to remain at her side constantly. Of itself he found no fault with this—but, dammit, things weren't happening as he thought they should. In his opinion Mister X should have already contacted Kleyr and made his pitch . . .

"I'm all right now," Kleyr said, smiling, as she reentered the kitchen. In evidence were only the faintest traces of the tears. "I'm a big baby, huh?"

"Of course not," Bucher told her thoughtfully, chewing over the new idea that had just that moment popped into his mind. "Listen. I'm going to be gone for a bit; I want your promise you won't leave the house."

She studied his bleak face for a moment before replying. "You have my promise, but why are you leaving? Where are you going?"

"Maybe to San Juan. I'm not sure. Big Jute Nappo has ten two-man crews here in Puerto Rico searching for you. I'm curious as hell as to why none of them have shown up here at your home. Where would the bums be looking for you at this time of day if not at your home?"

"I don't suppose it would do any good for me to ask if I might accompany you."

"Not a bit of good." He drew her close. "But I won't be gone long."

Outside a minute later he asked White Hat's director: "Any report from the teams you've got out searching for Big Jute Nappo's sharks?"

The director held up a staying hand, for at that moment one of the agents was talking over the radio phone on the Chinook. Half a minute more passed before the operator hung up, grinning.

"Big Jute Nappo is suddenly missing six gunsels," he grinned at his superior. "And the bodies won't be found for a few days at best. But that's only part of the good news. The rest is that all but four of his men have flown back to the mainland."

"Which four?" Bucher asked, suspecting the answer as he did so.

"Big Jute's brother Luigi, Surd Gulgar, Seeto Loyoka, and Mack McReady."

"But why would the others return to the mainland?" the director frowned in puzzlement.

"Because they were called," Bucher growled in perplex-

85

ity. "Somebody, and probably Big Jute, called them home. That's the only reason they'd return without accomplishing their mission."

The director rubbed his grizzled head. "But why? It doesn't make sense."

"I'll find out why," Bucher told him. "I need a pilot to fly me to San Juan. He'll come straight back. I want to rent a smaller helicopter, for myself. Do we know where Luigi Nappo and Surd Gulgar are putting up in San Juan?"

"At the Americana. Rooms 202 and 203; Nappo's in 202, Gulgar in 203. Seeto Loyoka and Mack McReady are registered at the Palamar, rooms 47 and 48 respectively."

6

An hour later at International Airport Bucher finished arrangements for renting a small four-passenger helicopter and hailed a cab for the Americana Hotel, his face grim. It was still too early for Luigi Nappo to be up and about—if the man got out at all today, considering the busted mug he had received at the Dainty Dish the night before. And, Bucher reflected as the cab made its way through the early morning traffic, Surd Gulgar would not be venturing out of the Americana except on orders from his boss, so . . .

Lady Luck beamed graciously on Bucher the instant he entered the Americana's lobby, for he caught ancient and withered Surd Gulgar at the tobacco counter in the act of paying for a morning paper. The old gunman started violently and turned as pale as very death at sight of Bucher striding purposefully toward him. Not unmindful of this stroke of luck, Bucher decided to play the score to the very hilt.

"Howsa boy, Surd, ol' buddy-buddy?" The breathy snarl in his quiet greeting gave the old gunnman another violent start; the Adam's Apple of his scrawny neck bobbed like a hysterical yo-yo, and he giggled foolishly in his fear.

"He-he-he! What you doing in this part of the world, B-B-Butchy?"

"I came to hear your last words."

"W-W-What!?" The yo-yoing Adam's Apple went crazy. "W-What, B-Butchy?"

"I'm here to hear your last words and confession," Bucher snarled with deadly implication. "And to learn what kind of headstone you want for your grave."

Gulgar's eyes drifted shut and the man would have collapsed on the spot had not Bucher gripped him by one arm and guided him to a nearby seat against the wall. A couple of minutes passed before Gulgar got his breath—but he was still pale as a corpse.

"B-B-Butchy, I got no hassle with you, Butchy."

"Then what's this crap about a five-mil hit contract on my woman?"

"A—*what?* A five-mil hit contract? On one person? Hell, Butchy, you gotta be kidding. Ain't *no*body ever put up five mils for a single hit. Five million dollars? Christ, a man could just about get the whole government tooken care of, near'bouts, for five million dollars."

Bucher's face did not reveal the sudden chill of alarm he felt. Either Gulgar was totally ignorant of the contract out on Kleyr, or he was a better actor than Bucher gave him credit for being, or—and this final alternative filled Bucher with a kind of frozen dread—he, Bucher, was completely, one hundred percent wrong in his approach to the entire problem.

"So what are you and kid brother Luigi Nappo doing down here in Puerto Rico?" Bucher growled.

"Layin' low until Big Jute can get a couple of things tooken care of back home."

"What about all the torpedoes Big Jute had here in Puerto Rico?"

Gulgar's eyes became shifty, which inclined Bucher to believe he had struck something important.

"Last night, after you bashed Luigi at the Dainty Dish, why, when the doctors got Luigi's face back in shape sort of, he called Big Jute, and Big Jute said send his men home."

"All his men?"

Gulgar started to lie by nodding, thought better of it, and shook his head vigorously. "Seeto Loyoka and Mack McReady stayed behind with me and Luigi. They're upstairs with Luigi right now."

"Why did Big Jute call his men home?"

Fear overcame Surd Gulgar, and he shook from it visibly. Once, twice, the third time he attempted to articulate he succeeded, his tone suggesting a prayer that he would be believed. "B-Butchy, I don't even know why Big Jute's men was in Puerto Rico."

After a long pause Bucher snarled softly: "As I told you before, I'm here to listen to your last words and confession."

Gulgur's yo-yoing Adam's Apple commenced to trip the frenetic fantastic and he neighed gently in terror as the full import of Bucher's words smote him. "B-B-Butchy, I swear to holy God I don't know what's goin' on." Tears showed in his ancient eyes. "First I get sidetracked into flunky for Luigi—I been a good soljer to Big Jute, I have—then we come down here to this godawful place on account of I don't know what—"

"You said Big Jute had to smooth over a couple of things for Luigi."

"I said till Big Jute could get a couple of things tooken care of," Gulgar said abruptly. "That's what I was told—that ain't sayin' I believe it."

For a long moment Bucher studied the aged mobster in stony silence; obviously something troubled the man, troubled him deeply—and suddenly Bucher knew what that something was. Gulgar was afraid he was being eased out of things, that details of Syndicate functions he was involved in were kept from him because he was no longer trusted, and was on his way to being given the rub. Without a second thought Bucher decided to play on the man's fear, then offer to pay generously for any information he might have.

"There's a rumor out on you, Surd," Bucher said in his

friendliest tone yet. "I was surprised to find you when I walked into the lobby here a while ago."

"Surprised to find me?"

"Alive. The rumor claimed Big Jute had put the word out on you."

"Alive?" Gulgar gobbled. "W-What sort of word?"

"Hell, Surd, you know what kind of word I mean. Claimed you had lost your usefulness and knew too much to be trusted outside the Syndicate, so . . ." Bucher sighed plaintively. "But we all got to go some time, one way or the other, don't we, whether it's a cement coffin or a bullet in the brain from behind—well, you know as much about it as I do. More, probably, since you been in the organization much longer than I was."

Gulgar did not speak, though his mouth worked desperately in effort to do so, and again his eyes faded shut, or would have, had not Bucher shaken him vigorously by the shoulders.

"Come out of it, Surd," Bucher growled. "What in hell did you expect—to end your days in a nice quiet old folks home somewhere? You been with the Syndicate all your life almost, and you're the same dog-robber you started out as, so what in hell did you expect? You don't think Big Jute'll put you out to pasture somewhere do you? Christ! You *know* better. And if you *don't*, maybe you *ought* to be deep-sixed at that." Bucher shook his head as if in silent ridicule of himself and sighed pensively. "And I was about to offer you a couple of Gs as a getaway stake just for old time's sake in case you had any usable information."

"W-What sort of information?" Gulgar mumbled carefully, at last alert.

"On this Puerto Rican caper Big Jute's working on. I know a fellow in the Syndicate who'd buy me a piece of the action on the Q-T for a little grease. I got wind Big Jute had something big and I mean *big* in the mill. Well, we both know Big Jute is no rum-dum when it comes to turning a tidy profit. But I don't intend to invest in something blind, so . . . I'm trying to learn what it is—you'd do the same, Surd."

89

"An-And you got a coupla Gs for what I know?" the old mobster asked. He had been planning to return to the land of his birth in central Europe for years, and two thousand additional dollars would round out his stake nicely.

"Yeah," Bucher told him flat out. "I've got a couple of thousand for what you know."

"It ain't much, Butchy, but . . ." His ancient, rheumy eyes studied Bucher's hard face, then watched until Bucher tugged a thick pad of hundred dollar bills from his money-belt.

"Okay," Bucher peeled twenty bills from the pad and shoved the remainder into his coat pocket for the time being. "There's your two thousand. Shoot."

"Well—I know Luigi ain't Big Jute's brother, ain't even no kin to Big Jute. And Big Jute claims he's got the biggest and the best angle, him and his partner, in all his life—"

"You know, for a fact, that Luigi isn't Big Jute's brother?" The chill of alarm Bucher had experienced minutes previously returned. "That Luigi didn't attend Harvard under the name of Oliver Dillingsworth?"

"Yes, I know it for a fact, Butchy, an' I ain't lyin'. His name also ain't Oliver Dillingsworth and ain't never been. The bastard's name, his *real* name, is Delaney Pryde, and he's a brain, Butchy, a big brain, the biggest brain, Big Jute claims, in the whole friggin' creation. Big Jute claims the guy's got one of these here computer kind of brains, like."

"A genius?" Bucher asked flatly.

"Yeah! 'At's it! A superstar from Geniusville, the biggest genius in the whole friggin' creation, Big Jute claims. Claims the guy can work miracles with figures—"

"A mathematician?"

"Yeah. 'At's right, Butchy, only he goes in for it—I—for it—" Gulgar's seamed face screwed into a grimace as he searched for the right words. "Like in a lab, like."

"A scientist?" Bucher was becoming more puzzled by the second.

90

© Lorillard 1975

Come for the filter...

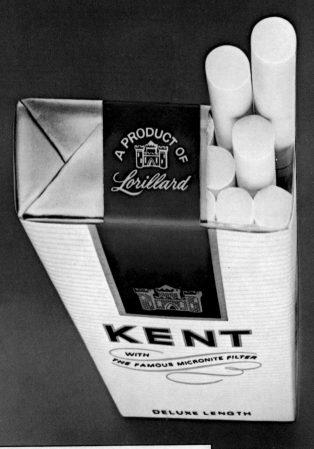

A PRODUCT OF
Lorillard

KENT

WITH
THE FAMOUS MICRONITE FILTER

DELUXE LENGTH

18 mg. "tar," 1.2 mg. nicotine av. per cigarette, FTC Report Oct. '74.

...you'll stay for the taste.

DELUXE LENGTH

WITH THE FAMOUS MICRONITE FILTER

KENT

A lot of good taste
that comes easy
through the
Micronite filter.

18 mg. "tar," 1.2 mg.
nicotine av. per cigarette,
FTC Report Oct. '74.

"A scientist, yeah!" Gulgar nodded vigorously. "Onlyest he does it with figures, Butchy, like one, two, three."

"And who's Big Jute's partner? This Delaney Pryde?"

"Huh-uh. Big Jute's got Delaney Pryde on the payroll onlyest to help his partner out on account of his partner is another one of these mathematician-scientist types. A broad as I understand it."

"A woman?" Bucher stared hard at the other man.

"Yeah. A female woman, only I don't know her name, but she's a doctor something-or-other just like Pryde is. And that's all I know, Butchy. I swear it." Gulgar studied Bucher's face half fearfully.

"Keep the goddamn money!" Bucher snapped angrily, thoughts in a turmoil. Then he grabbed rigid control of himself. "You've earned the two Gs, ol' buddy," he said in comradely fashion. "Keep it with my blessing. Who knows what you've just told me—besides you and Big Jute Nappo?"

"Delaney Pryde—he's from South Africa. You see, he come to the States on Big Jute's invite, but makin' like a tourist. I overheard him an' Big Jute makin' the whole yarn about Pryde supposed to be his brother and all. But Jute claimed this was necessary to prevent his Syndicate business associates from diggin' into Pryde's background and learnin' who he really is before Big Jute is ready for 'em to know. And Pryde didn't complain—hell! Big Jute's givin' the guy half a million a year for five years in nontaxable jeetus through some foreign bank. Ain't no bohunk gonna complain about nothin' for jeetus like that for nothin' but usin' his noodle. You know. Professional-wise, like. For usin' his genius-type brain on whatever Big Jute's got in mind." Revelation blossomed over Surd Gulgar's withered countenance. "By god, 'at's the reason Big Jute's about to put the rub on me!" he wheezed. "Somehow he's figured out I know somethin' I ortn't to know about his business with Pryde, so he's gonna have me rubbed, the ungrateful son of a bitch!"

"What's his partner's name?" Bucher asked urgently.

Gulgar shook his head.

"I've got another deuce of Gs for that name."

91

Gulgar stared in surprise and budding hope, then abruptly wilted. He was far in over his head with Big Jute Nappo as it was, but he didn't intend to venture in even ankle deep by lying to the Butcher! "I don't know her name, Butchy. I could use them other two Gs, but if I told you a name as hers, I'd only be tellin' you a lie, because I don't know her name. I swear I don't."

Bucher nodded—the name of Nappo's female partner had been a bit much to hope for, anyway. "You better get the hell out of Puerto Rico and as far away as you can, Surd," he told the other grimly. "I'm about to take the rag off the bush in this neck of the woods, and you might get caught in the cross-fire. If you've got a stash-out, go crawl in it, and stay there until I put Big Jute Nappo and his scheme on ice for keeps."

This, if nothing else, had informed Surd Gulgar that Bucher's interest in Big Jute Nappo's operations was not because he wanted to purchase a piece of the action, though at this stage of the game he did not know what Bucher's motives were and cared less. All he was concerned with at the moment was taking Bucher's advice of escaping Puerto Rico and the threat of his former boss' rub-out detail. His first act in hopes of accomplishing this was to jump to his feet with a hurried nod of gratitude and scurry for the front entrance of the Americana and the street.

After Gulgar left, Bucher remained seated in the Americana's lobby, with his back to the wall, not far from the tobacco counter. Big Words, he said to himself gloomily, referring to his comment of putting Big Jute Nappo and his scheme on ice for keeps. Hell, he couldn't even learn who Nappo's business associates were in the scheme—aside from Luigi Nappo-Oliver Dillingsworth-Delaney Pryde. And Pryde would be no problem to handle, because to Bucher Big Jute's reason for having the man parade under the alias of Luigi Nappo was crystal clear. After Delaney Pryde delivered whatever it was Big Jute wanted from the man, Nappo would have Pryde taken out in the boondocks some dark night and burned—the con game itself had been perfected years ago by Gyp the

92

Blood. This was the reason Big Jute had taken the trouble to create the third identity for Pryde, that of Oliver Dillingsworth, and paying the man through a foreign bank—a bank where, Bucher knew without being told, Big Jute already had money stashed. Each month a certain sum would be transferred from Big Jute's account into the account of one Luigi Nappo, where it would remain untouched by Pryde because Big Jute would be furnishing him with enough money, women, and other wherewithal for current use. Then, after Delaney Pryde was given the deep six, a member of the law firm handling Big Jute's affairs would notify the foreign bank of the death of Big Jute Nappo's kid brother Luigi and send along all necessary papers for returning the money from Luigi's account back to that of his only surviving relative's, Big Jute Nappo. It was a slick sceme that Bucher had seen worked, with variations, many times.

And so, Bucher continued to himself, his most sensible move right now would be to go upstairs to room 202 and try to coax Delaney Pryde to switch sides, by informing the man he was enroute to the graveyard by remaining with Nappo. Before rising to his feet, Bucher sat a moment longer and scanned the lobby of the hotel—it was far from impossible that either Seeto Loyoka or Mack McReady, or both, had left Pryde-Luigi's room and descended into the lobby. He saw nothing amiss, however, and seconds later was mounting the broad staircase beyond the elevator leading from the first floor of the hotel up to the second.

"How in hell," he muttered aloud, frowning in puzzlement, "could Surd Gulgar *not* have known of the five million dollar hit-price on Kleyr?" It simply didn't seem possible. Yet it was possible. It had happened! For Gulgar had not lied, had been too terrified to lie, about the five million dollar contract, about not knowing why he and Pryde had been sent to Puerto Rico, about why Big Jute Nappo had called his sharks home. Bucher's frown deepened on recalling that Big Jute's partner was a woman. The delightful image of Kleyr Boriquen had popped into his mind the instant Gulgar had told him this, though Bucher could discern no reason for it having done so, because for damn sure Kleyr was not in partnership with Big Jute Nappo. With Nappo holding a five mil kill-contract on her? A five mil contract with an irrevocable imperative clause in it? But if there was no kill-contract, Bucher was willing to lay his life on the line, any second, that Kleyr Boriquen would not be any kind of partner in any sort of undertaking with Big Jute Nappo! Bucher was no psychologist, but being a psychologist was not a pre-requisite to understanding human nature. Not where Kleyr was concerned.

On reaching the second floor, Bucher stopped cautiously at the head of the stairs. Immediately on his right was the elevator shaft, and down the hall twenty-five or thirty feet to his left was room 202. He surveyed the hall in both directions before continuing, and had taken only two or three steps toward his destination when the door of 202 opened suddenly and the hulking shouldered, florid-faced Mack McReady stepped into the hall and drew the door shut behind him. At first he did not see Bucher. The instant he did, shock and fear wreathed his meaty face, and he went for his gun.

"The Butcher!"

"Hold it, Mack!" Bucher snapped.

McReady ignored the command, whipped the .357 magnum from under his arm and—

"*Koosh!*"

The gentle death sigh of the ugly, silencered, Walther P-38 that appeared in Bucher's big mitt was the only sound in the hall—until McReady's .357 thumped to the carpeted floor when the man dropped it and stood there motionless for the space of a long heart beat, a neat 9mm hole at the top of his nose and squarely between his eyes, the rear of his head a gory mess where the 138-grain Parabellum dum-dum had exploded out the back of his skull. When McReady also dropped to the carpeted floor of the hall, there were other muffled thumping sounds and a gust of air forced from his dead lungs.

Bucher cursed under his breath in irritation over having been forced to kill the man—though he knew for a fact

Mack McReady had long ago forfeited his right to live. Bucher checked the hall once again, quickly, as he moved swiftly toward the corpse. According to Surd Gulgar, Seeto Loyoka would still be in room 202 with Delaney Pryde, and Bucher acted without hesitation when he reached the door by grabbing the knob, shoving the door inward and following with a long leap into the room, Walther palmed and ready. But the room was empty. The bed had been slept in, there was a large valise on a luggage stand near the closet door, but the room, including the bathroom, was empty of human life. Bucher returned to the corpse in the hall, seized the back of the coat at the neck and dragged the body into the room. Then he closed the door, locked it, and proceeded to search the valise. He found nothing in it unusual. Delaney Pryde and Seeto Loyoka, obviously, had taken their leave during the time he had been busy talking with Surd Gulgar in the lobby—unless they were in room 203, Gulgar's room, next door.

But they were not in Gulgar's room next door. The lock of 203 gave Bucher no trouble at all, and he found no more in the room than he had found in 202. He returned to the room with the man he had recently killed and went through McReady's pockets. Again nothing of any importance. When he rose to his feet, he frowned in disappointment. Bucher was about to leave the room for good when he noticed a tiny white triangle of a corner of a sheet of paper protruding less than an inch between the mattress and the box springs.

It was the Americana's stationery, he saw when he lifted the mattress. But the sheet was not by itself. There were several more sheets, all identical to the first, each covered on one side only with an intricate maze of signs and symbols that he did not recognize, much less understand. Nor were these sheets of stationery the only items between the mattress and the springs. With them was a small, narrow volume he thought at first to be some sort of a diary, though when he picked it up, he recognized it at once. For across the face of the book were the words: *Boriquen's Sylurgics*, by K. M. Boriquen.

"I be damned." Bucher chuckled in surprised amusement and flipped open the front of the book. Then he saw on the flyleaf, in ink and written in delicate, feminine script, the words: "With all my heart, Darling—Kleyr"; and his chuckle and his amusement faded swiftly. He stared hard at the words, in order to make certain he saw and understood them correctly, all the while knowing there was nothing at all wrong with either his vision or his understanding. A long, slow minute ticked past. A second minute did the same. And for not one single tick of either did Bucher remove his suddenly cold, hard eyes from the words: "With all my heart, Darling—Kleyr."

At last he snapped the cover shut and slipped the small volume into his coat pocket, with an indifferent shrug, craggy face emotionless. But inside he was not indifferent. Nor emotionless. Inside him rapidly building was a cold and deadly fury. And a dull, heavy ache. Goddamn it! Why? Bucher ground his teeth savagely. Why had Kleyr lied to him? He could understand her attempt to find a replacement for him in her emotions with the brief fling with Lyle Hardiman-Charles Everson. When she confessed the matter to him at the beach the night before, he had been surprised to learn she had made but the single attempt—or so she had said and he had believed her. And that was that. Until now!

Until: "With all my heart, Darling—Kleyr." These words unmistakably betrayed her falsehood, for a woman such as he knew Kleyr Boriquen to be did not write "With all my heart, Darling," unless she meant it sincerely! In addition, Kleyr would never write "Darling" to a woman. Such was not in her makeup, so whoever "darling" was, the son of a bitch was a man. Yet this in itself was not disturbing to Bucher. He was not jealous of "darling," couldn't be jealous of any one or all of several dozen "darlings" who might have passed through Kleyr's life since their affair eight years ago. He had no right to be jealous, for he had treated her shabbily enough when he walked off without a word of explanation or farewell. Moreover, there had been quite a few women in his life since Hibbings Summer Lodge in the Catskills. So from any angle of the compass he had no right to be jealous. And he wasn't jealous, goddamn it! Not because of "darling" written in the book. But he was goddamn well furious because Kleyr had lied to him. That he would not forgive easily—if at all. Bucher turned woodenly toward the door and almost stumbled over the corpse of Mack McReady—which caused him to pause, massage his face vigorously, and stand statue-still, staring toward the door but not seeing it, not until after he had cleared his mind thoroughly of its fury and calmed the emotions raging inside him. Then, and only then, did he permit himself to proceed—a man with a quarter of a million dollar dead-only reward hanging over his head was no less than stupid to venture out in public when not in complete control of his mind and emotions.

7

Thirty minutes after leaving the Americana Hotel, Bucher lifted off from the San Juan airport in the small rented helicopter, and less than thirty minutes after lifting off, he was gently setting the craft down beside the huge heavy-duty CH-47 Chinook helicopter White Hat's director used as his headquarters, at Kleyr's home on the edge of Arecibo. During the brief journey Bucher had decided to say nothing to anyone, yet, about finding a copy of *Boriquen's Sylurgics* at the Americana in the room that was registered in the name of Luigi Nappo. Later, on the small island twenty miles or so off the coast of Puerto Rico where he intended to take Kleyr for more certain protection tonight, if he deemed it necessary, he would mention finding the book to her then. But only if it was necessary. No, only if it was essential would he bring the matter to her attention. Then ... "Yeah," he muttered as the craft touched earth. "Then what, dumb-ass? What if you confront her with the lie, and she tells you to go take a flying frig at the moon? What will you do then?" He cut the helicopter's motor and crawled out of the small vehicle, answering his own question with, "Well, if she tells you that, I guess you'll just go take a flying frig at the moon, dumb-ass."

White Hat's director came striding up as Bucher stretched and straightened his clothes.

"Did you learn anything of value, Mr. Bucher?"

As briefly as possible Bucher recounted his conversation with Surd Gulgar and sketchily outlined his visit to the Americana's second floor, but mentioned no word of his finding a copy of Kleyr's book in Delaney Pryde's room. The director's face was filled with surprise when he finished.

"You say that Luigi Nappo's name is neither Luigi Nappo nor Oliver Dillingsworth, but Delaney Pryde?" the older man asked on recovering. "And he's from South Africa?"

"According to Surd Gulgar he is. And I believe Gulgar because he was too damn scared to think up a lie like that. Any info come in yet on Lyle Hardiman, Dr. J. Joiner Mull, and the rest of that list of names?" The remainder of the list had included doctors Samantha Bartlet and J. M. Philbrick, Martha Andrews, and the man Arnie-Dingus what's-his-name who'd got his throat cut in the Dainty Dish the night before.

"Nothing." The director shook his head.

"What about Kleyr's cousins?"

"Rachel and Nora Cordova were murdered some time around four o'clock yesterday afternoon, according to the police department's medical examiner in San Juan, and Homicide Captain Raymond Ortega seems to think the crimes were committed by a young woman."

"Come again?" Bucher frowned, as though having not heard right.

The director repeated his last statement, including: "Captain Ortega says an eight-year-old lad of a family neighboring the Cordova sisters claims to have seen a young woman leave the rear of the Cordova home yesterday afternoon; as best as he could pin down the time it was between four-thirty and six o'clock." He paused, squinting at the sun as he tugged at an earlobe. "Do you

98

suppose Delaney Pryde came down here to Puerto Rico to meet with Big Jute Nappo's female partner because this female partner is in Puerto Rico?"

"I don't know," Bucher grinned crookedly. "Could be, but the only female genius I know of in Puerto Rico is Kleyr, and I'll be damned if I'll consider her as a partner to Big Jute Nappo. How is Kleyr, by the way?"

"Asleep. We've got the telephone up in her lab building hooked up through our radio phone in the Chinook there now, and a few minutes after you took off for San Juan, she called to say she was taking a nap, but for me to call and awaken her when you returned."

"No." Bucher shook his head. "I'll wake her."

He approached the house from the front, going up the cement walkway, noting with satisfaction the great, glaring floodlights at the corners of the building, resembling the dead, blank eyes of some giant insect. But tonight when the lights were turned on, the area around the building would be lit up like Times Square. He went inside the house, and tiptoed silently into the bedroom, where he found Kleyr sprawled sound asleep on the large bed. Less the orchids, her slumber ensemble was precisely what it had been when he'd first seen her at the Dainty Dish the night before.

Making as little sound as possible, he shed his garments and crawled onto the bed beside her. Kleyr's only response was tiny sleep sounds. On the night prior to his flight from New York, Bucher had slept even less than the skimpy sleep he'd gotten on the beach with Kleyr last night, and though he was sorely tempted to awaken Kleyr to inform her of his return, the instant he stretched out full length beside her, he knew he would not, for at once the soft bed began doing delicious things to his relaxing muscles—in little more than sixty seconds he was as sound asleep as the young woman lying next to him.

Due to the White Hat task force guarding Kleyr's house, the heavy storm shutters of the windows were open, and the lengthening shadows of late afternoon were stretching across the bedroom floor when Bucher awakened. As was his habit, he awoke abruptly, instantly in command of all his faculties, yet not moving a muscle, not even so much as the flicker of an eyelid, nor in any other way betraying the fact that he was awake. He was alone on the huge bed, and faintly he heard sounds of the shower.

"Ooooeeee!" Kleyr squealed in delighted surprise, dropping the soap, when Bucher suddenly swept aside the curtain and joined her; then she knelt on one knee to retrieve the soap but instead took him, completely, unaware and he roared harshly in his own surprise and stood with feet apart, grimacing and gasping and helplessly pawing at the tiled wall until ... until ... three slow minutes ticked by and ...

Kleyr brandished the cake of soap under his nose impishly in triumph a second before she seized herself with both arms and, laughing in unrestrained, riotous abandon at his expression, did a little jig for joy.

"Wow!" Bucher gasped raggedly, weakly, for the moment sagging limply against the tiled wall. "You—you don't give a guy much warning, do you?"

"Not when the guy is you, lout." She flung both arms about his neck, pouted fetchingly, then drew herself up, butting noses with him and drawing her lips back in a caricature smile. "See, lout. All tooth enamel intact. So *you owe me*. Am I coming in loud and clear, Bucher? *You owe me.*"

"Hey—are you putting us on an exchange basis?" Bucher grinned.

"Of course not."

"Then why the 'you owe me' bit?"

"Well ..." She lowered herself, limpid eyes holding his, but standing hard against him. "You haven't done me— last night at the beach you didn't and, well, people *do* change you know, so if you have in that regard I'd like to know it, so I won't keep hoping."

"The answer is no. I haven't changed in that regard. But if you'll recall last night, when we were coming out of the water and headed—you mentioned a table—that's when we heard Loyoka and McReady and learned of the kill-contract on you."

After a moment of studying his craggy face, she nodded briefly and stepped back, eyes apologetic. "Darn," she said just above the noise of the shower. "You know something, Boo? I'd forgotten all about that kill-contract and subsequent mess until you mentioned it just now. I guess you really do turn me into a sex maniac if I'm letting sex take precedence over survival."

"Bull." Bucher took her by the arm, grinning. "I owe you, so let's hie ourselves to yon bedroom and—"

"Nope." She pulled free, but she was smiling vivaciously and had a sly glow of anticipation in her eyes. "No. Let's finish bathing first. Then we'll hie ourselves to yon bedroom. In the meantime tell me what you accomplished today."

He told her everything, except finding the volume of her *Sylurgics* in Delaney Pryde's hotel room, and as his account progressed her expression grew more puzzled. By the time he finished her lovely face reflected deep perplexity.

"But, Boo . . ." She paused in soaping his back to peer around his right shoulder. "If that Surd Gulgar didn't know anything about Big Jute Nappo's contract to have me killed, perhaps there never was such a contract."

False information about the contract could not have been purposely leaked to White Hat, Bucher well knew, since less than a dozen people outside the organization knew of its existence, but White Hat's source for the information could have been taken in by a false leak; Bucher well knew this. It had happened before, and there was no assurance it had not happened again. Nevertheless
. . .

"I can't buy that," Bucher told her honestly. "The same has occurred to me a few dozen times already and I simply can't buy it."

"What are you going on?"

"Experience. And instinct."

"Experience with the Syndicate?"

"Uh-huh."

"Then the contract on me was real?"

"It still is."

"But if Big Jute Nappo recalled all his killers from Puerto Rico—"

"I don't believe it." He turned to face her. "Lady, you're rubbing a hole in my back. You've been on that one spot five minutes."

"You don't believe the killers have been withdrawn then?"

"Oh, yes. I do believe the killers have been withdrawn, all but Seeto Loyoka. And Big Jute outfoxed himself. Sending all those gunsels down here to rub one teeny-weeny frau was stupid to begin with. If I didn't know Big Jute Nappo as well as I do, I'd swear an amateur had taken over his operation. And calling them back without the job done is stupider still; this is what betrayed Big Jute's hand. Calling them back. Sending twenty gunsels down here to kill one woman, when the reward is five million dollars, I can understand, especially when the contract has an 'irrevocable imperative,' but calling the gunsels back with you still alive is a dead giveaway. Goddamn it! I should have realized this before. The instant I heard it."

"Should have realized what, Boo?" Kleyr was all ears and eyes.

"The real killer is still here, in Puerto Rico, and still determined to kill you unless you cooperate with Mister X. Hell, the sonofabitch may *be* Mister X for all we know!" Bucher stepped under the full shower to rinse himself thoroughly, and Kleyr stepped through the curtain for a moment, returning with two large, thick towels. She waited until he cut the spray, then handed him one.

"Then—we're still waiting for a message from Mister X? Is that right, Boo?"

"A phone call. Your number's in the book, I take it. I mean, yours isn't an unlisted phone number is it?"

"It's in the book, but how do you know the message will come by phone?"

"I know because Mister X didn't have an ambush waiting for us—for you—when we arrived here last night. He wants you here. In this house. That way he can reach you, by phone, whenever he's ready to do so—I'm a bit surprised he hasn't phoned already."

"But—that twenty-five pound C-4 bomb you found in the pantry—"

"That was to kill you with if you failed to cooperate."

"But the person, the real killer, as you called him—"

"Is to get you in case the bomb was found, which it was."

After a long pause Kleyr shook her head in no little amazement. "Merciful heavens," she murmured in a mixture of awe and wonder. "I used to read of you—after the Catskills?—I used to read of your hair-raising exploits in first one magazine and then another and, honestly Boo, I'd wonder how you could manage to stay alive. How you always survived some of the situations you got into. She studied him solemnly a moment. "I'm beginning to think I understand. You're some sort of demon I believe, some—" She giggled impulsively. "Perhaps you're Satan himself. No! I mean it! Not Satan, silly. But I'm beginning to understand how ... Why didn't Sam and some of his men outside think of what you've just told me? About Mister X, the bomb, the phone, and the message and all?"

"I'll bite. Why didn't they?"

"See what I mean? Only you thought of it!"

"That's not to say some of them couldn't have—"

"But they *didn't*, Boo! They *didn't!* Don't you see what I mean?"

He grinned, unable not to. "Okay, but is it vital?"

"It's vital to me, lout." She biffed him on the chest. "It means I don't have to worry so darn much about my man winding up shot full of holes—damn you, Boo!" She biffed him again. "It's a wonder my hair isn't snow white! It's no thanks to you that it isn't! It's—" She stopped short at Bucher shaking his head in honest admiration, then asked: "Why?"

"You."

"Why me?"

"Lassie, because you've got more guts than a grizzly bear."

103

"Hmmmm. I think I like that." She turned toward the door.

"Be my guest." He thwacked her gently on the naked rump. "You're also about to be my guest elsewise. I owe you, remember? So hie thee to yon bedroom and—" He stopped, laughing, at the look she tossed over her shoulder; her face glowed with sudden, breathless anticipation, her eyes shone with it.

"And what?" she whispered tremulously.

He thwacked her a second time. "You know 'and what,' so scoot."

Several minutes later the telephone on the night stand at the head of Kleyr's bed pealed stridently. And was ignored—if it was heard. It pealed again. And again. And Again. And kept repeating its strident demand to be answered until the tenth peal, whereupon Bucher walked sideways over the thick rug on his knees to the night stand and lifted the instrument from its cradle. It was White Hat's director calling, his voice urgent, anxious, with concern.

"Mr. Bucher, is everything all right? The guards claim to hear sounds of terrible human suffering coming from inside the house."

"Just a minute." Bucher deadened the mouthpiece with a palm in order to give himself time to think of an answer, laughing and shaking his head and looking at Kleyr—who managed to struggle up on an elbow and return his look with dull, glazed eyes, face slack. After half a minute Bucher uncovered the mouthpiece and spoke into it.

"Tell the guards they're right," he said. "We're listening to a record Kleyr borrowed from the Institute of Puerto Rican Culture. It's an imitation of the ancient chant, if it can be called a chant, of a *Taino* Indian wife of a ball team captain whose team has lost a game. The penalty for losing, according to Kleyr, is that the captain of the losing team forfeits his head, and his wife becomes the concubine of the winning captain, so the guards were right. The recording does sound like terrible human suffering."

104

"I'm sorry I bothered you," the older man laughed in relief, hanging up at once.

"What was that all about?" Kleyr stiff-lipped the words in a hoarse voice.

"About all your screeching, shrieking, howling, gasping, sobbing, wailing, strangling, crying, babbling," Bucher laughed.

"W-What?"

"That was Sam White on the phone," he said, still laughing. "You heard what I told him about the *Taino* Indians; the guards thought someone was being tortured in here; terrible human suffering he said they called it." His laughter became uninhibited; at last he told her, "You make too much noise. You've had it, lassie."

Kleyr flopped flat off the elbow and straightened a knee quickly, kicking at him in play with the nearer foot hanging over the edge of the bed, then commenced lashing her head from side to side in unison with the syllables. "NO!-NO!-NO!-NO!-NO!" she intoned, pleading. "NO!-NO!-NO!-NO!-NO!" A long breath shuddered through her. "I've not had it enough, Boo. Please? Huh? *Please?* I won't make any noise, Boo." She reached for a pillow. "I promise. Now get busy, Boo." And she dropped the pillow across her face.

Bucher began drawing on his clothes in silence some forty minutes later—as yet he had told no one, including Kleyr, that he and she were not spending the night in her house, and it was getting late; plans had to be made. He was half dressed when he realized abruptly he was ravenous. He glanced at Kleyr, still on the bed.

"Kleyr. Are you conscious? Can you stand?" He noted the dull glaze was gone from her eyes when she opened them; her saucy smile told him the rest.

"Why, silver-tongue?" she giggled hoarsely.

"Dammit, woman, I'm starved. Get off that bed and rattle some pots and pans." After a moment's pause he added in softer tones. "I've an overnight trip to make."

"Where?" She snapped up into a sitting position. "Alone?"

Bucher pretended to mull over the question, at last answering her. "Tell you what, wench, if you can throw something to eat together within the next hour, I'll take you with me."

She bounced off the bed; her kiss missed his mouth and caught him on the right eye instead, after which, jabbering excitedly to herself as to what foods to prepare, she also began dressing.

"Listen, wench," Bucher told her before leaving for outside. "You ever let any of the guys outside hear you call me Boo or silver-tongue and it makes for bruises on your fanny. Get me?"

"Gotcha, sor." She aped a silly salute, offering with it a goofy grin, the fact that as yet she wore nothing but a blouse making the act seem all the more ludicrous, then barked sharply in pain and swung solidly when Bucher tweaked a small tuft and dodged out of reach toward the front door.

"Lout!" she yelled, darting after him. "Churl! Cur! Come back here and take your medici—!" She danced behind an overstuffed chair and hunkered, laughing helplessly, when he yanked open the door and hurried out.

The director frowned in perplexity at the chart he and Bucher studied in the Chinook. "Are you sure about this, Mr. Bucher? I don't see it on the map. Are you sure the island is there?" He chuckled inoffensively. "I'd hate like the very deuce for you and Kleyr to wind up in the Caribbean Sea in the dead of night. You say you've actually been to the island?"

"It's more of an atoll," Bucher said, nodding. "And I was there dozens of times years ago. The Syndicate used it as a drop for huge shipments of narcotics. The shipment would be broken down into smaller packets, smuggled into Puerto Rico by small boat, and once here it was concealed in a section of hollow superstructure of old World War II C-47s that ferried freight between here and Miami as a cover—the planes also belonged to the Syndicate. Barefoot, that's the name we called it; if the atoll has a name I don't know it. Anyway, Barefoot is only three or four

106

hundred yards long and a couple of hundred wide, and it's surrounded by coral reefs that stick a foot above the surface at low tide. Not even a small boat can get within a half mile of the place. It's only accessible by 'copter, and the closest land to it is the eastern tip of Puerto Rico."

"Twenty nautical miles, you say?"

"A fraction over twenty U.S.-International nautical miles. Exactly 37,070 meters, which makes it thirty meters over twenty nautical miles. I can find it in a 'copter on the darkest night of the year—by one of the most dependable systems of navigation in the world."

"How?" the director asked, completely absorbed with Bucher's plan.

"Compass and the stars."

"That's right. And I'm a hundred percent for your idea. What does Kleyr think of it?"

"You're the only one I've told. Kleyr knows only that we're going somewhere. I'll tell her where when we're airborne."

"You take this Chinook—you say Kleyr has a pilot's license?"

"Right."

"Then take the Chinook here. If things get hairy in flight, give her the controls and you man that .50 caliber machine gun a couple of the boys installed in the off cargo port. They improvised a five hundred round basket drum. If things get real hairy you can melt the .50's barrel if need be. Here now, let me show you something these 'copters also have." He moved to the instrument panel, pointing. "This toggle switch here, turn it on when you leave and any one or all of the other Chinooks will be able to follow you on one of these." He pointed to what appeared to be the blank face of a twelve-inch TV screen. "Radar, but with a small difference. We can follow you if you travel as low as a hundred feet above the surface of the water, and we also can spot any bandits that might get after you in case that damn Mister X gets wise. So if things do get hairy, you'll have help within minutes." He paused, looking hard at Bucher. "Mr. Bucher, something has passed

107

me somewhere. Big Jute Nappo's calling his men back to New York has me stumped, completely."

"Big Jute has slipped a cog and dropped down to amateur level it seems to me," Bucher said easily. "Big Jute's boys weren't even supposed to come after Kleyr, not seriously, when they came to Puerto Rico." He proceeded to explain as he had done to Kleyr earlier, and the director's seamed face reflected amazement increasing in proportion to his increasing understanding of the explanation. After Bucher finished, he simply stared—until Bucher said, rising to his feet: "Have a couple of the men back that rented Dodge van of mine over here and unload the gear and bottled water and other things here in the 'copter. We may need it on Barefoot." He turned toward the exit.

"You're returning tomorrow, aren't you?" the director asked, following behind. "In the morning?"

"That I can't say till the time comes. I'll call on the radio phone; how far does the Chinook's signal carry?"

"Over a thousand miles."

"Good. I'll call. What was that info you said came in on those background checkouts?"

"Lyle Hardiman has a kink in his psyche, and a bad one, about women. Likes to beat them. But he's clean otherwise. Dr. J. Joiner Mull is also clean, though the report says there may be more to come concerning him. Dr. J. M. Philbrick here in Arecibo is spotless. The way we got it, the old duffer's been tinkering around with some lass little more than a third his age, but his wife's been dead two decades so he can't be faulted for that. Dr. Samantha Bartlet at the Observatory is clean as a hound's tooth. Martha Andrews, who seems to have vanished since last night, is from Miami, Florida, as she told Kleyr she was, has three kids in boarding school there, and her husband, James Andrews, is in the Florida State Penitentiary for bank robbery, all exactly as she told Kleyr. The puzzler is: What happened to the woman?"

"Last night at the beach in Loiza Aldea, when we overheard Seeto Loyoka and Mack McReady talking, they were arguing about going to such extremes as hunting

108

Kleyr at Loiza Aldea when Loyoka told McReady: 'We wouldn't be in this fix'—of having to search for Kleyr all over—'if you hadn't glommed onto the wrong one at the Dish.' So I'm inclined to believe Martha Andrews probably got what they gave that poor devil who got his throat cut in his dressing room at the Dainty Dish last night. Loyoka and McReady went there after Kleyr, found the Arnie-Dingus character, slit his throat, and kidnapped Martha Andrews and did the same to her later. That's the way I've got it figured."

"Why didn't they slit her throat at the Dainty Dish?"

Bucher shook his head, tapping one temple with a forefinger.

"Loyoka and Hardiman have something in common about women, only Loyoka likes to hear them scream under lit cigars and the like. I've little doubt someone will stumble over Martha Andrews's body out in the boondocks some time soon. Has Arnie-Dingus been identified yet?"

The director nodded. "Name's Arnold Limpkin—English. He jumped ship a few months back, freighter out of Liverpool, and applied for citizenship. The name he was using at the time of his death, to prevent Immigration authorities from discovering what he did at the Dainty Dish, was Arnie Greenbaum. Oh, yes. Apparently Surd Gulgar told you the straight of it about Delaney Pryde. The man does have a third identity, under the name Oliver Dillingsworth, but we've been able to learn no more than Gulgar knew about his and Pryde's reason for coming to Puerto Rico—unless to make contact with this other female genius who is Big Jute Nappo's partner, as you suggested. And there's nothing new regarding Kleyr's two murdered cousins."

Bucher nodded. "Buzz me on the radio phone tonight if anything of importance comes in."

"By all means. Er, Mr. Bucher?"

Bucher, who had turned for the house, turned back. "Yes?"

"You're taking Kleyr to Barefoot tonight, I assume, because you don't trust the house being clean. May I ask why?"

Bucher chuckled, thinking a moment before answering. "Instinct."

"And that's all? Just instinct?" The director hurried on. "I'm not questioning your instinct, mind you." God knows he'd seen Bucher's instincts pay off many times, but ... "I'm just deucedly curious."

"That twenty-five pound C-4 bomb was a bit too obvious."

"I suspected that might be a contributing factor."

"Especially since Mister X has had plenty of time to phone. Maybe the bastard's got problems, I hope. What was on that tape from the recorder concealed in the floor of the lab building, by the way?"

"Bucher!" Kleyr called from the house. "Quickly!"

Bucher ran, fast, thinking Mister X might be calling at last, forgetting any phone call to Kleyr's number now would activate the phone in the Chinook as well, and stopped running only when he saw the mischievous smile on Kleyr's face as she stepped back, holding wide the door.

"You sounded urgent," he told her suspiciously, closing the door behind him.

"But you told me you were famished, ape," she insisted innocently. " 'Dammit, woman, I'm starved,' you said. 'Get off that bed and rattle some pots and pans' were your exact words. Only I goofed, Boo."

"Yeah?" he said, still suspiciously. "How'd you goof?"

"Well, I suppose I just got carried completely away with the idea of us going away for the night and, well, I forgot and packed the food in a large hamper I have." She took his wrist and towed him into the kitchen, pointing to a bushel-size splint hamper on the table when they reached it. "See. But here." She took half a fried chicken from a drainrack atop the stove, couched it in paper napkins and handed it to him. "Here, Boo. You can be munching on this till we get where we're going. Is it all right that I packed the food instead of us eating it here? Go on. Eat the chicken. Is it all right that I packed the hamper?"

Bucher nodded, knowing she had packed the hamper

110

thinking it was additional insurance of accompanying him—which Bucher found not only immensely flattering, it also made him feel like a damn louse, since she was the only reason that they were taking the trip. "My fault," he lied calmly, biting into the chicken half. "I meant to ask you to pack the meal anyway."

The steady, level look she gave said in effect: "I know you're fibbing, lout, but I also know why and I'm glad." Then, as if on cue, both burst into laughter, she coming into his arms, wriggling close.

"Hey-hey!" He retreated a quick step. "Ease up, wench, or we'll never make it out the door."

"Mmmm, goody. Where're we going?"

"San Juan," he lied again. But this one escaped her.

"Soon?"

He glanced toward the kitchen window. Dusk was beginning to settle in; night would soon be here. "Now," he told her, lifting the hamper off the table with his free hand. "My god, woman. What've you got in here? Lead weights?"

"Only a few, Boo," she replied happily. "No more than a dozen. Medium-size ones." She led the way from the kitchen, stopping at the couch in the living room. "May I take this also?" The pistol she took from the end of the couch was a Unique D. E. S. 69 match pistol, caliber .22, long rifle, ten-shot autoloading, one of most accurate match handguns in the world.

"Where the hell'd you get that?"

"Must I tell you?"

"No."

"Then I'll tell you—as if I wouldn't anyway, brute. Charl—Lyle Hardiman forgot it in my apartment. I lived closer in town then. He left in a hurry after he walloped me, and forgot this. *Now* may I take it along?"

"Can you use the thing?"

"I can hit a quarter-size spot six times out of ten at twenty-five meters, free style."

"The hell you say," Bucher intoned in blank amazement. "Then bring it by all means. We may need cannon and rockets before this rat race is over with." He waited

111

until she tucked the weapon behind the waistband of her slacks, concealed it behind her blouse, then led the way to the door.

"What's all this for?" Kleyr asked a minute later, as they entered the Chinook, indicating the canned food, bottled water, mattress, and other gear that had been transfered from the rented Dodge van into the helicopter.

"Just in case. Come on. Buckle in. Time's a-wastin', says Snuffy Smith. Let's move it."

Kleyr obeyed, not speaking again until they were airborne, or rather, as they became airborne, waving at the director who stood watching them ascend and calling once: "Bye, Sam." Then the gathering night swallowed them as they rose higher, Bucher angling the craft toward the general direction of the Cordillera Central Mountains.

"Boo, we aren't going to San Juan, are we?"

He grinned across at her. "Huh-uh. How can you tell?"

"Well, first by all that gear from the van in back of us. Second because we aren't going in the direction of San Juan."

"You know the direction we're going?" he asked in mild surprise. Kleyr Boriquen was a constant source of surprises.

"Of course, I know, nut." She pointed toward the instrument panel. "I can read a compass. Where are we going?"

Bucher told her, slowly, in detail, making sure she understood where their destination was and their reason for going there. The fact he suspected her house in Arecibo to still be mined fazed her not the minutest whit, for when he finished talking, she made no mention of it, instead slapping her hands and crying in delight:

"Ooooh-goody!-goody!-goody! That gives you all night!"

"Yeah? All night to do what?"

She pretended enormous chagrin. "All night to *knock me up*. You promised, you know."

"Yeah? I believe you are a sex maniac at that."

When her laughter subsided, the conversation lagged, Bucher concentrating on their route. Once over the Cordillera Central Mountains he swung the big craft due

112

east, heading straight for Rincon. Less than half an hour later they passed over Rincon, and he gradually let the helicopter down toward the Caribbean below. Once the altimeter was registering 400 feet, he slowed to a fast crawl, checking the compass repeatedly and frequently peering down toward the sea. After a while Kleyr spoke quietly.

"Is it much farther, dear?"

"That's genius for you," Bucher chuckled. "We're there."

"Really? So soon?" Her pleasure at the news was obvious.

"Madame, this noble aircraft is not a snail."

"Hear, hear. I—" She stopped as silhouettes of palm trees appeared between her and the starry sky. A second later the Chinook sank against the earth, and Bucher quickly cut the engine, then just as quickly turned out all interior lights.

"Boo, how in the world did you find this place in the dark, without outside lights or anything?"

"Practice," he grinned at her. "Experience."

"You've been here before?" Incredulity was written all over her lovely face. "I do declare, Sir Boo-Boo Bucher, but you beat all. And I suppose you landed us conveniently near the beach so we can go swimming and such."

"Depends on what you mean by 'and such,' but look." Their eyes were adjusted to the darkness now, so the light of the rising moon on the waves purling on the sandy beach not over twenty-five yards to their left made the beach easily visible.

"Humph," Kleyr feigned disdain. "So you work miracles. So what?" Then, contritely: "I guess I'm pretty coarse and crude for a lady, huh, Boo? A while ago I mean. I could've at least refined the statement to 'get me with child' or 'make me a mother' or some such, instead of 'knock me up'!"

"You could've said it several dozen ways I suppose," Bucher told her. "But I understood you perfectly the way you expressed it, and a lot can be said for clear communications, ma'am." He chuckled quietly. "Come on. Let's see what else you've got in that hamper."

"I think you're simply fabulous, Boo Bucher," she said a few minutes later, after they had unloaded her hamper, the mattress, and a few other items from the craft. Bucher, unaware until then that she still felt embarrassment over what she considered a gross statement, grabbed her and kissed her.

"Forget what you said." Then he chuckled again, though not so quietly this time. "And if I don't succeed at it tonight, well, there's always tomorrow, tomorrow night, maybe even years. Just hang in there and make me keep my promise to you, woman. I'll succeed or die trying. That's another promise."

"See, Boo." Now she kissed him. "Simply fabulous."

"You know something, wench? I don't know what happened to that half of fried chicken you gave me back at the house."

"You left it at the house. You placed it on the back of that big chair while we were talking about my pistol—I remember seeing you."

"I'm so hungry I'm getting left-handed. The hamper, Kleyr, the hamper."

He watched in silence as she spread a large table cloth beside the mattress and commenced laying out enough food to feed a dozen people.

"Here's what made it so heavy." She placed a gallon thermos jug on the edge of the cloth and handed him two large plastic cups. "Pour, please?" She continued spreading their moonlight repast as he complied, handing her a cup of the cold liquid when he finished.

"Here, and don't lose this one." She gave him another half of a fried chicken on a paper plate. "What else? You point and I'll serve." The plate was heaped in quick time, whereupon Bucher sank to a corner of the mattress with a sigh that is best defined as voluptuous. And ate. And ate. And gave Kleyr a look of pleased surprise.

"Champagne?" He held up the cup, Kleyr smiling in reply to his approval.

"Nothing but the very best for my one-man entourage." They ate in silence until Kleyr asked: "You have been here before, haven't you, Boo?"

114

"Many times." He followed with the account of the Syndicate's narcotic-smuggling use of the tiny atoll years ago, the same account he had given White Hat's director earlier.

"And you named the place Barefoot?" she marveled when he finished.

"Well, someone from among us at that time named it Barefoot, possibly because it's an ideal place to go without shoes, being mostly of sand aside from the vegetation. The place was constructed by the sea. The water here was very shallow, subsurface vegetation flourished, and gradually, as this vegetation became thicker, the sea began to build by lodging sand and particles of other solid matter among it. In time the atoll itself grew into what it now is, then over the years, or decades, or centuries, it was sown by wind-borne seeds. As far as I know the place has never been inhabited—too far out of the way, I guess, so there's none of the normal human debris like rusting cans, broken bottles, and whatnot to make going barefoot hazardous. So maybe that's the reason for us calling it Barefoot. Besides, Barefoot is as good a name as any."

They became silent after this, Kleyr devoting her attention to the meal, while Bucher sat looking at the purling waves without actually seeing them, a stern frown gradually maturing on his craggy features.

This frown was visible evidence of Bucher's efforts toward greater concentration in hopes of remembering something, though precisely what that "something" was, he did not know. Thus far he knew only, instinctively, that he was guilty of oversight, and that the knowledge of this oversight had been incubating in the periphery of his mind, gradually gaining strength sufficient to make itself understood, since last night not long after he and Kleyr had fled the Dainty Dish. He was trying to recall a trifling bit of evidence that pointed directly toward the identity of Mister X. Heretofore he had not been positive the evidence existed within his immediate framework of references, but only a few moments ago, while talking to Kleyr about the manner in which Barefoot came to be, the undeniable knowledge that he had encountered the evidence in person blossomed within his consciousness and flatly refused to budge. Which created a truly bizarre paradox: knowing he had encountered the evidence was of damn little value unless he could remember what the evidence was.

"Boo?"

"Humh?"

"Do you remember that alligator wallet you bought me?"

"Sure."

"I still have it. I guess I'm a sentimental boob or something, huh?"

"Why?"

"Oh, I don't know. I also have that stack of hundred dollar bills you left. All but a dollar and two cents of one." She began returning the remains of their meal to the splint hamper, except the champagne, then tucked the cloth around the top of the hamper and sat it back inside the Chinook. Bucher could almost feel her waiting for him to answer, but the topic of conversation was one he would not have chosen, therefore he hesitated, uncertain as to what he would say. Her attitude had changed, grown more serious, within the past few minutes, the change evidenced by the timbre of her voice, and because he now knew he had once almost been responsible for her taking her life.

"Boo, did you see that cat?"

"What cat?"

"The one that has your tongue."

"Oh-yeah-hummm, well, I guess I just might sue you for that dollar and two cents or something like that."

"I'll give you the rope I bought with it instead. I still have it also. But it's in two pieces; the Hibbings cut it in two taking me down, but the noose is still in it."

"Goddamn, Princess! Shut up!" Chills crept over him.

She plopped down beside him on the mattress. "Why?"

"Because the subject scares hell out of me, that's why!" He meant every word.

"Aren't you the good cowboy who cut a baddy off at the pass this morning at the Americana Hotel? Didn't killing a man scare hell out of you?"

"No! It didn't! That sonofabitch I killed wasn't you. Be-

116

sides, McReady got his jollies by drenching unconsciously drunk skid row winos with gasoline and 'torchin' 'em up' as he called it—"

"Boo, hush, please." She leaned her forehead against his shoulder. After a moment she raised her head, looking at him. "I'm sorry. Honest. But I was only teasing about the rope. It's far better to be able to talk openly and freely about something like that though, than to keep it locked inside. I'm rather proud of myself, really. Because I can speak of it without a twinge—such silly business, how foolish I was to do that. You reacted much more explosively than I'd thought you might." Her voice became gruff in imitation of his "Goddamn, Princess! Shut up!" "I'm also glad Sam let his tongue slip and told you about it. Now it's over and far behind us, and there's no reason to ever speak of it again. Are we going in swimming?"

"If you want. But not until after we give Barefoot a quick going over." He stood and gave her a hand. "Come on."

8

They could have circled the atoll in ten minutes easily but the night was balmy, the breeze from the sea gentle, the silvery moonlight from a magical, lovers' moon; therefore they circled it in thirty minutes instead, each carrying one of White Hat's new, experimental 9mm stainless steel submachine guns. As Bucher expected, they found nothing to cause alarm, though they discovered they were not Barefoot's sole inhabitants. On the beach at the east end of the atoll, they came across three giant green turtles, the largest a monster of several hundred pounds.

"Let's go play in the water, Boo," Kleyr suggested as they placed their weapons back inside the Chinook. "You want?"

"I want." Since having slept most of the remainder of the day after returning from San Juan, Bucher doubted if he would be able to sleep at all, which, all things consid-

117

ered, suited him perfectly. He had no reason to believe he and Kleyr would not be safe on Barefoot, but there was always the possibility of that one rare exception. Thus it was best that he remain awake.

After undressing, Bucher followed the nymphian grace of Kleyr's nude loveliness, and he shook his head in silent wonder, marveling at his libidinal energy and drive. Perhaps it was the Puerto Rican air, he grinned wryly. Perhaps he should cork up a few million bottles and place them on the market—with a picture of Kleyr on the label, of course. Christ! A man could become a jillionaire overnight—

"What's the joke, mug?" Until she spoke, Bucher had not known she was watching him. "Come on. Out with it." She took his hand as they waded into the surf. And when he explained what had been in his thoughts, she regarded him in enormous gladness, nodding approval.

"You like me in bed, don't you, Boo? No, let me rephrase that, I'm getting gross again. What I should have said was: 'You like me as a woman, don't you?' "

"Christ! Shouldn't I? No, let me rephrase that too: How couldn't I?"

She laughed merrily, much pleased, but sobering quickly. "You know something, Boo?"

"Sometimes I wonder."

"No, lout, I'm serious. You know what I'd be if I had a choice?"

Bucher nodded, aware suddenly that she was indeed very serious, more serious in fact than he'd ever before known her to be. "Go ahead. Tell me what you'd be if you had a choice." They were now in water reaching to his upper chest, which brought the level to just below Kleyr's chin, and he spatted water lightly in her direction with one hand as she moved to him before answering.

"First of all I would like not to be a damn superbrain," she said slowly, "as I used to be called, and still am on occasion. I do not mean I would like to be unintelligent, but to be only moderately intelligent. Second I would like to be a wife; nothing fancy mind you, just an ordinary common housewife with a comfortable, orderly routine of maintaining a comfortable, orderly home for my husband—who would father the twelve children I want to have. And that's all. Just these few, simple things are all I want from life. If ... Why is it, Boo, that simple things for some people are always the most difficult to come by?"

"I wish I knew," he said, now himself also very serious. The unspoken plea of her words touched him deeply, for it echoed his own secret desire for a tranquil, uncomplicated life. "But I don't."

"Do I ask too much?"

A long, thoughtful moment passed before Bucher answered, during which she threaded her arms through his, clasping them in back. "Yes. You ask too much."

"But why, Boo?"

"For you it's too much because it's impossible. You might as well dream of owning the moon or the sun, which is no less impossible to obtain than what you want. Unless you've invented some way to cease being a superbrain. The home, the husband, the kids? Why not? They're possible, entirely possible; but losing your smarts, Princess, there just isn't any way. If the second is contingent on the first, quit dreaming. Otherwise, have at it."

She studied his craggy face several long breaths in serious contemplation. "Padrino told me virtually the same thing half a dozen times. Almost verbatim."

"Kleyr, listen to me." He tilted her face up to his with a finger beneath her chin. "Unfortunately or otherwise, certain persons must go through life set apart from ordinary beings. No matter how hard they yearn or strive for happiness through commonality they cannot obtain it because they are not of the common people. There is something about them that makes them very special. Therefore they must find happiness among other special people. You are such a person, Kleyr. You are very special. In many ways—"

"Name one. Quickly."

"Your decision to not divulge any information about the manner you improved and perfected the Boston Experiment is one infinitely gigantic way, if I may strain at superlatives. Imagine a little half-pint angel come to earth protecting the entire world from only God knows what in the Fourth Dimension. And the world can't know about what she's doing, must never know; therefore she can never receive an iota of gratitude or a cent of money. Never. Under no circumstances. Her only recompense can be the knowledge that her superior intelligence daily, around the clock, with each individual passing tick of time, protects several hundred million people from the fiendish clutches of a monster in human form called Mister X—and this is only *one* way you are very, very special, Kleyr Boriquen."

She clung to him, motionless, arms up around his neck now, clung motionless with dark eyes in solemn fixity on his hard visage, and seemed to be trying to speak; yet she never uttered a word until the gentle lines and soft planes of her face trembled sharply, as though ready to collapse in tears. Her eyes did brim over, letting two great, glistening tears roll down her cheeks, and she said softly, so softly the words were a mere whisper: "I never thought of it like that before, Boo. Not really. You make me sound as if I were a saint."

He offered no immediate response, but continued looking at her in silence. Then, at last: "There must be at least one saint in every man's life."

She loosed a tremulous breath, at once inhaling deeply, the action lifting her cone-shaped, faintly up-jutting breasts a fraction above the surface. "You mean that, don't you, Boo?"

"Yes. I mean it." He grinned, winking hugely. "No worthy man ever lies to the saint in his life."

"No, Boo, please." Liquid diamonds fired by moonbeams burst to life in the droplets flung from her springy curls when she shook her head. "Please don't." She dashed away the tears, her entrancing vivacity commencing to again display itself, in her smile and in her eyes. "I'm not doing any of the noble and courageous things you described, so don't deify me. I'm no saint, Heaven forbid. I don't want to be a saint. If I were, you could not only never in propriety lie to me, but also never with me, lout;

120

and how's that for a vulgar play on meanings?" Soft laughter matched the gentle regard for Bucher in her eyes, albeit the regard was mingled with no little awe. "Mercy, lover, never have I had anyone appraise me with such stirring eloquence before."

"Perhaps no one knows you as well as I."

"That's true. Not even Padrino. Boo, did Sam say anything to you about Dr. Mull coming to the house today while you were gone? Or when we were asleep?" She drew herself up, clasping him about the waist.

"Nope. The only time he mentioned Mull was to tell me the man's background checkout came in clean, though it isn't yet quite complete. There's more to come. Why?"

"Well—for land's sake. Dr. Mull flies all the way from Massachusetts to Puerto Rico to discuss my sylurgics with me and he hasn't come to the house yet. Except that time when he was already there, this morning, when Sam told him you weren't letting anyone visit me, and he went to the Mir Hotel. Surely he doesn't suspect you might do the same to him as you did to that despicable Hardiman." At the flood of graphic remembrances of the beating Hardiman had received she made small sounds of pleasure, holding hard onto Bucher and wriggling closer. "It's mean of me, I know, but I'd still like to see you clobber that beast again. Perhaps only a little, but clobber him."

"Why don't I hold the bum while you clobber him?"

Implications of this were so unexpected, Kleyr's face for a moment went blank with surprise. But only for a moment, before she flung herself backward from the waist with a force that compelled Bucher to cup both big hands and support her as she squealed in high glee over prospects of realizing his suggestion.

"I'll do it!" she cried, rocking forward on his palms and wagging an impudent forefinger under his nose. "See if I don't. I'll get a stick and whale the living daylights out of that—that *thing*!" Abruptly she sobered. "You weren't teasing, were you? You will hold him, won't you? Promise?"

"I promise," Bucher assured her, meaning what he said. "Even if he's in the hospital. where I suspect he might be

121

for at least a day or two. I'll tie the bastard to the bed, and you'll wallop him to your heart's content, till you're exhausted."

Kleyr now believed. Knew he was serious. "What about the people at the hospital? Orderlies? Nurses? Doctors? What about them?"

"I'll tell you what about them. Either they pay a fee, say ten dollars a head, to watch you do your walloping, or I chase them out of the room. That's what about them."

Again Kleyr was smitten by the unexpected—of charging admission to see her thresh Hardiman with a stick rather than wait until all hospital staff were beyond his summons before threshing him—smitten anew so powerfully by the seizure of mirth after a minute or two her breathing grew troubled and her face alarmingly crimson. Bucher readjusted her circumstance by lowering them to the chin in the water for she, assuming he intended to take them under, seemingly miraculously recovered though continuing to laugh in spurts and starts of much less violence, sagged against his chest.

"Boo, you're—" she began at last, eyes on him filled with wonder. "You're fantastic. I'm beginning to suspect that I didn't come to know you too well at Ithaca and in the Catskills."

"As I recall, you were looking at the ceiling most of the time."

"At the ceiling?"

"Over my shoulder, ma'am," he grinned—and watched understanding blossom in her eyes.

"Humm, yes. I guess so. If we weren't in the midst of it, we were about to be, or had just finished and were resting for another go. Boy ..." She studied him obliquely with enigmatic eyes, a mischievous smile teasing her lips. "I died deliciously a million delicious times this afternoon at the house—before I got up to rattle pots and pans."

He laughed, feeling good. "You go for that like a million, don't you?"

"I go for it like a hundred million, Senor Silver Tongue." She reached herself upward, pecked his lips with hers. "Now hold still." A small grunt escaped her on

122

disengaging and she funny-faced him with a sigh, stepping back. "There now."

"So?" Bucher knew not what next to expect with Kleyr Boriquen, and thus was prepared, generally, in a manner of speaking, for anything.

"So let us discuss our remaining eleven children, Boo," she said seriously.

"I thought it was twelve."

"It is." She patted her tummy under the water. "But Boriquen Bucher, Junior, is already in the process."

Bucher chuckled, draping an arm around her shoulders as she began leading them slowly toward the Chinook. "You know for certain? Since only last night? You *know*?"

"I know I can read a calendar, lunk, and I know it's my time for conceiving."

"Humm. I be damned," he muttered, amazed at his reaction. Heretofore any prospect of fatherhood always filled him with a quiet terror, yet now, oddly, for the first time in his life it did not, which in itself was cause for surprise. "Humm. I be damned."

"You get one more, Boo. They're three for a dime."

". . ."

Her delighted laughter tinkled merrily around them.

"Thoughts of twelve squally brats sort of saps your zing, huh?" They emerged onto the beach, Kleyr still leading, and she dashed ahead to the Chinook for a towel.

"No," Bucher said honestly after her, though more to himself than to her, not yet recovered from surprise at realizing he just might like being a father after all—though only if Kleyr were the mother. Otherwise, nix.

By the time he reached the mattress, Kleyr had stepped down from the Chinook and was opening a clear plastic package containing three large candy-striped terry cloth towels. She tossed him one, dropped a second on to the mattress, and commenced drying herself with the third.

"Boo."

"Hum?"

"Will you continue to gallop hither and yon, saving the world while I raise the children?"

"No."

123

"But—*No?*" Obviously his "No" was unexpected. "I never realized . . . You like children that much?"

He ceased drying his hair to look at her. "I like my children's mother that much, dammit. Next question." When she said nothing in reply, but stood there regarding him in quiet, wondrous joy, he continued, "Then I've a few questions of my own, ma'am, on a different but necessary subject, so park thy fanny in comfort on the mattress whilst I pour two plastic tankards of grape from yon jug." Albeit Bucher's tone and choice of words implied a lack of gravity about whatever subject he had in mind, Kleyr was quick to detect an underlying seriousness of both and, therefore, obeyed without question, sitting near the center of the mattress with folded legs aside and bracing on one arm, watching as he poured champagne from the insulated jug into two of the plastic cups. She accepted hers without comment when he joined her. She was sipping, waiting, wondering what his questions were about.

"About that experiment of yours, Kleyr, the one going beyond the Boston Experiment—perfecting it, I believe you said. Where did you conduct the experiment?"

"At the lab, in that building above the house."

"The lab you share with Drs. Bartlet and Philbrick?"

"Yes."

"Were you alone when you conducted your experiment?"

"Naturally. Of course."

"Okay-okay," he laughed apologetically. "If some of my questions sound a bit stupid, please consider the source, huh? I'm not accustomed to dealing with genius-types."

"What is it you're after, Boo?"

"A link, however thin and trivial, between Bartlet and Philbrick and our Mister X. And don't protest the possibility of such a link existing out of loyalty, because believe me it is possible. Either one, or both, might be Mister X for all we know. Okay, dammit, go ahead and laugh. But who planted those tiny, highly sophisticated transceivers in the curtain rods to eavesdrop on every word said, every sound made, in the house? It wasn't a stranger who planted them, Princess. But a friend. A close friend. A friend close enough to be thoroughly familiar with your house, and with your living habits, at work, at home, wherever; close enough to have made a mold of your house keys in order to have your keys reproduced so this person, this friend, can come and go as he pleases whenever you're not around. What did you do with the equipment with which you performed your experiment? How many of these experiments did you do by the way?"

"Only one." Kleyr's levity of a moment ago was gone. Hearing that someone she assumed to be a friend had bugged her house had chased it away.

"And the equipment?"

"Boo, dear, there's something I'd better explain to you about that experiment."

"Have at it, lassie. I'm all ears."

She thought for a moment first, frowning slightly, then: "Boo, there isn't a scientist in the entire world, with one exception, who wouldn't give an arm, at least, to have his name recorded for posterity as the scientist who discovered, and therefore proved there existed, a fourth dimension. For good, bad, or indifferent, I happen to be that exception, and in this particular instance I think it good because it permits me to view the entire experiment through a perspective free of influence of anticipations of fame and glory in the world's scientific community, or expectations of vast wealth—my parents left me more money than any sensible person could ever spend in one lifetime. So you see, I am free of all these influences, including pride, ego, and whatnot, and can thus scrutinize my experiment in critical objectivity, so you—"

"Kleyr?" Bucher eyed her in curious speculation.

"Yes, Boo?"

"Are you by chance laying the groundwork to tell me your experiment was a flop? That, after all, you did not discover the Fourth Dimension because there isn't any Fourth Dimension?"

Impulsive laughter sprang from her lips and her limpid eyes sparkled with pleasure in the moonlight. "Boy, if you aren't a sharpy," she said in obvious admiration. "No, Boo, I'm not telling you I didn't discover the Fourth Dimension, because there isn't any Fourth Dimension. What I am telling you is that *I conducted only one experiment.*"

"But you told me that a while ago."

"Well, however many times I've told it, there was still only one experiment, and scientific proof cannot be established by one experiment alone."

"By god, that's right. And you quit after one because—" He waited expectantly.

"Because of only one reason—I was scared. I had produced an experiment the results of which terrified me— Fourth Dimension or no Fourth Dimension, it terrified me, so I quit."

"If not Fourth Dimension, then what?"

"Well, it is possible—I don't know how, but there is a lot I don't know—that instead of the experiment transfering my equipment into the Fourth Dimension, the equipment disintegrated into invisibility."

"But remained in this dimension."

"Oh, yes."

"Jesus Christ. How could anything disintegrate into invisibility?"

Kleyr shrugged, sipping from her cup. "Who knows? Perhaps through some laws of electromagnetism yet unknown; and heaven knows there can be plenty of those. Our universe operates on electromagnetism. So does this entire Milky Way Galaxy of ours. For that matter the whole cosmos, which extends from here, from our earth, into the unimaginable reaches of infinity and contains a hundred million billion trillion centillion centillion galaxies so large that our Milky Way Galaxy compared to one would look like a fly speck beside earth, and this, all of this, functions on electromagnetism. Yet did you know that man, with all his staggering scientific know-how, cannot explain why an iron magnet, which any child can purchase in a dime store, attracts metal? This is a very truth, Boo. So you see, there are many, many laws of electromagnetism that are unknown—and, if left up to me, will never be known. Truthfully, if it were an absolute must that I know my experiment resulted in either a disintegration into invisibility or the discovery of the Fourth Dimension, I'd

126

prefer the disintegration into invisibility. As I've told you, the Fourth Dimension scares me."

"Christ, don't feel lonesome. And you're never going to tell anyone else about your experiment?"

She nodded, winking hugely, over the rim of the large plastic cup—the bright moonlight allowed remarkably clear vision, and already Bucher had noted one or two little indications the champagne was beginning to affect her.

"Maybe I'll tell. One of these days. Some time fifty or sixty years from now, at a family reunion when all our children and grandchildren and great-grandchildren are gathered about. If you can get them quiet long enough to hear old Granny Kleyr's quavery, feeble voice, why, I might tell them. Okay Boo?"

"Okay," he grinned, wondering if he should pour her more champagne and deciding against it. Now, of all times, was no time to get intoxicated, neither him nor her. True, on the remote atoll Barefoot, out in the middle of nowhere, they were not likely to encounter any threat from Mister X & Company, but Bucher was alive not because he complied with the likely, but because he tolerated the likely while preparing for the unlikely. Therefore he poured neither of them any more champagne. Though more was unnecessary for Kleyr. She was already getting cozily rosy.

"Hi, Mister Moon." She saluted skyward toward the great silver light in the heavens, her tone having taken on the faintest slur. "You got any real good secrets tonight, Mister Moon?" She looked at Bucher, giggling foolishly. "You going to ecstasize me, Boo-Boo-Boo? Oh-boy, here comes my semantic articulitis. So much happening yesterday and today I've forgotten to remodelize—Boo, do you love your impressionized verbositoid? Will you please earthquake me, Boo? Hey, Mr. Moon, don't go 'way. Watch me get earthquaked in flagrante delecti, hokay? Boo-Boo is the earthquakingest dingus koonilingifier in se-se-seven states and Mexico, aren't you, Boo? And ... Saaaaaay, hmmmm, Whiew! Boy." She extended the hand holding the champagne cup out beyond the edge of the mattress and turned it upside down and, as if her decision to ab-

127

stain from drinking further had neutralized that already consumed, when she spoke she evinced no traces of inebriation. "Wow, I've had enough of that stuff." She tossed Bucher an exaggerated owlish wink and a feisty smile. "What was on your evil little mind, buster? Get this poor little innocent country girl drunk and take advantage of her?"

"Perhaps," he grinned hugely. "I enjoy watching you."

"Hummph! We can both enjoy something besides watching, if you'll come on and take advantage of poor little me, lout, and right now. After giving you that big build-up with my friend up there ..." she thumbed the moon, ". . . about you being a first-class number-one earthquaker, why, are you going to make this sex fiend of yours all aquiver with lust out to be a liar?" After thumbing the moon she continued to talk while reclining to face it, and during this time Bucher, anxious that his sex fiend not be made out a liar, responded to her desires with such alacrity that the instant after she uttered "liar," she gasped desperately, raggedly, a deep and soulful intake of breath.

And then to them the universe diminished to a tiny, private world for only two, a world of softly uttered sighs and gently flowing rhythms, a world of their deep affection that was close to worship.

Unfortunately it was also a world with factors identical to those of man's ordinary everyday humdrum world, one of which is time. Neither Bucher nor Kleyr were overmuch aware of time's passage. And thus it was that the first occasion Bucher consciously checked his chronograph for the express purpose of learning the time, he was flabbergasted to discover that dawn was not far off.

"We've got to get up."

"Why?" Kleyr purred.

"Because we're accomplishing nothing here." Yet when he began to rise, Kleyr's exceptionally adept bit of feminine maneuvering erased his inclination to do so.

"Not accomplishing anything," Kleyr mused, thoroughly enjoying herself. "Hmmm ..."

"Hush!"

128

This time feminine maneuvering could not have erased his inclination to rise; he was up in a flash, straining to hear. Kleyr was now off the mattress as well and hurriedly dressing. Already she knew of Bucher's exceptionally keen sense of hearing, and kept honed to a degree of efficiency almost beyond understanding, she suspected, by his enforced life style of never-ending danger. Therefore the fact that she heard nothing unusual concerned her little. Bucher would detect and intercept, and demolish probably, any danger threatening, so best she concern herself with matters of import falling within her sphere of capability. Such as the helicopter. She turned toward the Chinook and—

"Pssssst!"

When she looked quickly in Bucher's direction, he shook his head, said quietly:

"Don't start the Chinook. Not yet. Not till our visitor makes his intentions known."

Kleyr moved to stand beside him but still heard nothing. "What is it, Boo?"

"Helicopter. Small one, so it can't be any of our people, unless one of them decided to fly that little four-passenger job I rented yesterday, which I doubt."

"It's coming our way, Boo?"

"Straight at us. But it's not light enough yet for him to see us—unless he's looking for us especially and knows we're on Barefoot, which I also doubt. There's no use to worry, regardless. His 'copter is not over a four-passenger, so there can't be more than four people in it, and if there are no more than four, there's little point in working up a sweat."

Looking at him from the corner of her eye, Kleyr shook her head in joy and fierce pride. Just as when they'd been together four years ago, he never ceased to amaze her. Knowing four people might be coming to do him bodily harm, even to kill him, an ordinary man would now be shivering in his boots and shrieking for police protection. But Boo was calmly going about the routine function of putting on his clothes.

"Can you hear him yet, Princess?" Bucher spoke from

beside the Chinook, where the night before he'd put his garments, except his coat, which was inside the aircraft in the pilot's seat.

"No. Not yet." Kleyr shook her wealth of glistening, springy curls. "Once a moment past I thought I heard him but—yes! There he is! Now I hear!" With anxious eyes she scanned the speckled sky toward Puerto Rico, whence came the sound; the craft was coming low and coming fast.

"Don't make any motion," Bucher told her. The new arrival's sound was amplified because there were no other sounds about to act against it, which made it seem much lower, nearer than it really was, and also made it seem as if the craft were on a course to Barefoot. It was not. Bucher saw it first, south of Barefoot, flying east, two hundred fifty yards beyond the beach, yet hardly fifty feet above the surface of the sea. He might have missed it; the 'copter could have passed unseen, had not the faintest blush of dawn commenced to tint the east for day's approach.

"They don't know we're alive," Bucher said to Kleyr, who came to stand beside him at the Chinook. "And couldn't see us here, from where they are, even if they did." He frowned in puzzlement. "But why that altitude, or lack of it, so far out at sea? The nearest land, except here, is Puerto Rico, and yet that helicopter is no more than fifty feet above the water, flying low to keep from being silhouetted."

"Could it be smugglers?"

"Probably."

"Of what, do you suppose?"

"Who knows? And if not smuggling, then some other crooked enterprise. An altitude of only fifty feet is risky enough in daylight when the flight's a long one over water, but in darkness such as this the pilot hopes to miss detection or has lost his marbles. But either way it's none of our affair; not if he keeps his distance."

Last night shortly after landing on Barefoot, Bucher became aware of a disturbing paradox that stated he knew of evidence that existed in plain, open sight, evidence that pointed to the identity of Mister X, the paradoxical aspect being that he could now neither remember nor recognize what that evidence was, where he had encountered it, who had been with him at the time, or anything else except that it was in plain view for anyone who wanted to examine the case thus far. And now, as he and Kleyr stood gazing in the direction the strange helicopter had disappeared, Bucher was again brazenly confronted by the conviction he should recognize this evidence forthwith, speedily neutralize Mister X, and thereby remove the threat to Kleyr's life. But being confronted with the conviction and recognizing the evidence, or where to look for the evidence, were not horns of the same dilemma as they appeared to be, for they offered no alternate choice, nothing but an imperative either/or. Nevertheless, Bucher dared neglect no opportunity of solving the dilemma, and was about to give it full attention, when from inside the Chinook came the sound of the radio phone's buzzer, loud, angry, insistent. Bucher responded at once.

"Will that be Sam calling, Boo?" Kleyr asked as he entered the helicopter.

"It better be," he grinned over his shoulder. "No one else is supposed to have our frequency. Will you toss our gear back inside? We may be taking off soon."

Bucher removed his coat from the pilot's seat, where he had left it last evening, and, before answering the radio phone, spent ten seconds switching life into the Chinook's motors so they could be warming in case he and Kleyr decided to leave immediately after the conversation. As he had told Kleyr, the caller was White Hat's director, and after a brief identification code routine their conversation was conducted in Osco-Umbrian, the ancient dialect they had used the night before. The call was for the express purpose of informing Bucher, and Kleyr, that Mister X had called Kleyr at her home number.

"And he was using a mixer-baffle on the phone, Mr. Bucher, so I learned nothing from the quality of his voice. Or even if it was a man or woman calling, though I'm satisfied it was a man. And since I was talking through a mixer-baffle myself, I told him my name was Bucher, Dr.

Boriquen's consort-bodyguard, that she was out at the moment and that he would have to call back later."

"How did you know it was X calling?" Bucher asked, watching with interest the volume of Boriquen's *Sylurgics* found in Delaney Pryde's Americana Hotel room yesterday slide from the pocket of the coat he'd draped across his knee on taking the pilot's seat. It fell to his feet, hitting the deck in a manner that opened it at the back cover, which did not have written on it: "With all my heart, Darling—Kleyr," as the inside front cover did. But there was a photograph . . .

"I knew it was Mister X," White Hat's director replied, "because he wouldn't say anything except that he had to talk to Dr. Boriquen. That it was irrevocably imperative that he talk with her."

"He used the words 'irrevocably imperative'?"

"He did. You can listen to the tape when you come in, er, when will that be, by the way?"

"Soon," Bucher told him. "Very soon. We'll be leaving for Arecibo within half an hour."

When the radio phone conversation was concluded, Bucher picked up the volume of *Sylurgics* and studied the photograph of the young woman glued to the inside back cover, a color photograph.

The photo was four inches tall and three inches wide, giving a full-length view of the young woman. Unconsciously Bucher shook his head in masculine admiration; to judge by the photo she was almost as exquisite in form as Kleyr, though not quite. Her great mass of silver-blond hair looked strangely out of place, for one thing, though this was minor when compared to the thing he detected in her china-blue eyes when the cockpit light reflected off the photograph at a certain angle. The camera had captured something no camera is supposed to capture.

As Bucher sat frowning in perplexity at the photograph, he could not identify what it was he saw reflected in the young woman's eyes, though he did know he felt suddenly as if he were in the presence of some ancient, unholy evil; something spawned in the muck of primeval slime.

"You're crazier'n hell," he accused himself silently. "All

132

night with Kleyr has you addle-pated as a cockroach blind drunk on soured fly spray. Another night like that and you'll commence counting your fingers and toes, dumbass." Still, the feeling persisted.

An even more emphatic aspect of the photograph was its seemingly unintentional yet powerful eroticism. The picture had been shot with the sun behind her at an angle and not far above the horizon, the oblique rays not graphically outlining her physical charms, only suggesting them—and suggesting them in such a way as to prompt any virile male's imagination into endowing her with all remaining essentials necessary for creating the ultimate embodiment of eager, sex-oriented female, desperately anxious for his, and only his, particular techniques of appeasement and gratification.

"Jesus," Bucher muttered to himself. "The photographer, or the developer, happened upon a moment of genius, or else was a master at retouching."

Bucher stuck the book back inside his coat pocket at sounds of struggle from behind him, and turned to find Kleyr wrestling the cumbersome mattress into the Chinook. He moved swiftly to assist her, looking her a question when the mattress was inside. She nodded brightly.

"Yes," she told him. "That's all the gear, as you call it. Except that awful champagne. I poured that stuff out. Did you know I almost got zonked on it last night?"

"Oh, yes," Bucher grinned. "You even invited the moon to witness our flagrante delecti."

She turned away, shoulders shaking with laughter—but whirled to face him immediately, face fraught with shock. "Boo!" It was a horrified gasp.

"What is it?" He jumped from the aircraft to where she stood.

"Boo." Her lovely face was suddenly wreathed in shame. "Boo, I forgot to—so much has been happening— my poor cousins—I forgot to make arrangements for their funerals!" She scratched at her midsection, lifted the edge of her blouse, and readjusted the position of the unique 69 ten-shot French match pistol under the band of her slacks, covered it again, and repeated herself. "I forgot to make arrangements for poor Rachel's and Nora's funerals, Boo!"

"I'm not sure it would have accomplished much if you had."

"Why, for heaven's sake?"

"Homicide Captain Raymond Ortega of the San Juan police wanted a complete autopsy done on both, which in most cases takes over eighteen hours; so the bodies won't be released until some time today."

She stared at him painfully in hope: "You're sure?"

"No, but I'm almost sure—and your mentioning your cousins reminds me of something I forgot also. To tell you. It's powerful. Can you take it?"

"Tell me."

"Captain Ortega found a witness who claims to have seen a young woman leaving your cousins' home around four o'clock on the afternoon of the murders."

"A young woman?" Her eyes were aghast.

Bucher nodded. "Around four or a bit after."

"Why is Ortega having an autopsy?"

"Because, like a lot of men, he doesn't like to believe a woman is cold-blooded and inhuman enough to calmly slit another human being's throat. And doing it while the victim is bound, helpless, makes it even harder to believe."

Kleyr had opened her mouth, ready to speak, when they heard the second helicopter. Scant seconds thereafter, they heard the first returning. Bucher swore viciously, thankful the Chinook's powerful motors were warm.

"Inside!" He practically threw Kleyr into the craft. "They're trying to box us in, pen us down here on Barefoot! That first 'copter returning is a dead giveaway. You pilot—are you positive, absolutely positive you can handle this Chinook?"

"Don't worry, Boo, I can handle it," Kleyr told him with surprising calm. "Any particular way you want it done?"

"Burst-off. You understand burst-off?"

She nodded. "I hold it down tight, give it all the power it'll take, then feather-in wide open."

134

"Good girl. And don't forget to buckle in tight." Bucher was already arming the .50 caliber machine gun, which looked deformed due to the five-hundred round improvised basket on one side.

"You buckle in!" Kleyr called from the pilot's seat, the Chinook's motor gaining speed.

"Yeah!" The two White Hat agents who had installed the machine gun and improvised the enormous ammo basket apparently had forgotten a gunner's harness, but the gun mounting frame was secured firmly to the helicopter's superstructure, so there was no real danger unless he was thrown out through the cargo port over the top of the gun, which was hardly possible since it was so small above the weapon. The Chinook's blades were a dull semicircular streak in the weak light of dawn, they revolved so fast, and the huge craft was taking on a hard body quiver when Kleyr shouted over her shoulder: "Hang on!"

Bucher quickly sat, fortunately he felt sure, otherwise he might have been slammed against the deck when the Chinook literally shot into the air—but he'd told her burst-off. Through the bottom of the port, below the machine gun, he saw the Caribbean falling away beneath them at a dizzying rate—then he was on his feet, thumbs on the butterfly trips of the .50-caliber. The second strange helicopter, the one that had been approaching Barefoot from the direction of Puerto Rico, came into view a thousand yards away.

"Hold it!" Bucher yelled. "You see the first 'copter yet?"

"I just barely can; it's a long way off."

"Keep an eye on it and hold what you've got! We're about to have company!"

The second helicopter was still almost a thousand yards away, according to Bucher's estimation, was of the same dull color as the first and, as best as he could tell in the poor light, was also only a four-passenger craft. Actually, for a thousand yards the craft was little more than a dark outline, but it was coming fast and getting more distinct by the second. In another half minute—

"Kleyr!" Bucher yelled. "Flip that toggle above the radio phone's main switch to the 'On' position!" She obeyed promptly, and Bucher loosed a pent-up breath. He'd forgotten the combination distress beeper and radar the director had showed him. In case these two strange ships shot the Chinook into the sea, White Hat would at least know where to look for him and Kleyr. Then Bucher got a faint glimpse of the approaching 'copter's armament and felt a little sorry for the dumb-johns in it, and knew, also, that he should give the gunners of the other aircraft the first shot. There were two gunners, unless his eyes were tricking him, and it was still too far to make certain, but damned it if didn't look as though they were armed with M-16s. Still, he had no intention of giving anybody first shot at the Chinook, not with Kleyr aboard. The caliber of their weapons, the M-16s, signaled their tactics; the M-16s were far too small to shoot the Chinook itself down, so the approaching bandits intended to move in close, probably within fifty yards or less, and shoot the Chinook's pilot.

"I be damned if they do!" Bucher snarled savagely, swung the .50 caliber air-cooled machine gun on the other helicopter, which was still five hundred yards away but closing fast, and pressed the butterfly trips for a short burst to get the feel of the gun. Until that moment he had forgotten telling White Hat's director to be sure a certain percentage of the .50 caliber ammo was tracer, and after the burst he glanced quickly down into the improvised basket—small wonder the burst had appeared to be half tracers. Every other shell in the metal ammo belt had a red-tipped slug; the burst had been half tracers!

"Which makes the frog hair all the finer," Bucher snarled in immense satisfaction, not positive he would have fired on the other craft had not Kleyr been aboard the Chinook, but her presence made all the difference in the world to him. With her on board, mercy was a virtue he could not afford. Therefore he adjusted the muzzle of the .50 caliber machine gun toward the approaching bandit—with so many tracers in the ammo belt he could better zero the other ship after he began firing—and gently pressed the butterfly trips.

An intermittent streak of fiery hell stuttered from the side of the Chinook toward the bandit and beyond, streaked across the top of the other craft until Bucher elevated the receiver by both handles, butterflies down. The mindless mad thunder pounding from the big .50 in Bucher's iron grip never ceased its death staccato, not even after he found the range and hosed the intermittent streak into the thick plastic bubble in front of the pilot's seat. The bandit seemed to buck in midair, then it lurched violently sideways, halted abruptly only to slue in the opposite direction, after which it commenced a long, blazing plummet into the sea.

"Bucher! Are you all right?" In the contrasting silence when the .50 ceased, Kleyr's voice seemed exceptionally loud.

"Scratch one bandit!" His jubilance was unmistakable. "Where's the other 'copter?"

"Right there!" She pointed to the front. "It's almost upon us! But it's stopped. Hasn't it?"

"Swing me around to face it." When she did as he asked, he saw that the other craft was not quite "almost upon us" as Kleyr had said, but since it was higher than the Chinook, it was understandable how she would think so. Nor had the other bandit stopped. Not entirely. Only slowed momentarily, apparently, for when Bucher was swung around toward it, the craft started toward the Chinook with a vengeance. Or so it seemed to him. Regardless, he gave it no more mercy than he had the other one, which is to say no mercy at all. Nor did he wait until the craft got close enough for him to identify the caliber of guns it had aboard, for when he saw the heavier, thicker barrel of a weapon protruding from the off-pilot side of the helicopter, he knew it was much bigger, and thus more deadly, than any M-16. Gently his thumbs depressed the butterfly trip.

And this time he did not overshoot the mark, but undershot it; the bandit was still at a distance of five hundred yards; therefore, he gradually elevated the muzzle until the long, fiery arc formed by the tracers began vanishing into the other craft. It never had a chance. The tracers struck the gas tank and the ship exploded in a burst of flame. It, or its remains, disappeared so quickly below the lower rim of the port, Bucher never saw any of it again.

"Scratch bandit number two!" he yelled, no less jubilant than before. Kleyr's reply carried a frightened note.

"Boo! Come here!"

Bucher was quick to note the somewhat pasty hue of her complexion when he reached her. "Okay," he told her kindly. "I'll take the controls."

She relinquished them eagerly. "It's—I—you see—"

"Don't apologize. Not many people are so toughened they can stomach killing half a dozen or so fellow human beings when they first get up in the morning. Or any other time for that matter."

"Yes." She swallowed hard several times, nodding. "That's what I mean. Perhaps if they'd actually been shooting at us—no. I know if they had been shooting, it would have been different. I could have done it myself then." She punched his shoulder playfully. "Or if one of them had shot you, I could shoot them knowing they were out of bullets and couldn't shoot back. That doesn't say much for your belief that women are superior to men, does it?"

Bucher was about to tell her that when her offspring or mate was in grave danger, and killing was the only means of removing that danger, the female killed with far less compunction than the male, but he found himself staring at a tiny atoll far below. He assumed at first it might be Barefoot, then saw he was mistaken. Barefoot was visible from the opposite side of the helicopter. And once he saw Barefoot from the air for the first time in years, it was quite obvious that the other atoll had an entirely different type of vegetation growing on it, a vegetation far too uniformly green—unless the vegetation was of all the same plant, and this Bucher very much doubted.

"Kleyr, there's a small metal box bolted to the deck against the bulkhead in the rear, and there should be a pair of binoculars in the box. Will you bring them please?" The five helicopters and five pilots White Hat's director had brought with him to Arecibo had been airborne for Puerto Rico from southern Florida before the director and the twenty other agents left New York by jet, but since the 'copters were White Hat property, Bucher assumed there would be binoculars. A pair was standard equipment with each craft.

"What is it, Boo?" Kleyr asked when she returned, handing him the glasses.

"That atoll down there. Do you see anything peculiar about it?"

"No. Not really. Am I supposed to?"

"In the first damn place it's not supposed to be there. It's not five miles from Barefoot. And when the Syndicate used Barefoot as a base for smuggling narcotics, the closest land to Barefoot, in any direction, was Puerto Rico. I know. I was the one who picked Barefoot for the Syndicate, and I picked it for its isolation. That atoll there is not supposed to be there, dammit."

"But it *is* there, Boo. We both see it."

"Yeah, it's there, but something is screwy as hell somewhere. Mother Nature couldn't have built that atoll, and covered it with all that pretty green vegetation, the color of which is also screwy, in the few short years since the Syndicate quit using Barefoot." He laid the binoculars in his lap and put the Chinook into a moderate glide, slowing the craft and leveling off five hundred feet above the water only when the mysterious atoll was approximately five hundred yards dead ahead. It took him only seconds to adjust the binoculars to his vision, whereupon he promptly swore in surprise but continued to study the atoll a couple of minutes longer before handing the glasses to Kleyr. He made no comment in doing so, and if Kleyr noticed the slightly smug grin on his face, she said nothing. Yet after adjusting the glasses for her eyes she also evidenced surprise, hers in the form of a sharp gasp.

"Why," she said, still looking through the binoculars. "It's—they're—" She lowered the glasses and frowned at Bucher in perplexity. "Am I seeing right?"

"You're seeing right," he chuckled. "Or we're both seeing wrong, and I very much doubt that. Come on. Let's get the hell out of here, lady. We've done our good deed for the day."

"Oh, look, Boo, look!" Glad surprise was in Kleyr's tone. She pointed in the direction of Puerto Rico. There were four of them altogether, racing like bats out of hell and devil take the hindmost, all four of the White Hat Chinooks that had remained back at Kleyr's house in Arecibo last night. Bucher had not realized the fierce nervous tension Kleyr had been under since the shooting down of the two helicopters until he noticed the tears of relief in her eyes.

"Easy, Princess." He patted her knee. "We'll be home in a few minutes." He then got busy on the radio with White Hat's director, explaining about the two bandit craft he had shot into the sea.

"They found out some way we were on Barefoot," Bucher said. "Probably with a magnetic metal indicator. And we were far too close to their little secret, so they decided we had to be shot down to make certain we didn't spill the beans."

"What little secret, Mr. Bucher?"

"The two missing supertankers. They're anchored side by side and camouflaged as an atoll approximately five miles beyond Barefoot. But the vegetation-camouflage is too uniformly green. Probably plastic. Fly in to within four or five hundred yards, and with binoculars you'll be able to make out an outline of the prow of one of the tankers."

A long silence ensued, nothing coming over the radio but the faint frying sound of the carrier wave, until the director at last said: "One of the helicopters is going down to investigate, Mr. Bucher. The rest of us will follow you and Kleyr back to Arecibo."

9

Bucher flew straight to Kleyr's house on the edge of Arecibo, and because he did so, their return trip was made much faster than was the circuitous trip in reaching Barefoot the night before.

"Even after being gone only one night, home is so good

to come back to," Kleyr said, looking at her house through the window as Bucher sat the big craft down in the street near the end of the sidewalk. This time he did not search the grounds and the house before permitting her to enter. Guards were still stationed at each corner of the building; a fly couldn't have entered without their knowledge.

"And look at my poor yard," Kleyr said as they left the Chinook, referring to the brown spots showing where the Bouncing Betty personnel mines were buried. "But it's still a small price to pay."

The house inside was exactly as they had left it, even to the half of a fried chicken Bucher had forgotten on the back of an overstuffed chair in the living room.

"And now what, Boo?" Kleyr asked, busying herself with making a pot of coffee.

"We wait. Friend X will call again, and soon, unless I miss my guess. We pulled a sneaky on him when we suddenly pulled up stakes and flew off last night. I didn't think he'd be prepared for a move like that."

"I should call Padrino and tell him I'm all right," Kleyr said thoughtfully, taking a carton of eggs and a roll of Canadian bacon from the refrigerator, then lifting a toaster from a shelf to the kitchen work table. "He'll be worried sick; this hullabaloo going on here at my home, the guards around the clock, the weapons, the helicopters, and all. I know Sam's been in touch with the local authorities; otherwise this whole area would be surrounded by the curious, but the police can't control talk. I'll bet my house is the most talked about spot in Puerto Rico ... How many eggs, Boo, and how cooked?"

"Half a dozen and cook them any way you care to."

"Are you serious? Half a dozen?" She regarded him in disbelief, yet also with merriment in the depths of her eyes.

"Yeah, six," Bucher said automatically, thoughts on her use again, for the third time as he remembered, of the word "padrino." The word itself was the Spanish equivalent, a literal translation in fact, of the English word "godfather," the sense in which she had used it each time. But

141

he could not remember her ever having told him she had a godfather. He knew her parents had been killed in an accident when she was much younger, that she had been raised, in part, by her recently murdered cousins, Rachel and Nora Cordova, but he was certain she had never said anything to him about any godfather. Nor had White Hat's director made mention of a "godfather" being in her dossier.

"Who is your godfather, Kleyr?"

"Dr. Philbrick. Dr. J. M. Philbrick. I've told you of him ... Haven't I? Of course, I did. At Hibbings Summer Lodge in the Catskills. I know I told you there, Boo, because I told you absolutely every little tiny thing about me. And I also told you night before last ..." Uncertainty flickered across her lovely face. "I'm positive I told you; however, making up for eight long, lonely years in a single night, in more like three hours really, things did get a bit hectic and confused at times. But anyway, now you know. He did so much for me while I was growing up. It was Padrino who made Cornell possible. He told them about me, rather. Doing Cornell the great honor of bringing me to their attention, as he puts it. I dedicated—wait a sec. Be right back." And she was. In seconds. Disappeared from the kitchen looking very housewifey in apron and all, and reappeared almost at once with the volume of her *Sylurgics* from the library-study. "See?" She opened the book one page beyond the flyleaf, to the dedication page, pointing to the words near the center of it, which read: "To Dr. John Malcolm Philbrick; my mentor and godfather."

"He's a darling, Boo, honestly. You'll love him. You'd better, lout, because I do." She left the book with him and busied herself about the stove. "Aside from Rachel and Nora, since my parents died, Padrino has been my teacher—I *know* I told you he is a famous psychiatrist and writes these huge books on all phases of psychiatry— my family, my guardian, he even managed the estate my parents left me until I was old enough, and there was not one single copper cent out of place when he turned the books over to me. Anyway, he is an old dear. So after

142

breakfast I must phone—" The phone rang, interrupting her. Bucher answered at the wall phone extention beside the kitchen door.

"Yeah?"

"Mr. Bucher," the director's voice came over the wire. "We just got word from the police stake-out at the San Juan International Airport that Big Jute Nappo has just arrived in Puerto Rico. Not over fifteen minutes ago."

"Wonderful!" Bucher almost shouted the word. "Those six torpedoes of Nappo's our boys iced down and failed to return have got the superstitious sonofabitch walking around with all pockets full of chicken guts, probably. Did he come alone?"

"Two of his murderous crew are with him. Equalizer Alberts and Candy Dancer."

"Jesus! That broad? Nappo's got grisly work in mind to bring her along."

Kleyr, at the work table, paused in breaking eggs into a bowl and stood regarding Bucher with an expression of near-worship. She had never even heard of, nor read of, any man like him before. Watching him now, just standing there looking at his broad back as he talked on the phone, she experienced a distinct impression of tremendous and savage power held in masterly restraint—she knew for a fact he could be as gentle, as tender as it was possible for a man to be—and her face flushed a deep crimson with a fierce, adoring pride.

"Now maybe we'll get some action," Bucher continued. "This not knowing which way to move is getting my goat; I'm about ready to start feeling like a resolution seeking a temptation. We've got a tail on Nappo and friends, I take it."

"Oh-yes. Oh-yes. I've no doubt he'll lead us to Delaney Pryde and Seeto Loyoko. Pryde I want to get my hands on. I've a notion that scutter will open up like an oyster once he is made aware of the situation."

"Pryde," Bucher said as if to himself. "That's Scottish, isn't it? Delaney sure as hell didn't sound like a Scot the other night at the Dainty Dish. It's just a thought. Being from South Africa, the bastard could be a Zulu in disguise.

143

The way this caper keeps flip-flopping around, nothing surprises me any more. Let me know where Big Jute Nappo lights. I want him for myself; I'll learn the name of the bastard's female partner genius or wring his damn neck."

"What's this about a female genius?" Kleyr asked.

"The same one I told you about last night," Bucher told her, hanging up the phone. "You think you can restrain your Latin temper if I pass along a bit of gossip Sam gave me about your Padrino?"

Kleyr ceased beating the eggs she was preparing for scrambling. "What kind of gossip? About Padrino?"

"How old is he?"

"Sixty-one. And his birthday is March 7. I know. I always remember it."

"He's got a girlfriend. In her early twenties, according to Sam."

"Wh-What?" Disbelief wreathed her features. "Padrino? My Padrino has a girlfriend?" The disbelief gradually gave way to mirth and she laughed happily. "I think that's *wonderful*! Don't you, Boo?"

"Yeah," Bucher chuckled. "As a matter of fact I guess it is, especially with him sixty-one—wait a goddamn minute!" He whirled out of the kitchen for the bedroom where his coat lay on the big bed and took from the coat pocket the copy of *Sylurgics* he'd found in Delaney Pryde's Americana Hotel room the day before. Two or three times already he had intended to show it to Kleyr, but something had always popped up. "Here." He extended the volume to her, open at the flyleaf on which were the words: "With all my heart, Darling—Kleyr." "This looks like one you gave to someone. Can you recall to whom?"

"Certainly. Padrino."

"What about this?" He opened the back cover of the book, showing her the photograph of the young woman he'd discovered to be in it back on Barefoot. "Do you know who she is?"

Kleyr studied the photo a dozen long, slow heartbeats, a deep frown gradually creasing her flawless brow. "No," she said at last, tone colored by puzzled irritation. "But

144

darn it, I have the odd feeling I *should* know who she is. I—Boo, what's wrong with that photograph? It gives me a sort of unwholesome feeling. As if I'd been too close to something unspeakably filthy. Where'd you get Padrino's copy of my *Sylurgics*, anyway?"

"In Delaney Pryde's room at the Americana Hotel in San Juan yesterday."

She still frowned, and now she searched his face meticulously in attempt to find some clue that he was joking and when she found none, she echoed barely above a whisper: "In Delaney Pryde's room at the Americana Hotel in San Juan yesterday? Boo, do you understand what you're saying?"

"I understand. Now if you're going to scramble those eggs, please do so. I'm famished."

Their meal was almost over before Kleyr referred to Dr. Philbrick again. "No!" she said with heat, shaking her curly head stubbornly. "Boo, Padrino is *not*, repeat *not*, involved in this plot against me. I won't believe that, Boo."

"Good. Very good. That leaves the young woman."

"You mean—you believe me? Just like that?"

For convenience they were breakfasting in the kitchen nook, and Bucher looked across the table, nonplussed she should think exceptional his taking her word without question. "I seem to remember something you said about sincerity, that if a relationship between two people didn't have a foundation of sincerity, they didn't have much— something like that. Princess, if I can't believe you I might as well take one of the Chinooks up to ten thousand feet and dive out without a 'chute. Sure, I believe you. Just like that. So we've got to find out the identity of that young woman in the photograph."

"But how in the world could Pryde get a copy of the *Sylurgics* I gave Padrino?"

"The young woman in the photo."

"You mean she has been—"

"Yep. That's exactly what I mean. She's been laying a little discreet nooky on Padrino, not a lot I daresay, with

145

him sixty-one, but enough to get what she wanted from the old boy."

"And what did she want, Boo?"

"Information about you. Anything that Padrino could supply in that vein. And, of course, that volume of your *Sylurgics* for Delaney Pryde. Chances are that young woman in the photo is Big Jute Nappo's partner." Without further ado he burst into gladsome laughter; experience told him the end of this baffling case was drawing nigh, and he sensed it as well, yet the cause of his laughter was not this entirely, but from knowing the why behind: "With all my heart, Darling—Kleyr."

"For shame, Boo," Kleyr said with a straight face. "Why do you find it so funny that Padrino found solace in the young woman's company?"

"I'm not laughing at that."

"Then why do you laugh?"

He told her, and when she understood his seizure of rage at finding a copy of her book in Delaney Pryde's Americana Hotel room was rooted in plain old-fashioned everyday garden variety jealousy, she squealed in delight.

"You thought I had another lover?" she queried saucily, beside herself with joy. "But I should slug you, lout, for not knowing me better than that by this time."

"I thought you'd lied to me," Bucher insisted doggedly, enjoying her pleasure nonetheless. "Now let's get back to the woman in that photograph. You say you almost know her? Does that mean you believe you should know her? That you might recognize her under different circumstances? Or what?"

"It means just what I told you, Boo. I have the odd feeling I should know her, that I should recognize her."

"But you don't?"

"Obviously not, nut. Otherwise I'd have said so before now."

"I see," Bucher said, thinking hard, in no wise liking the conclusion that forced itself on him. And Kleyr's earlier observation that all of Arecibo now knew of strange goings-on at her place did not help matters, either. "What is Dr. Philbrick's home address here in Arecibo?" he asked, getting to his feet. Kleyr followed suit, limpid eyes suddenly large with alarm.

Again Bucher went no farther than the kitchen wall phone, where he dialed White Hat's director outside, repeating the address of Dr. J. M. Philbrick's home in Arecibo, which Kleyr had just given him.

"There's bad news for Kleyr from that corner, I'm afraid," the director said quietly over the wire. "A couple of our people just came from Dr. Philbrick's home. I sent them last night to see Philbrick, but they got no response to their knocking, so right after we landed a bit ago I sent them back, this time accompanied by Arecibo police. They found the doctor bound hand and foot to a chair in the kitchen, and you can guess the rest. It was a repeat of what the police found at Kleyr's cousins' home. Give Kleyr my sympathies."

Bucher was slowly returning the phone to its hook when, without forethought, acting impulsively and with no prior consideration of the act, he caught himself and shouted into the instrument:

"What did Dr. Samantha Bartlet give as her reason for setting up a meeting between Kleyr and me at the Dainty Dish?" A lengthy pause ensued, during which Bucher wondered at himself for shouting into the phone, but wondering more at the question he'd asked the older man—revelation sweeping across his mind in the manner of sunlight bursting across the horizon following a stormy night. He groaned aloud, knowing what the director was about to say even before he said it.

"I haven't seen Dr. Bartlet." The words coming over the wire exactly as Bucher knew they would. "I assumed you'd taken care of that chore yourself, with Dr. Bartlet being such a close friend of Kleyr's and all."

The director still stood outside the second Chinook he had made into his headquarters after releasing the first for Bucher to fly to Barefoot the night before, still stood with telephone to his ear and looking in the direction of the house in puzzlement when Bucher dashed out the front door, Kleyr following at his heel, untying the apron about

147

her tiny waist and flinging it to the yard. Only then did the director hand the phone to the agent inside the Chinook.

"What's up?" Sam White asked, obviously at a loss regarding Bucher's strange conduct.

"I made the same mistake you did," Bucher told him in passing, headed for the small four-passenger helicopter he'd rented in San Juan the day before. "We've both been assuming the other checked Bartlet out in person, when as a result neither of us has."

"I'm not sure I get the connection." The director frowned heavily, following Bucher to the smaller craft, where both men, and Kleyr, stopped.

"Remember me telling you of Seeto Loyoka and Mack McReady searching for Kleyr near the Loiza Aldea beach, and what Loyoka said to McReady about glomming onto the wrong one—?"

The director snapped his fingers, recalling. "It went something like this: 'We wouldn't be in this fix if you hadn't glommed onto the wrong one at the Dish.'"

"That's it!" Bucher said. "And the wrong one they glommed onto was Martha Andrews, not knowing the difference between her and Kleyr's appearance. Loyoka and McReady assumed the Andrews woman was Kleyr—whom they were sent there to kidnap."

The older man's face went blank with surprise, but he recovered in a hurry and commenced an almost violent stuttering in his anxiety to articulate. He at last managed a truncated blast. "To kidnap Kleyr?"

"Damn right to kidnap Kleyr! And who the hell besides Kleyr herself knew she was to be at the Dainty Dish that night?"

"Why, the one who set up the meeting, of course."

"Of course." Bucher could not prevent the acid bite of his tone, though it was for himself, for what he deemed his incredible laxity; perhaps he was getting stupid in his old age. Or should he say stupider? Christ! The solution to the enigma had been right under his nose the whole time, but with him too damn dumb to see it! Until now. "And the one who set the meeting up was Kleyr's superior at the Arecibo Observatory; Dr. Samantha Bartlet."

"You're going to the Observatory? I'm going too!" Kleyr did not wait for a reply, but climbed into the small helicopter, waiting impatiently while Bucher quickly explained to Sam White about the copy of her *Sylurgics*, which she had given to Dr. Philbrick, that he had found in Delaney Pryde's hotel room at the Americana.

"And you say Kleyr did not recognize the young woman in the photograph you found in the book?" the director asked. When Bucher shook his head, the older man continued: "Have you told her about Philbrick's death yet?" This last was not intended for Kleyr's ears, but she overheard.

"Send a team to check out Bartlet's home here in Arecibo," Bucher said, entering the craft and taking the pilot's position, then turning to Kleyr. "Do you know Bartlet's schedule?"

"She should be at the Observatory now, especially with me not on duty these days."

"You check her house; I'll check the Observatory," Bucher told the director. "And if she's at neither place, let's bring in the local police and launch a massive search."

"I'm for that." The director turned to one of his men who came rushing up with a square of yellow foolscap extended, but Bucher was in too much of a rush to wait and learn the contents of the message. Kleyr remained silent until they were airborne.

"I heard what Sam said about Padrino," she at last said in a strained, little-girl voice. "Padrino is dead, then, Boo?"

"I intended to tell you later, at a more appropriate time, but since you must know, now is as good a time as any; there is no appropriate time to tell of death." Seemingly, suddenly, all around Bucher was evidence of death, his nostrils filled with the fetid odor, and powerfully the biting, galling bitter taste of defeat came into his mouth.

Beside him Kleyr sat hunkered in a small ball, eyes stark as she stared fixedly ahead at nothing in particular. "First that Arnie-Dingus person at the Dainty Dish; he was the first to die from a slashed throat. Then my cousins, both murdered in the same fashion. And now Padrino—did he die as the others did, Boo?"

Bucher nodded. "Bound securely to a chair." He reached across and patted her knee comfortingly. "Don't worry, Princess. We'll get the bastard. This is one time I'll enjoy deep-sixing a murdering sonofabitch."

"You'd better be quick in doing it, Boo Bucher," she gritted in a flash of fury, one hand at her midsection. "I've still got that French match pistol, the Unique 69, so you better be quick in doing it."

To alter the course of their conversation, Bucher said: "Tell me about the Arecibo Observatory; are we nearing the place?"

"Yes. That's Rio Abajo State Forest down there. We're above the Krast Region—it's named after a similar region in Krast, Yugoslavia—a limestone plateau filled with sinkholes and weirdly shaped hills. The reflector of the telescope is the world's largest, the collecting area nearly twenty acres in size. It's a giant bowl a thousand feet wide and covered with nearly forty thousand individual aluminum panels, each capable of being separately adjusted to keep the surface perfectly spherical. Hanging over this dish—we'll be able to see it in a moment—hanging over it at a height of sixty stories is a steel triangular platform where radio waves from space are received and amplified before being sent to the control building below for computer analysis. The platform weighs over six hundred tons and hangs by steel cables from three concrete towers located in the nearby hills almost six hundred feet above the bottom of the bowl.

"The telescope's effective radar output is a hundred times greater than the total power production of all electrical generating plants in the world. It is the strongest signal now leaving earth. To the radio eyes of some creature on a distant star, the Arecibo telescope gleams from the darkness of space with a brilliance ten billion times greater than the fire of our sun."

"Ten billion times greater than the sun?" Understandably, Bucher's thoughts of the moment had little to do with the sun—or anything else save the neutralizing of the

150

deadly, inhuman Mister X, or Ms. X as it should now be since he was convinced Dr. Samantha Bartlet and X were one and the same person, but the words "ten billion times greater than the fire of our sun" had a power of themselves that demanded surprised attention, if only for a moment.

"I guess I'm beginning to sound like a tourist brochure, huh?" Kleyr asked in a lackluster tone, atremble with tears, which informed Bucher her run-on discourse concerning the Observatory was a means of restraining further evidence of grief over the death of her beloved Padrino. When she spoke again, however, her tone had more spirit.

"There." She pointed earthward toward the great silver-hued dish that was the Observatory's twenty-acre telescope. "There's Arecibo Observatory."

"How many people can we expect to find there?" Bucher asked, putting the 'copter into a descent angle that would bring them to the cluster of buildings on the telescope's south side.

"No more than one at this time of day," Kleyr replied. "One of the scientists, I mean, and it should be Sam, though there may be several technicians and a janitor or two about the place. And Igor Boshnikov, of course. If Sam is there, Igor will be with her."

Bucher saw no one when he set the craft down at the intersection of two roads between the telescope and the buildings. He made no effort to get Kleyr to remain behind in the helicopter, knowing any attempt to do so would only be a waste of breath. And in spite of the gravity of the situation, he stifled a grin at sight of her lovely features cast in lines of grim determination. Yep, the kid had more guts than you could hang on a fence, and spunk also. The all of which informed Bucher he must remain especially alert if he meant to take Samantha Bartlet alive, which he wanted to do in hopes of extracting information from the woman, for little half-pint Kleyr Boriquen, to judge by her expression, was on the prowl to avenge the senseless death of her Padrino. By extracting blood, not information.

151

Bucher also saw no one after they entered the cluster of buildings; a fact that caused danger-warning hackles to rise on the back of his neck.

"Oh, now I know where everyone is," Kleyr said at last. "Isn't this Wednesday?" Bucher shrugged; he had no idea what day of the week it was. "Come." Kleyr continued, taking his arm. "Let's go to the lab." She pointed to a low and long stone structure with a beautiful slate roof. "If Sam is here, she'll be in the lab—all the maintenance crew are off on Wednesday. So are the janitors and all, except the scientist on duty. And if Sam is here, Igor Boshnikov will be also." A plaintive note entered her voice. "Boo, I hope Sam isn't Mister X, or Madame X, or mixed up in this icky mess in any way."

Kleyr got her wish. Samantha Bartlet was not mixed up in the icky mess in the way Bucher and Kleyr had suspected she might be. She was a part of the icky mess itself, though they did not discover this when they first entered the low stone building with the slate roof. One side of the building was plain wall, the unsurfaced inside wall of the building itself. On the other side, from floor to ceiling, stood row upon row of electronic gadgetry—the sight of it reminded Bucher of the transmitter room of a Mexican 50,000-watt commercial broadcasting station across the border from Del Rio, Texas, which he had had occasion to visit some years ago. Except this was infinitely more sophisticated and extensive, with enough electronic gear to complete several dozen such transmitter rooms as had the Mexican station. Yet there was a great similarity, aside from the banks of computers, even to the smell of electrified ozone, and—

Bucher tensed, though only for a moment, and began scanning the place from where he stood, Walther palmed. Despite the vast similarity, the smell of ozone now, here, in the lab room of the Arecibo Observatory, contained a difference. A striking difference. And that difference was the unmistakable, faintly sweetish, sickening smell of fresh human blood!

"W-What is it, Boo?" Kleyr's large whisper was barely above the hum of electricity about the place.

152

They found him in a small editing room behind an impressive array of self-servicing tape recorders.

"It's Igor," Kleyr gasped in horror. "Igor Boshnikov."

"Russian?"

"Yes. He was one of the team of international scientists working, and studying, at the Observatory." Kleyr's large eyes, now larger than Bucher had ever before seen them, stared at the corpse of Igor Boshnikov bound fast, hand and foot, to a swivel chair at a cutting table in front of an array of splicing equipment. The killer had first gagged the young Russian by stuffing his mouth full of strips of cloth, which were held fast by another strip around his mouth and knotted in back. And then the killer had gone about his grisly business by cutting Igor Boshnikov's throat from ear to ear, the gory gash so neat and thorough that decapitation had almost been accomplished, for the dead man's head virtually hung upside down back between his shoulders.

"O-Oh, my G-God!" Kleyr gasped, wheeling aside and struggling not to, but retching in spite of herself. Bucher's cold eyes searched the long room.

"You mentioned Boshnikov in connection with Dr. Bartlet a bit ago," he said gently to Kleyr when she recovered. "What was the connection?"

"They were lovers. They were to be married soon, with Sam returning to Russia with Igor when his studies here at the Observatory were completed."

To this Bucher had no comment, for he was already beginning to suspect that his assumption that Dr. Samantha Bartlet was the mysterious X was a mistake. A minute later, when he entered a small office filled with storage files far down at the opposite end of the room, he discovered proof of the mistake; proof in the form of Dr. Samantha Bartlet herself—who would never marry anyone nor ever be anyone's lover again, nor ever go anywhere again except the graveyard. The manner of her death was identical to all the others; she had been securely bound in a chair, gagged, then her throat slit from ear to ear. As with Boshnikov, blood was all over the floor. The impact

153

of this close contact with the double murder of two people she had known well and worked with was a bit much for Kleyr, to the extent Bucher had to support her as they returned to the helicopter. Yet she was not long so helplessly stricken.

"Why?" she stormed at the world at large as Bucher sent the small craft skyward. "It's all so senseless!" She stared at Bucher, limpid eyes begging for an answer. "You've had experience before with—such horrors as this. Why all these senseless killings?"

Bucher gave it to her straight from the shoulder. "To work you into such a state of hysteria that you'll be easily manageable."

Kleyr gaped at him momentarily in shocked fixity. Then her small jaw clenched decisively. "To manipulate me into becoming a blob of emotional putty?" It was a statement of understanding, yet also a question.

"That's my opinion."

"So I'll cooperate with this madman X when he contacts me?"

"Right. Look at it this way. With the exception of that Arnie-Dingus character who teamed up with Martha Andrews for their act at the Dainty Dish—his name was Arnold Limpkin—with the exception of him, the first murder victim, all the other murder victims were either very close to you or well known to you. The way I see it, the killer hopes by these killings to have you not only cooperative, but eagerly cooperative the next time he gets in touch with you."

"You . . . Do you think that he'll try again soon?"

"I'm surprised he hasn't tried more than that one time. Yes, I think he'll try again soon. For damn sure something is about to happen soon, otherwise Big Jute Nappo wouldn't have brought Equalizer Alberts and Candy Dancer to Puerto Rico with him."

"Are they—" involuntarily, Kleyr gulped, "—bad people, Boo? That Equalizer Alberts and Candy Dancer, I mean."

"Alberts is nothing but another punk goon, but he's a

154

dimwit who idolizes Big Jute Nappo, which helps keep Nappo's gargantuan ego inflated, so Nappo takes him wherever he goes. Candy Dancer is cut from an entirely different bolt of cloth."

"How?"

"Aggressive, destructive sadism."

"She's insane?"

"She sure as hell isn't normal. One of these rare subhuman types who derive enormous erotic stimulation from watching another person die, the pleasure amplified many-fold if she is the cause of the death."

A sound of loathing sprang spontaneously from Kleyr's lips. "I—I've heard of such people, but . . ." Her voice faded, and she sat frowning in silence as Arecibo came into view far below them.

As they began their descent, Bucher counted only four of the huge CH-47 Chinook helicopters about Kleyr's house on the edge of the city, and fanned the sky hurriedly with his eyes; the fifth Chinook hovered at two thousand feet above the main highway between Arecibo and San Juan, and when Bucher noted this, that the Chinook hung in the air as if in observation, he slowed his smaller craft and studied the scene below. After a moment he became aware of the airborne Chinook's object of interest; or rather, objects of interest, for there were two large black sedans. About a hundred yards apart they were and creeping toward Arecibo at a snail's pace, their present location approximately one mile from the city limits.

"I wonder . . ." Bucher spoke as if to himself, putting the small 'copter into a steep swoop toward the four remaining Chinooks outside Kleyr's place.

"You wonder what, Boo?" By force of will Kleyr had recovered enormously from the gruesome ordeal at the Observatory and news of the murder of her beloved Padrino.

"I wonder about those two black sedans creeping along the highway toward Arecibo." For a reason he was unable to define, it had occurred to him a moment ago the two

155

sedans were in some way connected with the threat against Kleyr's life.

"Could the sedans be Big Jute Nappo and his henchmen?" Kleyr asked, again displaying an almost uncanny knowledge regarding the direction of his thoughts.

Busy as he was fitting their small craft between two of the large Chinooks, Bucher did not answer, and when the little 'copter sighed against the earth, White Hat's director came briskly toward them, a yellow square of foolscap in one hand.

"The two-man team I dispatched to Dr. Samantha Bartlet's home in Arecibo just phoned in the report that her place is empty," the older man said as Bucher and Kleyr dismounted.

Bucher nodded. "I know." And Kleyr stood quietly by, listening as he gave the director a brief but detailed account of their findings at the Observatory. Before the director could comment on the two additional and senseless murders Kleyr burst out:

"Boo! Sam!"

The three of them stood in a rather close huddle beside the small helicopter, and now Kleyr placed a hand on the arm of each of the men as she stood looking back and forth from one to the other in stricken dismay.

"What is it, Princess?" Bucher asked in low voice, instinctively knowing they had arrived at a definite juncture in the case of the mysterious X character.

"Boo." Kleyr's voice was scarcely above a whisper. "That photograph in that volume of my *Sylurgics* you found in the Americana Hotel. Where is that photograph, Boo?"

Without a word Bucher plucked the book from inside his coat pocket, handed it to her and stood waiting in tense silence while she studied the photograph of the young woman, brow furrowed in concentration.

"Boo," she whispered hoarsely at last. "Her coloring in this picture . . . I . . . That's what threw me off the first time I saw the photograph—her coloring, I mean. That great mass of silver-blond hair and those china-blue eyes . . ."

156

"Go on, Princess," Bucher urged quietly. "What do you know about her? Who is she?"

Slowly Kleyr closed the thin volume, as slowly as one might have done so in a dream, the dismay reflected through her concentration now strongly mingled with elements of incredulity—but Kleyr Maria Boriquen was far too much the disciplined scientist to long abide dismay and incredulity when confronted by irrefutable fact; thus when she handed the book back to Bucher there was neither doubt nor uncertainty in the look she gave him.

"Kleyr, please." The vibrant urgency in Bucher's tone was now much more pronounced, and the director's seamed face was taut with hope. "Do you know anything about the girl in the photo? Do you know who she is?"

"Of course. It's Martha Andrews."

"The Martha Andrews—Mary Jo Philasheo of the Dainty Dish?"

"Yes." Kleyr nodded thoughtfully. "But as Martha Andrews she always had chestnut brown hair and clear brown eyes—and in the photograph her face is a bit fuller, somehow, and her brows different."

"Wigs and contact lenses," the director said, relief evident in his tone. "And a bit of plastic sponge correctly placed inside the mouth, and false brows. With all the available materials and disguising gadgetry on the market these days, disguising oneself from one's own mother is simple as mud."

"But why would she be having an affair, in a blonde wig and with blue eyes, with Padrino—unless—unless—?"

Bucher saw chilly horror spring alive in her eyes as the truth reached her, and her mouth sounded raspy dry when she continued:

"—unless Martha Andrews is Madame X?"

"No." White Hat's director shook his head, handing Bucher the square of yellow foolscap he carried. "The woman you know as Martha Andrews is Madame X as I figure it, Kleyr, but she's not the real Martha Andrews." He indicated by a nod the message Bucher was reading. "It arrived from the Dade County sheriff's office just as you left for the Observatory."

"And according to this, the real Martha Andrews was found murdered in a swamp south of Miami—"

"Bound hand and foot and her throat cut," Kleyr interrupted, reading aloud from the message around Bucher's shoulder.

"Christ," Bucher muttered grimly. "That bitch goes for the throat every time, doesn't she?"

"But, Boo . . . how could she have known I was to be at the Dainty Dish the night of our reunion? Was it only the night before last? Dear God above, suddenly it seems ages ago. Tell me, Boo. How could Martha have known I would be at the Dainty Dish? You said McReady and Seeto Loyoka knew beforehand that I would be there and went there expressly to kidnap me, but how could Martha have known I would be there?"

"Apparently she learned of it from Dr. Samantha Bartlet. I don't know the details, but if only you and Dr. Bartlet knew you were to be at the Dainty Dish, she had to have learned it from Bartlet, somehow." At the start of surprise flickering across Kleyr's face, Bucher added: "You and she were the only two who knew you'd be at the Dainty Dish, were you not?"

"So I've been thinking," Kleyr said slowly. "But only this moment it occurred to me that I might have told Padrino; I kept no secrets from him, Boo. Not even you."

"Then this Martha friend of yours could have wheedled it out of the old boy with little trouble."

"Boo, please." Kleyr shuddered. "Don't be calling that—that monster my friend. But how can you be positive she and X are one?"

"I'm not positive. Not by way of proof; I just know it's her, would bet my last dime on it being her."

"She could have gotten her information from Dr. Samantha Bartlet," White Hat's director mused reflectively. "That is, if a budding suspicion of mine holds up." At Bucher's and Kleyr's inquisitive looks he continued hurriedly. "When our people were running a background check on Dr. Samantha Bartlet, they uncovered the existence of a half-sister, Janis Bartlet, whose name shows up nowhere in any of the information Dr. Bartlet gave about

158

herself and her family to the various agencies governing the Observatory when she applied for her position there."

"A half-sister?" Bucher asked.

The director nodded. "Same father, different mothers, and the way we got it, this Janis was the family genius, in a manner of speaking. Extremely high IQ, photographic memory with total recall, and . . ." The older man glanced at Kleyr quickly, as if in apology, but continued nonetheless. "And a compulsive, insatiable nymphomaniac. Her family kicked her out because of it—in spite of all her enviable talents, or gifts, or blessings, or whatever. All except her father, but he's been dead now something over ten years, as I recall."

"Compulsive, insatiable nympho." Bucher winked at Kleyr. "I told you any person who'd cavort around naked like that, even if it was supposed to be a nightclub act at the Dainty Dish, had to have kinks between her ears."

"Boo, compulsive, insatiable nymphomania is no more of a 'kink,' as you term it, than alcoholism is. With proper treatment it can be corrected." A fetching giggle escaped her. "But what woman in her right mind would want it corrected?" At Sam White's startled expression at this, her giggle blossomed swiftly into warm laughter and she winked surreptitiously at Bucher, lacing an arm through the director's arm and purring cozily. "Sam, can you guess what that awful Boo Bucher did to me in less than two hours after we met at the Dainty Dish night before last?"

Being taken unaware, the director articulated on cue automatically, the perfect straight man. "No, what did he do to you?"

"Humph." Her feigned miff was perfect. "He got me pregnant, that's what; and us having not seen each other in over eight years. Can you imagine such a thing? With all the jillions of things we had to say to each other, and Boo with his one-track mind—" She broke up, utterly, unable to maintain the put-on in face of Sam White's blank gape, which a second later was transformed by laughter wrinkles as he joined her merriment.

"You seem very positive," he at last told her.

159

"Well, he had better have." Kleyr brandished a fist in Bucher's direction. "And if he didn't I've got every single minute of his six months' Puerto Rican vacation planned for him, and never you doubt it."

"What six months' Puerto Rican vacation?" Bucher demanded in surprise, knowing they had not really discussed him taking a six months' vacation here with her when this case was over, though he was in no wise adverse to the idea. But what might have been Kleyr's rejoinder they were never to learn, for at that moment one of the White Hat agents approached from the direction of the headquarters Chinook and spoke respectfully to the director.

"Mr. White?"

"What is it, Mike?" The director faced him.

"The Chinook upstairs just phoned in to report that Big Jute Nappo and his gang are less than half a mile away."

The director acknowledged with a nod and faced Bucher again. "We've got company coming, it seems."

"Those two black sedans we saw returning from the Observatory?"

The older man nodded, though frowning in perplexity. "But why is Nappo paying us this visit? That's what I can't figure out. Our tail on Nappo radioed in just after you left for the Observatory that Big Jute & Company left San Juan airport burning rubber and were headed for Arecibo hell bent for leather, then again radioed in later saying the sedan slowed to a creep four or five miles out. But why? That's the puzzler. For what reason would Big Jute Nappo land at San Juan and smoke up the road for Arecibo?"

"And come here?" Bucher asked. "To Kleyr's place?"

"My guess, yes, but it's only a guess."

"Then we're in trouble." A harsh savagery had edged into Bucher's tone.

"You're sure?" The director and Kleyr asked in unison, showing alarm.

"I'm positive," Bucher snarled.

10

Bucher's bleak eyes swept the highway connecting Arecibo with San Juan. The highway entered Arecibo only half a dozen blocks away, where the big Ronrico Rum sign stood at the intersection, and even now, as he viewed the area beyond the intersection, two big black sedans swept swiftly into view, roaring forward now at top speed. "Big Jute Nappo wouldn't dare expose himself by coming here in open daylight—unless the bastard knows something about our immediate situation we don't know, something that'll give him a wide edge of safety if the hair gets short." Bucher glanced sideways, looking at Kleyr, who stood watching the approaching sedans, and an icy trickle of apprehension for her safety crept up his spine. She was in grave danger, of this he was certain without any proof other than Big Jute's coming here. And not only Kleyr alone, but all who stood here with her were in equal danger. Yet for his own welfare and that of the other White Hat agents present he gave not a second thought.

You're a selfish bastard, he grimaced wryly to himself as the two sedans drew closer, and again he glanced at Kleyr. But why in hell shouldn't I be? She's the very best thing ever to happen to you, dumb-ass, and never you forget it. Moreover, she hadn't volunteered to risk her life, or to knowingly place herself in jeopardy for the cause of justice as he and the other rum-dums present had, so the other rum-dums knew the score and could hustle for themselves—while he concentrated on taking care of Kleyr and himself.

"Princess?" he asked quickly on inspiration in a low voice.

"Yes, Boo?" She moved over to stand close beside him.

"Has the city of Arecibo done any work in this immediate area any time recently? Like fix the sewer lines or repair the streets and things like that?"

"Oh, mercy, yes. Both the sewer and the streets for that

matter. The sewer was backing up in my bath, so the city laid an auxiliary line right down the center of the street after fixing the main one." She pointed. "See that line of sparse grass leading from the house straight across the lawn? That's the main line. They replaced it completely, new tubing and everything. Why?"

Bucher shrugged—he hoped indifferently, not trusting his voice, fearful the silent groan of despair lowing in his ears would make itself known to the others. Now he knew Big Jute Nappo's ace in the hole. In all probability the phony street gangs and sewer crews had buried enough high explosives about the place to destroy the entire neighborhood in a single blast.

Now the two sedans arrived at the intersection, one hard behind the other so much so that instead of two separate sounds from the tires of both vehicles, there was only one prolonged sound of screeching protest from rubber as each sedan two-wheeled it around the corner in a sort of mechanical desperation and roared blindly toward Kleyr's place. Exactly, or so it appeared to Bucher, as though the front vehicle were trying to escape.

And escape, Bucher and the others watching learned scant seconds later, was precisely what the front vehicle was trying to do. Not only trying. It did escape—at least from the pursuing second sedan, though for whatever reason the first sedan sought escape, in Bucher's opinion it had accomplished little more than jump from the frying pan into the fire—assuming his suspicions were correct about the entire area around Kleyr's house being murderously mined. Regardless, one way or the other they would soon know.

At the three-block mark between the house and the intersection the second sedan commenced an abrupt wild ride, recklessly careening all over the street, its determination to stop short of the house evidenced by twin black roils of rubber-smoke from agonized tires' screams of protest. The vehicle succeeded in its aim. It stopped short of the house, all right, but less than a block and a half short, which, if the house and grounds were mined as Bucher suspected, would offer scant protection should Martha An-

162

drews-X or whatever her real name was decided to have a big bang. As for the lead vehicle, which at the last minute Bucher discerned to be driven by none other than one Surd Gulgar, it managed to stop within a dozen feet of where Bucher, Kleyr, and White Hat's director stood observing. And the instant the vehicle came to a halt the withered and seamed Gulgar seemed to literally explode from it through the driver's door, tears of thanksgiving streaming down over his leathery, wrinkled-parchment face, which reflected that disturbing hue known as morgue-white, his hands those of a man beset by a fierce seizure of palsy. He lurched drunkenly in the general direction of Bucher and the others, his desperate but unsuccessful effort to communicate vocally with Bucher producing noises not unlike the frenzied gobbles of a psychotic turkey on Thanksgiving Eve.

"The poor man," Kleyr said in tender compassion. "What ails him, Boo?"

"Nothing," Bucher told her. "Except fear." He made a gesture that he knew Gulgar would interpret as him about to draw his Walther, whereupon the palsied Gulgar instantly found his voice.

"No!-Butchy!-fer chrissake!-no!" He sagged, limply, and would have fallen had not the small 'copter been at hand for him to lean against.

"I thought you were leaving Puerto Rico," Bucher snarled.

Gulgar rolled terrified eyes toward the second sedan, from which the squat, menacing form of Seeto Loyoka was just emerging a hundred yards away.

"You was right, Butchy," Gulgar declared, tone heavy with hopeless desperation. "Big Jute was keepin' me in the dark about that five mil contract and all on account of he learned somehow I overheard him and Delaney Pryde scheme to palm Pryde off as Big Jute's brother. I was supposed to be deep-sixed here in Puerto Rico soon as this ruckus here is settled. Deep-sixed by *him*." Gulgar pointed toward the second sedan, beside which Seeto Loyoka now stood in full view, but his fear was so great, and he had

163

come so very close to certain death, he would not look at the gunsel assigned to kill him.

"Clue me in real good on why Big Jute came to Arecibo and I'll handle Loyoka for you—I owe the sonofabitch one for a little Chinese-American girl he butchered for pastime in Frisco years ago."

Until now neither Kleyr nor the director had made a sound since Gulgar's unusual arrival, but at "butchered for pastime" Kleyr gasped in horror, shuddering, at which Bucher gestured quickly for her to remain silent—for an incredible if not miraculous transformation was taking place with Surd Gulgar as the ancient, withered gunman's here-and-now swiftly evolved from watery-gut terror of eternal death to assurance of the blessing of continued life, at least for the present, and all this because of Bucher's offer to take care of Seeto Loyoka in return for cooperation.

"I was h-h-hopin' you'd deal, Butchy," Gulgar blubbered, tears starting afresh. "You just ask me, ol' buddy, and if I don't tell it, it'll be because I don't know it."

"Why did Big Jute head straight for Arecibo post-haste the minute he landed at San Juan?" Bucher asked.

"On account of if he hadn't a done it, Delaney Pryde woulda killed him by now: That's where Loyoka and Pryde glommed onto me. At the airport. And since Loyoka didn't have any orders concerning me, except to ice me down for keeps, when he spotted me at the airport, he knew I was cutting out on the Syndicate. So they grabbed me. Then Pryde read Big Jute the score while Loyoka coaxed Equalizer Alberts into the men's room at the airport and burned him good."

"Alberts is dead?"

Gulgar nodded vigorously, his color almost normal again. "That's what Loyoka told Pryde after Loyoka come back from the men's room at the airport."

"How come they didn't ice you down in the men's room?"

"On account of they needed me to drive along in front of them from San Juan to Arecibo, they said."

"They who?"

164

"Delaney Pryde, Seeto Loyoka, and Candy Dancer."

"Nappo's in the sedan you drove?" Bucher barked in surprise, read an affirmative answer in Gulgar's face, and quickly turned, but White Hat's director had read the same answer and was already issuing quiet orders to the several young agents of his team who had gathered around.

"What kind of word did Pryde read Big Jute at the airport while Loyoka was killing Alberts in the men's room, Surd?" Bucher asked the ancient gunman, hoping to hear what the expression implied. "The double?"

Again Gulgar nodded vigorously, rheumy eyes reflecting pleasure that the man who had ordered his death had been marked by his most trusted henchmen to meet the same grim reaper. "Yeah," he breathed, and almost voluptuously, tears and other traces of his former terror rapidly faded. "Yeah. The double. Big Jute walked right smack-dab into the sweetest little double-cross you ever did see. Every little detail had been tooken care of in advance. And from what I overheard between Pryde and Loyoka, it was Candy Dancer who did it, who arranged everything."

"Candy Dancer?" Bucher frowned. Perhaps he wasn't receiving complete and authentic information over the Syndicate grapevine these days; Candy Dancer had been Big Jute Nappo's moll for several years and—

"Huh-uh, Butchy." Gulgar shook his head, having read the question forming in Bucher's eyes. "That's what everybody else thought too, including me, but that ain't the way it was. The way I overheard it, Candy was some sort of a plant in Big Jute's organization. Put there on purpose, like, to femme fatale it with Big Jute and finagle herself in close to him, which she succeeded in doing by playing hard to get, I reckon, seein' as how Big Jute used to have to tie her up to screw—" The old gangster proffered a feeble smile of apology in Kleyr's general direction.

"Why the double-cross, Surd?" Bucher asked, impatient with the other for digressing.

"On account of they don't need him no more, I reckon, since Candy's just about tooken everything he owns, one way or another. And then conned him, some way, into fronting for this whatever-it-is that they call the Puerto Rican operation—"

"Big Jute a front?" Bucher's surprise was unmistakable. Dame Fortune must have turned her back on Jute Nappo altogether for big-thinking, big-talking, big-scheming Big Jute Nappo to pose as a front for ... "A front for what Puerto Rican operation?"

But Gulgar was already shaking his head before the question was completed. "I ain't got even a little bitty idea, Butchy. I swear I ain't. Like I told you, I was tagged to be deep-sixed right here in Puerto Rico, and from what I learned at the airport in San Juan since Pryde and Loyoka and Dancer glommed onto me, why, you know yourself they made sure they kept me from learning anything; I didn't even know about the five mil contract when you first ast me about it in the Americana Hotel, nor what was behind it."

"You know now what was behind it?" Bucher waited in breathless expectancy, nor did he wait in vain.

Surd Gulgar's head bobbed as he replied. "It was supposed to scare hell out of somebody, only nobody in Big Jute's organization, includin' Big Jute himself, knew this to begin with, only that some pill-roller was to be hit for a five million dollar contract. According to Candy Dancer, Big Jute pulled his tiger sharks out of Puerto Rico, all but Loyoka and McReady, who are with Candy in the double-cross, when she told him the contract was a gimmick to soften up some pill-roller so's he'd get real easy to handle. I never did learn who the pill-roller is though." To Surd Gulgar a pill-roller was a doctor and all doctors were of the medical profession, which accounted for his seamed face going blank with surprise when Bucher indicated Kleyr beside him and said:

"This is the pill-roller right here, but she doesn't scare easily." And after a second or so of Gulgar's jaw sagging in surprise, Bucher continued: "Who planted Candy Dancer in Big Jute's organization? And who was Big Jute fronting for?"

"You got me, Butchy. I don't know them either. From

166

the gist of the talk at the airport I ain't sure Big Jute himself even knows who's using him as a front."

From the corner of his eye Bucher had been able to keep track of what took place at the black sedan Gulgar had been driving, and now he glanced in the direction of the vehicle to see several White Hat agents help Big Jute Nappo out of it. As it always had in the past, now also sight of the runty five-foot tall mass of quivering obesity aroused in Bucher strong feelings of disgust; big-thinking big-talking big-scheming Big Jute Nappo was in addition a big glutton who seldom ceased, while awake, to glut. However, now was one of those rare exceptions. The mass of quivering obesity that was Big Jute Nappo was at the moment simply that: a mass of quivering obesity but little else. Unless one added fear. Though fear only made the obesity quiver with more determined vigor. And wear a sickish green about the gills. Bucher was about to speak to Kleyr regarding Nappo, but the ugly lash of Seeto Loyoka's angry voice caught him.

"Gulgar!" Loyoka stood beside the second black sedan, squat, menacing, deadly as a blind rattler during dog days with the .357 magnum he carried under his left arm. "Come and get it, Gulgar!" This followed by explosive, idiotic giggles that caused Bucher to glance at Surd Gulgar quickly. "Come and get the goodies I got for you, Surdy Gulgar-boy! Come Surdy-Surdy-Surdy-Surdy-boy! Come get the goodies Daddy Seeto's got for you."

"What's wrong with the sonofabitch?" Bucher snarled softly to the gunsel beside him. "Does he mainline?" The distance, in Bucher's judgment, between him and Seeto Loyoka was very close to one hundred yards, and the Walther's serrated dum-dums dropped four inches the first hundred yards, which meant he must aim a fraction high—there being no question whatsoever in Bucher's mind that a blood-gutsy between him and Seeto Loyoka was swiftly coming to a head. Nor did the thought ever occur to Bucher that he could evade the kill-quick-or-die hassle with Loyoka by feeding Gulgar to the sharks, as it were, for he had committed himself to the aged torpedo standing with him and Kleyr at the small helicopter, and to renege on that commitment would be to violate one of the foremost principles over which he had left the Syndicate. Besides, there was his long-unsettled debt with Seeto Loyoka; he had not lied about owing Loyoka just retribution for the man's hideous butchery of a Chinese-American friend in San Francisco some years ago.

"Naw, Butchy," Surd Gulgar drawled without fear and in complete assurance. "Seeto don't take the needle. Or hard drugs in any other way I know of. It's some sort of pills he takes. They get him all hyped up and real weird sometimes. They're what's got him all wound up right now."

Bucher took a step away from the small helicopter, to draw Loyoka's fire away from Kleyr and the others, but only one step before Kleyr grabbed him by the arm.

"Where do you think you're going?" Her words were not loud, but they were fraught with alarm.

"To shoot a mad dog," Bucher replied, not looking at her and pulling free. "And without giving the sonofabitch the chance for a final prayer."

Kleyr simply stared, transfixed by incredulity, on the verge of screaming protests, though not because of the shoot-out, per se, but because of the personal danger to Bucher for his involvement with the shoot-out. Two or three times it appeared as if she would speak again, but she did not, at last taking a slow, deep breath and relaxing a tiny measure, looking at Surd Gulgar with unfeigned loathing and contempt as she addressed him.

"That should be you going out there in the street to do your own killing, you slimy old worm." The unmistakable hatred in her voice did not alter the smug satisfaction on the old gunman's face.

"Lady, I couldn't win a shoot-out with Seeto Loyoka the fastest day of my life."

"But he shouldn't have gone," Kleyr insisted with quiet hopelessness. "He doesn't have to."

Surd Gulgar eyed her in a moment of heavy silence before replying, then said with absolute finality: "He had to go once he give me his word."

168

11

"Kleyr." It was Sam White, calling to her from under the nose of a Chinook some yards away. "It's safer over here; you could be hit by a ricochet."

Kleyr only shook her curly head stubbornly, looking after the scurrying figure of Gulgar as he departed to join those at the larger helicopter. Then she looked back toward Bucher, who was making his way nonchalantly toward the street leading to the big intersection six blocks away, stopping on the sidewalk even with her and directly in front of the menacing, squatty Loyoka beside the second black sedan. Unconsciously her right hand fingered the tailored grip of the French-made Unique 69 match pistol through the material of her blouse, the .22 caliber ten-shot still inside the waistband of her slacks. She stood very still, eyes going back and forth between Bucher and the gunman, not unmindful of the fact she was the cause of all this unpleasantness and that if that vile creature facing Bucher a hundred yards won the upcoming shoot-out, she would be directly responsible for Bucher's death—a possibility that caught the breath in her throat and fostered a numbing ache in her heart. She chanced a quick glance toward the Chinook where Sam White and his men had their attention focused on the disgusting glob of blubber taken a few minutes ago from the first sedan, and impulsively almost cried out for some of the inconsiderate, cowardly louts to go to her lover's aid. But she hesitated a fraction of a second, wondering if Bucher would be shamed or humiliated by having her demand assistance from the others on his behalf, and within that fraction of a second's hesitation, barely within the periphery of her vision, she detected unexpected action at the point where Loyoka stood. Quickly she looked hard in that direction—and saw the lissome, nymphian graceful, and utterly captivating young woman not more than a very few years her senior emerge from the black sedan beside which Loyoka stood.

"Candy Dancer," Kleyr said silently to herself. The woman had to be Candy Dancer, for Surd Gulgar had mentioned no other woman besides her in connection with all this mess. Kleyr studied the young woman with critical eyes, thinking surely one so lovely as she could not be the depraved creature Bucher had spoken of during their return flight from the Observatory. Then Kleyr saw the ugly automatic in the woman's hand and knew at once she was, in fact, the depraved creature Bucher had told her about.

A quick burst of animal hate flushed through Kleyr Boriquen, fiercely protective, at seeing her mate's life threatened. Without giving any more thought to the act than she might have given taking a breath, her right hand vanished beneath the lower edge of her blouse and her small fingers fitted neatly into the sculptured grip of the Unique 69. The French match pistol was in her hand in plain view of all when she moved toward Bucher.

Some twenty yards away Sam White, leaning forward, attention centered on the run-on, fear-inspired monologue of the revolting Big Jute Nappo, was inexplicably yanked erect, he knew not by what—save a sudden distinct impression history passed him by, and it was then he saw the esteemed, world-renowned genius, Dr. Kleyr Maria Boriquen, vicious-looking match pistol in hand and headed toward Bucher, obviously determined, now that Candy Dancer was a threat on the scene, to take the place she considered rightfully hers beside Bucher and thus equalize the odds he faced. Sam White's mouth flew open to cry out a warning, but he did not cry out nor make a sound except hiss in quiet command, and those with him at the Chinook fell silent to watch Kleyr also, fascinated, spellbound, for about her was a certain not readily definable aura of purpose, of inflexible determination, of irrevocable resolution. Perhaps it was the classic, age-old picture of the female rushing fearlessly in to do battle beside her beleaguered mate, but whatever it was it smote each man watching powerfully with a sense of awe, an admiration of which they were justly proud, and a touch of harmless

170

jealousy of Bucher, but only for a moment, envious that they had none such as Kleyr to respond for them in a like situation.

Kleyr approached Bucher at an angle at which he could not see her, not wanting him to know of her presence as yet because such might prove a distraction and thereby his undoing, for in spite of her lack of experience with the bludgeoning, bloody art of killing her fellow man, she was not unaware of the almost stifling high-voltage nervous strain charging the scene. Thus it was that she drew up on Bucher from the rear and slightly to one side, halting a couple of paces behind and to the right of him.

Seeto Loyoka, as yet having evinced no reaction to Bucher's acceptance of his challenge to Surd Gulgar, now said something in a low aside to Candy Dancer and erupted in nasal guffaws, holding himself with both arms and jiggling in frenetic glee—portrait in life of conceited imbecile. But as such a portrait misleading all the more. This Bucher knew for a fact.

Loyoka's lip-smacking zest for inhuman butchery was well known throughout the Syndicate. Not so well known was his practice of the technique he termed "psyching-out" an opponent prior to attempting the kill, psyching-out Loyoka's private definition for indulging in disarming diversion during which he suddenly struck, taking the opponent by surprise. Thus far those who had braced Seeto Loyoka and learned of this practice always learned of it too late. Bucher had no intention of being taken unaware, neither by Loyoka nor by his lovely companion. Albeit Candy Dancer was a woman, and though the most nauseating and repulsive thing in life to Bucher was killing a member of the opposite sex, his knowledge of Candy Dancer's heinous proclivity made her an exception.

The automatic in her hand was an Erma KGP six-shot .32 ACP and, if Syndicate scuttlebutt was to be believed, she was a wizard at shooting it, her philosophy based on the very valid premise that unless one hit what one shot at, one could not be effective. As a consequence of this, according to rumor, Candy Dancer rarely missed.

"I'm gonna think of ol' Butchy-boy every time I spend

one of the quarter-million clams I get for burning you," Loyoka suddenly chortled loudly, greasily, rubbing his crotch vulgarly in anticipation.

"You're a lying, slant-eyed son of a bitch," Bucher replied slowly, distinctly, making sure the other heard and understood all he said. "Your mother was a whore, your sisters sluts of the gutter, and your father a pimp for the lot, you included. You've got a big mouth because you're hyped on pills and because sounding off in the presence of that diseased chippy beside you shores up your sagging courage. If you had the guts of a slimy worm, you'd already be going for your—"

A howl of mindless rage tore from Loyoka's throat at the deluge of unbearable insults—which Bucher had employed to hasten the action. Loyoka's gun hand vanished behind the loosely hanging side of the light coat he wore, flashed into view half a thought later gripping his metal blue Colt .357 German-made magnum, which he lined on Bucher—as Candy Dancer snapped her Erma .32 up on Bucher also.

"Koosh!"

"Spat!"

The ungainly, silencered and deadly Walther P-38 that appeared magically in Bucher's big mitt rendered its gentle death sigh, the sigh followed by a foreign "Spat!" that Bucher found mystifying at the moment but that he ignored as the sound of Candy Dancer's small bore weapon modified by acoustical influence. He kept his cold eyes on Seeto Loyoka, though unnecessarily, for hardly had the Walther's sigh and the odd "Spat!" faded before Loyoka had lurched wildly, drunkenly, weapon unconsciously flung aside, a gory cavity where his left eye had been a second previously, brains exploded by the P-38's serrated dumdum out the right rear of his skull in a shower of splintered bone and shreds of flesh. Then Bucher flicked his cold gaze to Candy Dancer—and very gradually an expression of mingled wonder and disbelief overspread his craggy features.

The lovely and youthful female psychotic murderer stood gazing rather placidly in his general direction, yet with a somewhat enigmatic cast also on her face, serving to reflect no less wonder and disbelief than Bucher's, through the aspect of enigma created by an additional ingredient. This ingredient itself was engendered by the sure knowledge, and the inevitability, of swiftly approaching death. Her death, a phenomenon she had never before given serious consideration, death from the wound through which a deep crimson was gradually spreading over the left breast area of her thin middy. Her arm aiming the Erma .32 dropped abruptly to hang at her side, the pistol itself not ceasing in its descent until it struck the concrete with a metallic clatter. Very gradually, at first almost imperceptibly, her knees began to fail, and both White Hat's director and the young agent named Mike had dashed past Bucher in her direction at full speed and were within less than ten yards of her when she gently crumpled to the street.

Bucher reached the spot where she lay only a second or two behind the others, not from sympathy nor from any hope of altering her fading state, but from an honest desire to learn what in hell had happened. And yet, when he stopped and stood there above Sam White and Mike kneeling beside her, Bucher at once discerned in her eyes a sanity never present in them the few times they had met in the past, and with the sanity—a chill touched Bucher when he recognized it, yet there was little use denying it was in her eyes also—with the sanity a quiet and gentle serenity about death's approach. My god, he thought in grim surprise, she's glad to be dying, glad it's all over for her.

"Candy," Sam White asked in quiet urgency, "who's behind this operation that brought you, Nappo, and the others to Puerto Rico?"

"Janis." Her tone was quiet and gentle as the serenity of her eyes.

"Janis Bartlet? Samantha Bartlet's half-sister?"

"Yes." Obviously the young woman on the street was surprised that White should possess this knowledge. "How long have you known?"

173

"Only strongly suspected for some time, though not certain until now."

"It was Janis who played the part of Martha Andrews, wasn't it?" Bucher asked, going to one knee. "And Mary Jo Philasheo at the Dainty Dish?"

A smile touched the dying woman's parted lips. "The same old Butcher. You never miss a trick, do you?"

Bucher saw no point in wasting the time to explain he had been ignorant of Samantha Bartlet's half-sister's existence until only a while ago, asking instead: "Was it Janis, as Mary Jo, who wrecked her dressing room at the Dainty Dish and killed Arnie Limpkin in preparation for Loyoka and McReady to kidnap Dr. Kleyr Boriquen?"

Candy Dancer smiled weakly but affirmatively. "Like I said, the Butcher never misses a trick. The trouble began when Loyoka and McReady, not knowing what Janis looked like, mistook her for Dr. Boriquen, kidnapping her instead. And that's when she began slitting throats left and right, even her half-sister, who'd posted her on the time Dr. Boriquen was supposed to show at the Dainty Dish."

"What was her theory behind killing so many people who'd been close to Dr. Boriquen? To frighten the doctor into cooperating after the snatch at the Dainty Dish failed?" This was from the director, and after Candy Dancer's noticeably weaker nod, she looked past the older man, above and between where he and Bucher knelt, at last managing:

"Are you Dr. Boriquen?"

Bucher looked up and around, unaware that Kleyr had joined them.

"Yes," Kleyr nodded, a stricken look about her limpid eyes. "I'm Dr. Boriquen."

"Boy, for a doctor you're some shot with that freaky-looking little pistol." They were the last words Candy Dancer was ever to utter, and not until Bucher had risen to his feet and digested them thoroughly did he understand the dead woman's meaning. He looked at Kleyr in wonder and no little admiration.

"You?" He grinned so hard his face hurt. "So your little

174

.22 made the 'Spat!' I heard. I didn't know you fired, or where you fired from for that matter."

"I was behind you and to the right, almost within arm's reach." Her tone carried a flat, vapid timbre; she smiled limply. "Boo, I don't believe killing people is my cup of tea."

Beaming grandly on Kleyr, White Hat's director made an inarticulate sound in his throat, following with one of the rare instances Bucher ever heard the man use strong language; the first instance in the presence of a lady, but he did so, albeit unconsciously, forgetting himself in reaction to Kleyr's unhesitating, courageous stand in facing Loyoka and Dancer. "Mr. Bucher—" His voice literally quivered with unvarnished admiration and a little envy. "Mr. Bucher, if there was any one woman anywhere in the whole cockeyed world who held me in only half the regard Kleyr holds you, I'm a son of a bitch if I wouldn't consider myself to be the luckiest man on the face of God's green earth—and I'll sign a written statement to that effect, damned if I won't!"

This did it for Kleyr, paradoxically. One instant she suffered acute remorse for having killed Candy Dancer, the next she hung onto Bucher's arm, shoulders shaking with laughter.

The director spoke to the agent, Mike, who was rising to his feet, indicating Dancer and Loyoka with a gesture: "Have Gustavo and Heinrich take them into the police station in Arecibo and give the chief of police a full report."

"Right, Chief." Mike spun away at once but was back less than a minute later, as Bucher, Kleyr, and Sam White walked back to the helicopters. "Chief, there's a man trying to hide in the rear seat of the second sedan. He fits the description of Delaney Pryde, sir."

It was Delaney Pryde, all right; huge, hulking, heavy-shouldered, heavily muscled arms, and from Bucher's deadly brass knucks two nights past at the Dainty Dish a face looking tromped on by a mule; a Delaney Pryde who not only did not look like himself, but who also did not even *know* himself, his sanity having been temporarily sidetracked by bulge-eyed, gutless terror into hysteria by drinking half a liter of rum. But with the rum in his pumping gut, and some time to regain his senses, his eyes discontinued most of their alarming bulge and his screeches, snorts, and groans faded gradually into clarity.

"These people!" he gasped, pointing toward the Dodge van the bodies of Candy Dancer and Seeto Loyoka were being hauled to Arecibo police station in, then stared about in mumbly horror. "They *kill* people! It's their *profession*! To them it's a *business*!" His wild cackle of laughter bore traces of hysteria returning and Bucher shoved the bottle of rum back into his quaking hands.

"Drink!" Bucher snarled. "And quit gobbling like a dumb-ass."

Pryde obeyed, and when he lowered the bottle this time, there was a more rational look about him.

"Where's Janis Bartlet?" White Hat's director asked the man after a surreptitious wink at Bucher.

"Who?" Pryde asked, nonplussed.

"Janis Bartlet."

The South African stared at the director in wonder, gulping several times during the process, at last managing: "But—you just saw Janis Bartlet's body hauled away in that van."

At this the director glanced at Bucher, but Bucher said nothing. Even so, his thoughts were racing a mile a minute. His jungle animal instincts, those same instincts that had so fascinated Tino Orazio in Chicago years ago, were already clamoring at him that all here was not as it appeared to be—and without obviously doing so, Bucher changed his position in order to see the entire area of the helicopters and where the action had recently taken place. Nothing was amiss, as far as he saw, but something was amiss nonetheless. It was not necessary that he see it, immediately, to know of its presence, but something was way to hell out of kilter.

"Who told you the dead woman was Janis Bartlet, Pryde?" the director asked, again glancing in Bucher's direction, apparently the only one aware of Bucher's changed position, and why.

176

"Well ... she was introduced to me as Janis Bartlet," Pryde blurted.

"Introduced by whom?"

"Him." Pryde pointed toward the obscenely blubbery Big Jute Nappo, still near the nose of the Chinook with Surd Gulgar, the gesture simultaneous with Nappo's slowly toppling to the ground to lie without moving, Gulgar gaping first at Nappo, then at Bucher, in astonishment. Then Gulgar squatted quickly beside the fallen man, feeling beneath Nappo's coat among rolls and lumps and pads of suet over the general area of the heart.

"His ticker!" He called to Bucher in unfeigned dismay. "It ain't tickin'! It's quit! He was eatin' something, kept puttin' pills of some kind in his mouth and crunchin' 'em, then all of a sudden he made a sort of punctured noise and let go all over." Gulgar's rheumy eyes found Kleyr. "You wanta look at him, Doc?"

"Stay here!" Bucher cautioned Kleyr in a low voice, as Mike, who for some few minutes had been scrutinizing the first sedan, the vehicle Surd Gulgar had driven, from all angles as he repeatedly circled it in successively smaller circles, halted at last at the rear of the car, attitude one of extreme caution. After a moment's listening, bent forward, ear toward the closed turtle shell, he pointed toward the shell with an exaggerated gesture, indicating the object of his curiosity was in the rear of the vehicle. White Hat's director, with surprising power for one so small, spun the hulking Delaney Pryde by the shoulder and planted a polished brogan forcefully on the seat of the South African's learned britches.

"Move, crud!" the small, elderly man said angrily, Bucher recognizing the rise in temper as a hint of confusion the director was beginning to labor under. Nor was Bucher himself untouched by the confusion, though he betrayed no hint of it, nor was it of any bothersome strength. Nor did he intend to let it become bothersome, he assured himself, walking along slowly behind the director and Pryde and slightly to the rear of Kleyr. Once she stopped to wait for him to move up and walk beside her, but he motioned her on, shaking his head. The rear gave

177

him the vantage point of being in a position to see everything in front, and instinct, the same survival instinct warning him of a danger present, now warned him that the black sedan they were approaching, in some way, represented that danger. When the four of them reached the point where Mike still stood at the rear of the vehicle, the director motioned for the young man to open the rear turtle shell—which Mike proceeded to do with a pick from a small leather packet of stainless steel tools he took from a rear pocket. Bucher, Walther palmed, instinctively stepped in front of Kleyr protectively when Mike raised the shell.

"I be goddamned!" Bucher spat spontaneously. The director muttered something unintelligible in surprise, and Delaney Pryde merely gawked stupidly, the enormous quantity of rum the man had been forced to consume in order to subdue his hysteria beginning to take effect now that the hysteria was gone. At sight of the near-naked young woman heavily gagged and bound hand and foot in the trunk of the sedan, only Kleyr responded to her plight—or tried to respond.

"Martha!" Kleyr exclaimed in alarm, stepping around Bucher to go to the woman's aid—Bucher hooked an arm neatly about her tiny waist and swung her back behind him in a single gesture. "But that's Martha Andrews!"

"No." His tone was low yet forceful, nor was he disturbed she had so soon forgotten her Padrino, the Russian, Samantha Bartlet, her two cousins, and all the others with their throats deftly, cleanly slit from ear to ear, for the stage had been cunningly set, every tiny detail meticulously in place to make her forget. And not only her; the rest of them as well. "You stay away from her, Princess. Understand?" Her move to go to Martha Andrews' assistance had been an impulsive one, and now her face clouded as remembrances returned in an avalanche.

"Oh, yes, Boo," she quavered in trembly voice. "I—I—For a moment I forgot. That's all."

Now that the turtle shell was up and the woman in the trunk of the car saw herself about to be rescued, she commenced squirming and grunting and twisting, struggling mightily against her bonds, but even in her unusual cir-

178

cumstances, and without her silver-blond wig and the contact lenses that gave her china-blue eyes in the photo in that volume of Kleyr's *Sylurgics*, he had no difficulty at all in identifying her as one and the same person. As Kleyr had described her, she had brown hair and eyes to match, and currently had a beautiful tan, virtually all of which was visible except that partially concealed by whisper-thin Bikini panties and a bra that revealed much more than it concealed. Aside from these two trifling garments she was stark naked, though her lack of dress bothered her not at all, as Mike and the director lifted her bodily from the trunk and placed her delicately on her feet, then began cutting at the wide bands of white adhesive tape binding her wrists and ankles. She removed the tape from around her mouth herself, spitting out an enormous wad of soggy cotton with an equally enormous, "Ugh!"

The instant the gag cleared her mouth, Bucher stepped forward, swung powerfully, all four fingers of the hand lashing her viciously across the mouth.

"That's number one for the real Martha Andrews you left dead in a Florida swamp, slut!" he snarled as viciously as he had struck, but waited until she regained her feet from being flung by the blow against the side of the car. From Mike came a sound of protest while Sam White literally boggled at his ace operator, boggled because he knew the Iceman's private code regarding women, which demanded that he protect them whenever possible but never harm one and especially never strike one savagely with no provocation whatsoever. And yet he knew the Iceman too well to interfere. So did Kleyr Boriquen. Kleyr not only suspected Bucher had an ulterior motive behind his peculiar conduct, she was absolutely positive of it—for she knew him far, far better than Sam White ever could. The other White Hat agents, albeit junior agents with the larger number on their first field assignment, stood quietly watching but making no sound. Often they had heard and more often read of the hardly believable exploits of the granite-faced ex-gang lord called Bucher, and not a one of those present thought of going to the semi-nude woman's aid, for if they had learned one thing about this man the underworld knew as the dread Butcher, it was that he never did anything without definite purpose. Bucher's purpose of the moment was to rekindle in the woman's eyes the thing he had glimpsed but fleetingly when Mike first raised the trunk lid, and unless he succeeded, he might well be in for making the goat of himself—but he had no intention of not succeeding.

"I'm going to kill you, slut!"

The breathy snarl accompanying these words caused her to flinch involuntarily and faintly dodge. "Why?" She swallowed hard.

"The real Martha Andrews, Rachel and Nora Cordova, Dr. John Malcolm Philbrick, the elderly man you murdered—after shacking with him in order to glean information about Kleyr Boriquen, whose volume of *Sylurgics* you stole from Philbrick and sent to Pryde here because you couldn't master the mathematics yourself; for your half-sister Dr. Samantha Bartlet—"

"How did you know my name?" she screamed.

"I haven't mentioned your name. I said your half-sister Dr. Samantha Bartlet." Bucher knew he had her then; it didn't show on his hard face but he knew he had her. He lied boldly. "I've known you were Janis Bartlet from the beginning."

"Who told you?" The hoarse demand carried a threat of evil—and prompted Bucher to take a shot in the dark.

"Lyle Hardiman told me. He told us all, in fact." And Bucher watched the blind shot bear fruit, watched the madness he'd seen in her eyes before struggle against the remaining few shreds of her better self, dominate it and rush to the surface a hellfire furnace of blazing madness.

"L-Lyle told you?" It was a little girl voice that asked the question. "When?" She squirmed and wriggled her voluptuous body, stretching upward, threading tapered fingers through silken chestnut tresses, acting exactly as if their conversation dealt with topics no more grave than the time of day or the weather.

"That's right," Bucher said. "Lyle told me." He indicated Delaney Pryde. "But old rum-dum here would have told me if Lyle had not, because Pryde knew he was being patsied the minute you killed Arnie Limpkin, your sex partner at the Dainty Dish, wrecked your own dressing room to make it appear to have been wrecked while being searched, and attempted to palm Candy Dancer off on him as Janis Bartlet." Bucher continued the lie with all the conviction he could muster. Nor was Pryde likely to protest it; the man was too stupefied by rum to be much more than conscious. "You see, Candy's full name was Candy Dancer Pryde; she and Pryde here had once been married in South Africa but couldn't hack it, so Candy returned to the States, leaving Pryde in Transvaal. Neither bothered with a divorce, though Candy returned to using her maiden name." Bucher's reason behind this seeming rigamarole was a hope of infuriating Janis Bartlet into talking freely. Also, Pryde had claimed he believed Candy Dancer to be Janis Bartlet, and Bucher preferred the mad woman's words to either condemn or exonerate the South African. Janis Bartlet laughed softly.

"I think you're lying, Bucher. Old rum-dum there, as you call him, didn't know much of anything about my scheme to—" She stopped, features altering imperceptibly yet becoming a mask of unwholesome obscenity as she continued, staring fixedly at Kleyr, voice laden with a withering evil and hatred. "Old rum-dum didn't know anything about my scheme to make Puerto Rico's blinding genius give up her secret of the Fourth Dimension." She made a vulgar sound with her mouth, looking back at Bucher. "But even if you are telling the truth, Lyle Hardiman won't be snitching to anyone else. Not ever again. Nor his uncle, Dr. J. Joiner Mull, either, for that matter."

"Oh, Jesus!" Sam White, White Hat's director, muttered just above a whisper. "So that's why Mull hasn't been back around to see Kleyr." He spoke to Mike. "Take a couple of the boys and go cart Mull's and Hardiman's bodies to the police station also. And better take gasmasks along. In this heat they'll be ripe already." To the mad woman he said: "How'd you get Hardiman out of the hospital?"

She chuckled fulsomely. "I could get Lyle Hardiman to wade through knee-deep coals of fire for me any day of

181

the week; the poor dear didn't even know I was in Puerto Rico. Nor I he, to be truthful, until I chanced to encounter his rut-minded old uncle in San Juan yesterday." She tossed Bucher a fetching smile. "I saved your life, Bucher. Lyle swore he intended to kill you the minute he was up and around again."

"That's right," Bucher replied. "Look how close he came to killing me his first try." To Bucher's way of thinking, Janis Bartlet was far too self-confident to be any other than positive she was in complete command of the situation—which she damn well might be, considering all the high explosives he was certain the phoney street repair and sewer crews had buried in the area of Kleyr's home. His one advantage, if advantage it could be called, lay in the fact that the mad woman was unaware that he knew of the explosives. Now, Bucher reasoned swiftly, if he waited until precisely the most propitious moment to disclose his knowledge of the explosives, handling the disclosure with proper tact and subterfuge, and falsehood, he just might be able to get Janis Bartlet's complete story—of her attempt to force Kleyr into revealing her knowledge related to the Fourth Dimension—from Janis Bartlet herself. Trouble was, since he did not know how Janis Bartlet could detonate the explosives, though he was convinced it was by remote control, if his little scheme failed, her insane thought processes might well conclude the time to trigger the blast was now. Yet he had little choice as he saw it. There was no other way.

"The thing that puzzles me," Bucher said with great seriousness, "is how a genius-type dynamite chick like you got mixed up with a herd of dumb-asses like Big Jute Nappo and his worthless do-nothing, know-nothing punks."

The woman had been about to speak when Bucher said this, but now, instead, she became very still, studying him closely, with obvious interest, and when she did speak, Bucher knew at once he had penetrated her guard.

"You honestly think I'm a dynamite chick, Bucher?"

At first Bucher doubted his ears, yet recovered quickly enough. "I've heard from numerous sources you're a genius, and nobody but a blind man could deny you're a dynamite—no, change that." He chuckled good-naturedly. "Make that a nitro-chick. Nitroglycerin makes the bigger bang."

The effect produced on the mad Janis Bartlet by this gross, sledgehammer type compliment was remarkable to say the least. She did not wilt in Bucher's arms, nor even move from where she stood some two yards away for that matter, but the inclination was present and obvious nonetheless.

"You think I'd make a better bang than her?" The evil obscenity was again in her voice. She looked past Bucher to Kleyr, once again stretching voluptuously and threading long, tapered fingers through her chestnut hair. Bucher, eyes never for one instant leaving the mad woman, shrugged with vast indifference, indicating Kleyr with a movement of his head.

"There's no thinking about it. Dr. Boriquen is far too establishmentized. Likes too well to go by the book. You'd never find her doing the hanky-panky before a nightclub audience in such as the Dainty Dish. No imagination. By the way, was that Dainty Dish act necessary to your plan of making Kleyr cooperate?"

"No," the woman replied coquettishly. "But I have imagination." Her eyes changed as they found Kleyr again. "Just what is the mysterious ingredient in your experiments with the Fourth Dimension, bitch? Joiner Mull told me about the Boston Experiment, which you attended, and my stupid half-sister Samantha wondered to Dr. Philbrick at your experiments in that lab you share with them, and Philly expressed the belief you had succeeded in unraveling the mystery of the Boston Experiment, and perfected a technique for entering and leaving the Fourth Dimension."

Sam White released a long, slow breath at this, and the look he gave Bucher said he now understood the powerful and terrible secret Kleyr possessed and that Janis Bartlet wanted.

"What's the secret, bitch?" Janis Bartlet said with deadly calm. "I have a means of making you talk—or blowing you to Kingdom Come."

183

"Psssst! Huh-uh!" Bucher shook his head quickly in warning, pretending to believe only she heard it. "They found the explosives in the sewer line and beneath the road and removed them."

"Did they now?" she purred throatily.

"Tell me something," Bucher continued quickly. "How come a smart cookie like you let a couple of two-bit yeggs like Seeto Loyoka and Mack McReady kidnap you at the Dainty Dish instead of Kleyr? Didn't the bums know who their boss was?"

"Because that stupid half-sister of mine gave them my description on purpose, hoping to louse my operation up. Getting information out of her was almost like getting blood out of a turnip, anyway. But she cooperated after I told her who it was that killed Arnie Limpkin. And the Cordova sisters and the others."

"Then the five million dollar contract was not real after all?" Bucher asked, returning to the subject again.

"Oh, it was real enough for a while. To those who believed it. But Big Jute went into a double tizzy when six of his guns failed to return home, and I had to tell him then there was nothing to it." The glare she gave Kleyr was alive with maggoty hatred. "Why waste five million dollars on the tart when I can have the pleasure of killing her myself and also save five million dollars?"

It was here Bucher began to suspect it was he who was being toyed with; that he, not she, was the mouse in their little game of cat and mouse—and icy chills flushed in successive waves up his spine. He fixed the mad woman with cold eyes, suddenly anxious to terminate their confrontation with all possible dispatch. Killing a woman went powerfully against his grain—but Janis Bartlet was no longer a woman, or even human, only human-shaped insanity bent on death and destruction.

"Nobody kills Kleyr Boriquen," he snarled softly. "And especially not an insane slut like you."

"Oh, come now, Boo," she said, purring again. "Isn't that what the bitch calls you? Boo?" She laughed throatily, stretching a third time, combing her long fingers through her silken hair and—too quick almost to see, she sprang,

184

screaming, the Puerto Rican sun glinting brightly off the deadly straight razor that appeared in her hand.

Bucher cursed in surprise, and could have foiled her had she sprung at him or at Kleyr. But she didn't. Inexplicably, unless it can be accounted to the cunning of the insane, she sprang in the direction Bucher least expected. Toward Delaney Pryde. Not at Pryde, only toward him, in Pryde's direction, for she passed him, and Pryde grunted drunkenly in surprise though never seeing the glittering sweep her deadly razor made, nor, in his sodden state, aware he was its mark until he strangled for air on inhaling and coughed a crimson plume, eyes bulging as he suffocated on his own blood though never coming to know the extent of his injury. He did not live long enough.

Fiendish female laughter crackled insanely about the black sedan as she danced past White Hat's director, who wheeled away from her, staggering, and then she was at Kleyr, swifter than a streak of lightning.

Multiple sounds of alarm burst from those witnessing on the side—White Hat's training manuals offered nothing to cover such a situation as this, but Bucher gave them no heed. He watched, Walther palmed and ready, as the incredibly quick mad woman spun in behind Kleyr Boriquen, snatched her head rearward by a handful of hair, and slid the murderous razor—

"Drop, Kleyr!" But Kleyr couldn't drop.

"Koosh!"

Janis Bartlet screamed in pain when the P-38's 138 grain serrated dum-dum shattered her elbow and the razor fell to the street, Kleyr falling with it.

Janis Bartlet screamed a second time, fangs bared and—

"Koosh-Koosh!"

—never made another sound. As with Delaney Pryde, she did not live long enough, but died before she was flung into an ungainly lurching back-flip, two gory cavities where her eyes had been, back of her head a shapeless, squashy mass of bloody splintered bone and shreds of flesh with bloody, mangled hair—which would never again conceal another straight razor.

Bucher swore in futile despair as he glared about. The agents Sam White had brought to Puerto Rico ignored Delaney Pryde, for Pryde was dead, instead gathering in a tight, tense knot around the director and their superior, but they might as well have ignored him too, for White was dead also. Wasn't he? Bucher shook his head in dismay. The director was *not* dead! That insane slut he'd just killed had not been as proficient with her razor as he'd thought! He turned toward Kleyr. She lay as she had fallen, on her back, her lovely face unnaturally white, a specter of death, not moving. Not until Bucher reached her side, whereupon she grinned at him feebly but with returning color, extending a hand for him to help her to her feet.

She came directly into his arms, not looking at the dead lying about, not wanting to see the grisly havoc of which she had been inadvertently the prime mover.

"Come on," she said in an almost normal voice. "Let's go inside."

"Huh-uh," Bucher told her, thinking of the high explosives the area was mined with. "We're flying to San Juan. I might as well start my vacation now as later."